There's Blood in This Brew

A Books & Brews Anthology

MADAXEMEDIA.COM

There's Blood in This Brew
Published by Mad Axe Media

All rights reserved.

"Loophole"© 2025 by Clay McLeod Chapman
"A Little Drop of Poison"© 2025 by Christina Henry
"Jimmy Donaldson's Last Call"© 2025 by Brandon Eldridge
"Regulars"© 2025 by Robert Essig
"Ladies Night"© 2025 by Ruthann Jagge
"The Fifty Yard Fox"© 2025 by DE McCluskey
"Death Walks Into a Bar"© 2025 by Paul Avery Tindol
"True Believers"© 2025 by Chris Jones
"The Red Thirst"© 2025 by Steven Pajak
"Mulligan"© 2025 by Andrew Najberg
"The Special on Tap"© 2025 by Jay Bower
"The Special"© 2025 by Elizabeth Devecchi
"The Band Played On"© 2025 by Lance Dale
"Vintage"© 2025 by Elizabeth J. Brown
"The Wood-Man's Tavern"© 2025 by William Gray
"Last Night at Dead Moose"© 2025 by D.W. Hitz
"Cheers"© 2025 by Alexandrea Christianson
"Serenity Box© 2025 by MJ Mars
"Don't Knock Back"© 2025 by Mike Salt
"Bar & Grill"© 2025 by Joe Scipione
"Linger Longer Lounge"© 2025 by Ben Young
"The Godfall Taproom"© 2025 by Cassandra Celia
"Ahoy, Matey!"© 2025 by Viggy Parr Hampton
"Looks That Kill"© 2025 by R.E. Sargent
"The Slasher Swizzle!"© 2025 by Sean McDonough

No part of this publication may be reproduced, distributed, or transmitted in any form or by any means, including photocopying, recording, or other electronic or mechanical methods, without the prior written permission of the publisher, except as permitted by U.S. copyright law. For permission requests, contact info@madaxemedia.com.

The story, all names, characters, and incidents portrayed in this production are used fictitiously. No identification with actual persons (living or deceased), places, buildings, and products is intended or should be inferred.

Edited by Nico Bell & Joey Powell
Cover & Interior Design by Joey Powell
Interior Illustrations by Alexandrea Christianson

Print ISBN: 978-1-966497-08-0
E-Book ISBN: 9 978-1-966497-09-7

Acknowledgements

The individuals below helped make this project possible and had a direct financial impact on Books & Brews 2.0 through their contributions. We are enormously grateful for their generosity and for their enthusiasm for the horror genre.

**Renee Blair | Steffany Kurilovitch | Jamie Young
Andrea Johnson | Karen Larsen | Sophia McIntyre
Tiqua Lovett | Sara Rose | Erica Fields
Kathryn Bell | James Gass IV | Jordan Triplett
Rosina Elizabeth Simpson | April Stapleton | Jay Bower
Shanda Langley | Kristina | Stephanie Neitzel
Steve Pattee | Colleen Feeney | Meredith Livingston
Kayla | Trisha Smith | Samantha | Kristin Myers
Sean & Shawna Millott | Alicia Toothman**

Thank you to the volunteers below for dedicating your time and energy into Books & Brews 2.0 and making the event a reality:

**Alexandrea Christianson | Alicia Dale | Alicia Toothman
Alison Hodyna | Amber Reed | Becky Burgess
Becky Lawrence | Ben Young | Brad Ricks
Brandon Eldridge | Brandon McNulty | Chris Landis
Derek Austin | Emmie Stone | Heather Larson
Holly Landis | Jae Mazer | Jay Bower | Joey Powell
Jordan Triplett | Kate Forsman | Kathy Gordon
Kendra Allen | Lance Dale | Lauren Young
Leigh Kenny | Leyla Zmeskal | Rhonda Lynn Bobbitt
Robin Watts | Sam Allen | Sean McDonough
Shannon Jack | Staci Mae | Steven Pajak
Tricia Baert | Tricia Smith**

And, of course, thank you to Tiffany Koplin for bringing so many amazing individuals together.

Table of Contents

The Slasher Swizzle!

Sean McDonough

Enjoy the following stories with this simple drink recipe from author Sean McDonough.

Equal parts:

Dark Rum
Pineapple Juice
Mango Juice
A splash of grenadine
A splash of lime juice
A splash of falernum

Mix and serve over ice.

Loophole

Clay McLeod Chapman

My recruitment officer called. Said he bought me a bus ticket straight to boot camp. But that was three bottles ago. It's all numb under the knees for me now. I'm working up the nerve to move onto the rest of my legs next. Then my fingers. Hands. Couple more shots and I won't feel anything outside the Johnnie Walker running through my blood. Medium-bodied. Creamy and peaty. A salt-tinged finish. My body may as well be a distillery. I could open a vein and put myself on tap, serving up shooters from whichever artery I siphon. Next round's on me! It's happy hour ... I got nine pints left within me. *Line 'em up and knock 'em down*! 'Cause tomorrow, we're shipping off to South Carolina.

Did you know the first recruiting station for the Marines was in a bar just like this? They'd enlist tipsy kids all night. Have them sign on the dotted line right at the bar, toasting to their good fortune, only to wake them the next morning by splashing a bucket of cold water in their face, dragging them off to basic training with one hell of a hangover.

But times have changed. The Marines can't coerce new recruits anymore. Now they have what's called the *Delayed Entry Program*, giving you a year to forget all about ever signing some contract that says they can come knocking on your door and haul you off to Paris Island. *Use the year to reflect*, they say. *Be seeing you soon, son ...*

They brought Ronnie Thompson's body back this week. Buried him with his family. Me and Ronnie used to play kickball in the street when we were just kids. Ronnie had a crush on my sister, so he'd always let me play, even if I was younger. Got my ass scrapped every game. But Ronnie never complained. Never gave me lip for making his team lose.

To Ronnie Thompson. Casualty number one thousand eight hundred and fifty-six.

And he wanted to go over. He enlisted the day he turned seventeen. He stepped on that bus and never looked back. My sister saw him off, sobbing away as his Greyhound pulled out. Her mascara's streaked her cheeks, leaving her looking like that bus sped off over her face, leaving skid marks clear across her skin. And I remember thinking—*She loves him. Why's he running off when he's got such a good thing going for him?*

So I signed up. I went straight to the recruiting office and filled out my own application, thinking—*If it's good enough for Ronnie Thompson, it's good enough for me.*

Wanna know what I've done with the last year of my life?

Nothing.

Not a damn thing.

I'm thinking about the girlfriend I never asked out.

The job I never applied for.

I'm thinking about all the things I was supposed to do with myself that I never got around to. Only now ...

Now it's too late. They're coming for me tomorrow. *Zero six-hundred hours.* Two men in uniform are personally escorting me to the bus station, making sure I'm onboard.

Too late to back out now. No cold feet for me.

I'm thinking about the girlfriend I never had seeing me off tomorrow, kissing me. I'm thinking about how she's going to wrap her arms around my shoulders. Bury her face in my neck. Only she won't let go, determined to keep her grip on me, even after everybody else has gotten on board the bus. Those officers will have to take an arm and try prying her off. She may not look like much, but she's got enough piss and vinegar in her to bite the hand of any Marine that comes close enough. She'll scratch and claw at anyone who tries separating the two of us. She'll never let me go.

Canada's not an option. Crossing the border isn't as easy as it used to be. Can't get a college deferral. I'd only be able to postpone service until the end of my first semester.

I figured if I failed my drug test, they'd kick me out, so I went through my mom's medicine cabinet, swallowing as many different prescriptions as I could find. Began with this bottle of *magnesium hydroxide*? Only to end up shitting all over myself right there in the bathroom. Mom rushes me to the hospital. Gets my stomach pumped. When the doctor comes in, I begged him to write me a note. Said I'd pay him a hundred bucks to tell my recruiting officer that I had some kind of physical defect. Webbed feet or something like that. Anything.

There's nothing I can do for you, he said. *Do you know how difficult it is to convince a recruiting officer that you can handle your life on a daily basis but can't sacrifice it for your country?* He looked over his shoulder, making sure no one was in the room. *When I was your age, a friend of mine dodged the draft by shooting himself in the foot. He lost a few toes, but it kept him out of service.*

The room's spinning a bit. I'm seeing stars. The floor's all red underneath me. Each plank's rippling, flapping at my heels. An American flag. I'm sitting in a pool of the red, white, and blue.

I'm playing a little drinking game. The rules are simple: *Take a shot for each toe.*

Here's the hatchet, here's the Johnnie Walker. You get a sip of whiskey for each little piggy you free. No nipping the nail, now. We're talking about the whole toe. Once you get to the fifth piggy, it's all downhill. You won't feel a thing.

I've got a head start, so I'm hopping onto my left now.

This little piggy went into the service ...

This little piggy stayed at home ...

This little piggy had cold feet ...

This little piggy had none ...

And this little piggy went wee! wee! wee! all the way —

A Little Drop of Poison

Christina Henry

M ellie smelled the tablet the man had dropped in his date's strawberry margarita from across the room. It wasn't the sort of thing that one could normally smell, but then Mellie wasn't a normal person. And she *was* on the lookout for exactly this kind of man.

He looked like the kind of guy you'd want to bring home to Mom—moderately successful (Tissot watch, Prada leather sneakers) with moderate good looks (brown hair, blue eyes, straight nose, some artful stubble). Probably had a job as a commodities trader or an investment banker or something similarly boring. He presented as a safe, respectable sort. That was the type you always had to watch out for. That was the type that carried around a little bottle of white tablets, tablets that were palmed and dropped into a drink while their date went off to the ladies' room to freshen up her lipstick.

Mellie made a beeline for the table, holding an empty tray. The bar was all bright lights and warm, gleaming wood, with a slightly upscale feel for those who weren't fond of sticky floors and cut-rate beer. Despite all that, the lanes between tables were narrow, usually requiring some side-to-side movement if two people were passing one another. She just had to time her entrance correctly.

The man had ordered a fresh round of drinks right before the woman—a little blonde with a slightly hesitant smile—had left the table. Another server had delivered them, and that's when the guy did his little party trick with the tablet. Mellie didn't know how many times he'd done it before, but she was going to make absolutely certain that he never did it again.

She sped up a little as someone approached the man's table. In a regular situation, she would step into an empty space and allow the other person to pass. Not this time. She wanted to be forced to slide by the man's table, too close.

The tray was in front of her and held just a little too low and loose, so that when she passed by, the tray just brushed the tainted strawberry margarita and spilled in the direction of the guy's lap.

"Watch it, you stupid bitch!" he snarled as liquid poured over the table and onto his brand-name jeans.

She let the insult pass—she was already planning to punish him, so no need to lecture him on polite behavior—and played mortified as she wiped at the table with the rag she carried in her back pocket. "Aww, I'm so sorry! Let me get you another round, on me."

"Jesus Christ, these jeans are brand-new," he said, and stood up just as his date returned. "I gotta go wash up."

His date hovered uncertainly, taking in the mess. "What happened?"

"This dummy knocked over your drink. I'll be right back." He went off in a huff, muttering curses.

Mellie noted the little furrow between his date's brow. She obviously didn't like the way he'd acted, and a second later she said, "Gosh, I'm sorry. He didn't mean it."

"No problem, hon. It was my fault anyway," Mellie said. *Of course he meant it, and more.* "I'll get you a new round, okay?"

She deftly scooped up both drinks, even though he'd hardly touched his old-fashioned. Then she returned to the bar and put in the couple's order. When the two filled glasses came up, she placed the strawberry margarita on the tray and then did a little party trick of her own over his old-fashioned, quickly snapping open the clasp on the ruby ring she wore on her right hand and just as quickly snapping it closed again.

She hummed a certain Tom Waits song to herself as she walked back to the table. The man had returned and scowled at Mellie as she placed the drinks down.

"On me," Mellie said. "Sorry about that again."

"Thank you," the blonde said.

"Least you can do," the man said.

Mellie swiftly leaned down close to the man's ear and spoke in a low tone. "It would be a real shame if your date knew what kind of person you are. I think people's outsides should match their insides, don't you?"

Then she stood, and smiled, and let him see her eyes shift. He stared at her, his brow puckered, uncertain nerves prickling in his gaze. The man picked up the old-fashioned and gulped it down in one fast swallow, which meant he'd done exactly what she wanted him to do. Mellie glanced at her watch. It should be about a half hour, give or take, until this jerk's evening ended in a way that he had not planned.

"Another old-fashioned," he said, slamming the glass down.

Mellie collected the empty one, and her smile widened as she noted that his date had pushed her chair away from the table, just a touch. The little blonde looked like she was reconsidering this evening out.

The bar hummed along, patrons coming, patrons going. Balls clattered together on the pool table, followed by shouts of encouragement. Someone laughed loudly, and someone else set the jukebox to Chappell Roan. Three twentysomething girls at a table in the corner immediately began singing along.

Mellie kept a sideways eye on the man and his date. He'd regathered his equanimity after the spilled drink incident and appeared to have turned on the charm offensive. The blonde had a polite look of interest on her face, but nothing more. She hadn't touched the replacement margarita at all.

Then the man's face contorted, like he had a stomach cramp. Mellie placed her tray down on the bar, untied her apron, and slid into a shadow in the corner, watching.

The man tried to continue speaking, then halted. He put both hands over his own throat and coughed hard, then gagged.

"Hey, what's wrong?" the blonde said.

A second later, he keeled over and fell to the floor, writhing and contorting. Several people nearby pushed away from their chairs and stood, shouting for a doctor, wondering if he was having a seizure, for someone to call 911. Because it is the 21st century, four people just pulled out their phones and started filming.

Mellie knew when the man started to change. The little blonde screamed, "Oh, my god! His face! What's happening to his face?"

The smell of rank meat burning filled the air, and a couple of patrons retched. More of them pushed out of the bar and into the cold November air outside.

The man twisted and screamed, and as his face changed, more people ran from him, including the little blonde. The phone-filmers stayed, even though all of them looked ill. At least some were probably live streaming, and you couldn't run out when something so crazy was happening. Your followers would never forgive you.

It was down to maybe ten or so people, all standing in frozen horror, when the man's contortions finally stopped. He drew himself up to one knee, and one of the people filming said, "I think I'm going to be sick," and promptly followed words with action.

"What?" the man said.

He sounded groggy, like he'd just woken from a long sleep. He stumbled forward, knocking over chairs, until he reached the bar. Like so many of their ilk, there was a long mirror behind the rows of bottles on the back counter.

"What the—" he said, and touched his face, and screamed.

The man's face had melted, stretched, become the visage of the monster under the bed, the demon that lurks just out of sight, the horror that creeps in the woods. Whoever looked at him from now until the day he died would see only their worst nightmare. He'd never be able to hide what he was again.

His eyes darted, found Mellie in the corner.

"What did you do to me? What did you *do* to me?"

Mellie smiled and shifted. Before she disappeared, she whispered, and her whisper floated through the air.

"Just making sure your outsides match your insides."

Then she slipped between the shadows and out into the night. There were four more bars on this street, after all, and she had a lot of work to do.

Jimmy Donaldson's Last Call

Brandon Eldridge

"**I**'m going to slide this across the table to you, Jimmy. I know you're not going to like it, but this is where you're at."

Troy Lemke could barely look at me as he said it. His hand trembled as he slid it across, and I wondered—for some ridiculous reason—how many times he had done this. Maybe not a lot, I assumed, noticing how his hand nervously pushed the paper.

I held it out. The older I got, the worse my eyes were at reading things up close.

To Tenant, James "Jimmy" Donaldson, in possession of the premises located at 1141 South Broadway Street, Farriden, Indiana, 40293. Company name: The Thirsty Pig.

You are hereby notified that the undersigned intends to foreclose under provisions of that certain agreement executed by you on September 26, 2025.

You are hereby further notified that unless you pay the sum of $2 6,491.38 within FIFTEEN business days from receiving this notice, Financial Holdings, LLC, shall take possession of said property.

"Hell, Troy, how am I going to be able to pay that in three weeks?" I asked.

"You're going to have to figure that out, Jimmy."

"But my parents owned this bar for seventeen years—"

"Yeah, and your parents made some terrible financial decisions in that time. Look, I really wish I could help, but unless you come up with the ... what is it?" he asked, taking the paper from me, "Twenty-six grand, you're SOL."

"They'd be rolling over in their graves if they knew what was going on," I said, sighing.

More than anything, I wanted to cry. I wasn't going to give him that satisfaction, that was for damn sure. The last thing I'd do was break down in front of Troy Lemke.

I'd known Troy since high school; we both graduated from Farriden High. Troy was a lot thinner then and a hell of a quarterback, but he was likable enough. He didn't make fun of me the way the other kids did, although I am sure that may have been different behind closed doors.

Oh, it was brutal. Try being a severely overweight kid with diabetes and red, inflamed, itch-until-you-want-to-cry patches of psoriasis that would find new places of your body to invade every week.

When my parents passed away, both dying from massive heart attacks, the rumor around town was that I had dismembered them and eaten their remains. I am sure it started as a joke, but you wouldn't believe the looks I got all over town. Some people *believed* it. That was what hurt worse than anything.

The next day, I opened the bar at the same time I always did: 2 PM. My first customer, an unemployed drunk named Greg, who usually slept down at Harper's Bridge, walked in the door, smelling of body odor and cigarettes.

"Hi, Jimmy," he said, sitting down at the bar. "I heard your fat ass is about to lose the place. Maybe you should have paid the bills instead of eating your parents who *supported* you, by the way!" He roared into a maniacal laughter.

"Not today, Greg," I said, wiping dust from the back counter. "In fact, get out of my bar."

"You can't throw me out."

"I can, and I will, if you don't shut up."

"Just get me a beer, Jimmy," he said.

I opened a bottle, set it down angrily in front of him, and continued to clean the counters. I used to love the smell of lemon and spilled whiskey. Strange, I know. It meant people. It meant laughter, I was making people happy, and during that time I wasn't the butt of their jokes.

Lately, though, the lemon-scented cleaner couldn't cover the smell of the mildew. Or the fact that the ceiling tiles were sagging in the corners. Or that no matter how much I scrubbed, no matter what cream I used, the psoriasis on my elbows and scalp never went away.

And people would notice. It was a ritual to call it out. It wasn't even creative anymore.

"Hey barkeep, snowing in here?" Funny.

"Jesus, Jimmy, do you actually eat the profits from this place?" Good one.

The worst part wasn't the mockery. It was the normalcy of it. How they thought it was okay because I never really pushed back.

I just went on, cleaning glasses and pouring drinks, thinking about how unattainable twenty-six thousand dollars was.

I closed early that night. No one noticed. No one cared. They left drunk and cackling, same as always. I stayed behind, just me and the hum of the cooler in the back and the smell of lemon-scented cleaner.

Twenty-six thousand dollars.

My whole life, measured in debt. My whole life, slipping away.

When I got home, I sat in front of the computer screen for hours, convincing myself this was the only way out. The internet had answers to questions no one should ask.

I read. I learned. I planned.

The next night, I gave them the drinks they ordered—exactly how they liked them. I kept my face blank.

"Hey, Jimmy. Got an extra keg under that shirt?" the man said as I poured his drink.

He wouldn't be laughing later.

No one noticed a thing. Not the extra seconds behind the bar. Not the hint of something different in my eyes.

A group at the front table toasted to something stupid. They laughed at nothing. One of them made another crack about my skin. This time, I smiled. Big and wide.

And then I looked around the room. I watched the hands on the glasses. I saw the liquid disappear from the clear glass down their throats.

I smiled as the confusion began to flicker behind their eyes. One man began coughing violently.

The internet didn't mention how quickly the stuff would work. It was a pleasant surprise.

My face gave way to another big grin, then I poured one for myself. It *almost* tasted like it always did.

Bitter.

Warm.

Final.

Regulars

Robert Essig

In memory of Cheers 'N' Beers
Lakeside, California

All dive bars have their regulars. My local watering hole, Cheers 'N' Beers, was no different. The early afternoon crowd consisted of older gentlemen wetting their collective whistles while reminiscing on old times and catching a ball game. The music on the juke was low and fitting. Old country or classic rock. By nightfall, the old timers grabbed a blue plate special at Mort's on the other end of the strip and headed home to finish the evening with some canned brew while the younger crowd took over. The music shifted to dance hits and modern country and the decibel level increased steadily through the night.

I was no regular at Cheers 'N' Beers but I knew the bartender pretty well, mostly because I would wander in there around the time the old timers were slipping out. I'd have a few drinks after work and chat with Denise while she started her shift. Sometimes I thought there was a connection between us but I didn't want a misjudgment on my part to interfere with our rapport, and thus I never confessed my feelings or detected a strong enough attraction on her side of the equation.

Denise was a failed molecular biologist of all things, a subject she wasn't quick to discuss no matter how many times I tried to shoehorn it into our conversations. It was a part of her past she was ashamed of for reasons I just didn't understand. I always wondered how someone with her smarts ended up tending bar in some rinky-dink shithole like Cheers 'N' Beers. She claimed the tips were good and it was walking distance from her home. Fair enough.

I had a late night at work followed by dinner with a few colleagues and needed to take the edge off before heading home so I dropped in quite a bit later than usual. The place was pretty loud so I found a spot at the end of the bar furthest from the stage where people were singing karaoke. I'd never been into either listening to horrible renditions of burnt out songs or participating, so I figured my time here was limited to one drink if I could even get through that.

"Hey there, Denise," I said with a smile.

She looked at me and gave a wink. "Be right there, Vince." She was pouring vodka into three highball glasses and topping it with cranberry juice. She looked back at me while pouring. "A little late for you, isn't it? Didn't think I'd see you tonight."

Her attention was directed back at the drinks, but her ears were on me. "Had dinner with some people from work." I raised my voice to be heard over the din. "You know how that is. Conversation always goes right back to fucking work."

Finished making the drinks, Denise said, "Enjoy," as she slid them across the bar with a smile. The contempt in her eyes did not match the smile.

The three girls who took said drinks were pretty sloppy as it was, with their eyes glossy and sinister grins on their lips like they were in on some evil prank. I could spot the type a mile away. Regulars. Bar flies. They buzzed around the place like they owned it. They were loud and proud, especially when their vodka-cranberries kicked in. They were the reason I never came to Cheers 'N' Beers this late.

"I hope it's strong," one of them said. She slurred 'it's strong' into one word connected with several S's. Her make up was caked on like spackle and cracking at the curves of her cheeks. Too much eyeliner gave her a raccoon appearance that she was damn proud of.

"I always make 'em strong for you," Denise said, smiling though I could tell it was as fake as the plants in a Denny's.

The girls walked away from the bar, drinks in hand. One of them said, loudly, "Who's singing next, bitches!"

I sighed.

"Not my crowd," I said as Denise approached me holding the vodka bottle. "Maybe you should make me one of whatever it is they're having just so I can fit in." I offered a smile that barely hid the weariness of my evening. Things were changing at work again, as they seemed to do every year or so. Changes implemented to justify some unnecessary position. Fixing things that don't need fixing. Exhausting stuff.

Denise gave me a strange look I was too tired to decipher and then the bottle slipped from her grasp and shattered on the floor causing the patrons in our vicinity to all turn and share a mix of laughter, rude comments, and flimsy offers to help that were thinly veiled attempts by drunk frat boys to get close to Denise.

"Oh shit, I'm sorry," I said as if it was somehow my fault.

She shook her head. "It happens. How about your usual?"

I hesitated. "Maybe I should go. It's a little stuffy in here and I'm pretty fried." I shrugged. "It's not my scene, you know?"

Denise's eyes shifted away from me to the small stage where people sang karaoke.

"No, stick around for one drink." She winked. "You'll regret it if you don't."

I opened my mouth to protest but the look in her eyes spoke to me on a deeper level. I'd never seen anything quite like it. There was passion there. Intrigue. She didn't exactly hate tending bar, but it didn't bring her great enjoyment either. It was a means to live. Her passion was molecular biology. From what she'd told me on those slow evenings when we talked and I sipped a few drinks, she knew her shit. I mean, it wasn't like I knew a damn thing about molecular biology, but she could talk about the subject ad nauseum and it always made her smile. Even though I could hardly follow her scientific mind, I appreciated listening to her pontificate on anything that brought her such pleasure. But I knew better than to ask why she hadn't made molecular biology her career.

"Just one," I said, and I saw, as she made a simple Jack and ginger ale, that the girls who had just been served were taking the stage, strong-arming another young lady at the very moment her song finished. It was an aggressive act that made me cringe. They thought they were hot shots in this tiny microcosm of the world where their beer goggles had a strong prescription that made stars out of mere dust motes. This was the one place in their shitty little lives where they had some modicum of control, and like so many in a position of power, they took complete advantage of it by making an ass of themselves night after drunken night.

I took the drink from Denise. "Thank you."

"On the house," she said.

"Oh, you know I'm good for it—"

"Enjoy the show."

What the hell does that mean?

She stood back, her attention zeroed in on the three girls upon the stage. I'd never been to Cheers 'N' Beers this late before. I loathed a bustling bar scene. Really, the only reason I frequented this bar as much as I did was to talk with Denise. I could just as easily have a drink or two at home to let off some steam. I'd heard, on those evenings when we talked and she served drinks to the lingering old timers who lamented, in equal measures, their wives and the loneliness of being widowers, that the worst thing about working at a bar were the regulars. Not me, she said, or even the retirees shooting the shit all day.

It was the night crowd regulars she loathed.

The three sloppy chicks on stage bitched at the karaoke guy about getting the song right. "Don't fuck it up again, Carl," one of them snarled. Carl smiled with his mouth but glared with his eyes. He knew what to expect from these bar hogs. Anyone who'd spent more than two or three nights here did. They dominated. They were loud. And you knew that this was *their* dive damn it!

One of them was wavering, another giggling, and their bitchy leader talking shit into the mic, pointing at someone in the crowd. Maybe an ex, or someone she took home and fucked one night. Maybe a rival barfly who seemed like a proper threat. Who knows?

The song started. The music was a generic rendition, but the place screamed and hollered, as they were apt to do night after ear-bleeding night when this tune was played, sometimes two or three times.

I glanced at Denise, and she shook her head but never wavered from her gaze upon the stage, the slightest hint of a smile on her lips. This confounded me about as much as her dropping that bottle, for she had been here so many nights seeing the same tired play and yet, on this night, she was enthralled for some reason, which caused me to sip my drink and watch too, as if clued in on something exclusive that I had to be a part of.

It was halfway into a slaughtering of some poppy country hit when one of the girls twitched so violently I thought she was having a seizure on stage. The loud one who'd been hogging the mic laughed and pointed. That's when the twitching girl's back opened up as something thrust through her skin, ripping her shirt. Bloody wings emerged like a butterfly from a human chrysalis. She screamed so loud it seemed as if her larynx would explode. That's when her eyes grew wide, bulging from her face and popping from her skull, trailed by bloody optic nerves and lost somewhere in the shocked crowd of drunkards. Her ocular cavities cracked and split as new eyes took the place of her human ones. These new eyes were rather large and coated in blood but, in some strange way, familiar.

The girl with the mic dropped it and said, "Jesus fucking Christ, Gina! What the fuck is up with you?" As if Gina was making her grand transformation on purpose to disrupt karaoke.

That's when the other girls started twitching and screaming as their bodies pulsated. Flesh split as pressure increased within their bodies, blood seeping from the wounds, dripping off their appendages and pooling around them onto the battered and creaky stage. Wings burst from ripped backs, flesh flayed off their human faces, revealing something alien beneath, but oddly familiar with large, bulbous eyes sprouting on the sides of their heads.

They writhed on the stage with shreds of clothing and flesh dangling from their slick new bodies. They buzzed and flapped their soiled wings. Proboscises reached from their insect heads like party favors as they rubbed their new hands together as if trying to get the remnants of blood and muscle tissue from the thousands of coarse black hairs.

I couldn't believe what I was seeing. The crowd screamed and rushed for the door. The faint chorus from the shitty karaoke rendition of a tired hit serenaded. I just sat there on my bar stool and watched from a good distance. When I pivoted to see Denise, she was absentmindedly wiping a glass with a dirty rag and staring in awe. The grin told me something I'd rather not consider, and the way she nodded confirmed my suspicions.

Ladies Night

Ruthann Jagge

J oel Tanner dropped the beer glass he was polishing when he saw her stepping out of the battered sports utility rideshare out front. Trying to see better through the smudges on the windows, it took him three seconds to realize that the girl he dreamed of was about to enter his bar. It was a first, but he was ready for it. His involuntary low whistle drew attention from a couple of regulars down at the other end, and they turned in unison as her scent filled the room. *Will you look at her? Damn.*

Ella Martel's clicking heels on the worn wooden floor signaled her annoyance. Her thumbs flew over the screen of her phone, making the inconvenient situation clear. Her light brown hair bounced with each stomp, but her tight black skirt made a full-on rage walk impossible. Not even her harsh frown could diminish how pretty she was, and Joel, pretending to sweep up shards of broken glass, prayed to whatever god watched over barkeeps that she would stick around.

Tossing off her tailored jacket, she slid one long leg over the cracked leather barstool like a pro and glared into Joel's kind brown eyes. Her cool green ones shot out multi-colored sparks. Or so he thought. No words came to him, only an involuntary trickle of saliva betrayed his shock.

"Can I get you something, Miss? I have a decent selection of imported and domestic on tap if you want a cold one. And a few bottles of hard stuff that's not too bad. What's your pleasure?" Hoping to charm a smile from the sophisticated stranger, Joel winked, a friendly gesture, not suggestive.

"Bourbon. Best you've got. Three cubes." Flipping back her hair, Ella resumed tapping on the small screen, making it clear she wasn't in the mood for conversation. A few more locals entered after six o'clock. The Come Back Inn, a decent establishment miles from town, offered reasonably priced drinks, weekend live music, and excellent pool tables.

"First one's on the house. I'm Joel Tanner. J.T. unless you owe me money, and this is my place. What did you say your name was?" Joel flushed at his cliché' attempt to learn more about the stunning female as he set a napkin and glass of whiskey before her. "If you're hungry, Ginny knows her way around a burger." Joel nods to the older woman in a hairnet, staring through the kitchen opening and making obscene gestures at him. "Music starts at nine, and I expect a full house." he was stirring the ice with one manicured finger while clicking away with her other hand. She stopped, and then Ella tossed back the drink in one gulp, pushing the empty glass towards Joel.

"Another." A quick flash of her green gems at him. Blinking approval, Joel grabbed the bottle and poured a generous refill, trying not to stare at her flawless face or the curves under her white silk blouse. *Why am I so damn nervous? Get a grip.*

"This one's on me, Buddy." The slight man in a plaid shirt wearing a WWII cap pointed at the bottle and winked at Ella. "My pleasure." She nodded in his direction, acknowledging the gift. Joel smirked. *Ol' Sammy's got better skills with the ladies than I do.*

"He's harmless. The poor guy lost his wife last year; he visits daily for drinks and conversation. 'Gotta' love the ones who never quit trying."

"He's not bothering me. Your hovering is." Polishing off the second drink, Ella sighs. "I'm stuck here for the night, and the only way I can cope until my car's fixed is if I'm numb."

"Did you break down? Are you okay? I'm guessing Wes has your car. He's the only mechanic in town. Do you need me to call him? Do you have a place to stay?" Joel's rapid-fire but genuine concerns amuse Ella, and she looks at him for the first time. Joel melts. He hasn't felt this way since high school when Sara Mosely sat next to him in homeroom. *Stay calm. Don't be a dumbass!*

"I'm fine. I hit a pothole, and my car protested. A guy in a red truck passed by, and yes, his name was Wes. He offered a tow, and his sister runs a B&B. I'm set for bed but missing a critical meeting. Apologies if I'm not in the mood."

"You'll be fine. Marnie Lowe runs a nice place. Sorry about the meeting, but it's Friday night, and I'm guessing not much will happen until Monday. I hope you stick around."

"Sitting under granny's quilt sipping tea while scrolling isn't my style. I'm having trouble connecting with my colleagues; cell service here is awful." Joel's head nods up and down like a goofy jack-in-the-box. But at least she's responsive. "So, keep them coming, and tell Ginny I'm all about that burger." Ella slides a bill from her shoe, crumples it into a perfect little ball, and then tosses it over to the cook, who grab-catches it mid-air with a childish whoop.

"I've got you. How would you like it?" *I'm giving this my best shot. Girls like her are rare, and I deserve some fun.*

"Burn it until she screams, then flip her once for good measure." Ginny grins, giving Ella a double thumbs up. The smell of sizzling beef pervades the bar. After work, the boys arrive, hoping to snag Happy Hour prices or a barstool before the music starts. The Come Back has tables lining the walls, surrounding a small dancefloor. As the night goes on, the area becomes gossip for the next week, and the evening's entertainment and alcohol make outstanding dancers out of the clumsiest patrons.

"Don't be stingy, Joel." Ella's on her third, with no signs of a slowdown. Joel focuses for the first time since the beauty arrived. She can hold her liquor, but there is something odd about tapping her long pink nails on the bar as if signaling in code. He places a hand on top of hers, intending to calm her.

"Don't be nervous. You're among friends, and I'll make sure you're comfortable and safe." With a single movement, the young woman flips his wrist over onto the bar, and the pain causes Joel to wince.

"Don't touch me." Ella's eyes narrow to menacing green slits. "You're a nice guy, but we aren't friends. I'm here because there's no better option. So, thanks, but I'm fine. It's them you need to worry about." Ella tilts her head to one side. Ten overdressed and giggling women are gathering at a table near the door.

"Let's get this party started! Five pitchers of margaritas and ten shots!" A short blonde girl wearing a tight red dress and a satin "Bridesmaid" sash snapped her fingers and waved a credit card. "It's Ladies' Night!"

"All good, Mary Lynne." Joel shakes his head. He's not a fan of bachelorette parties, but they're a business necessity. "Let me call for backup, and we'll take care of you. Devin's on his way in." Three girls pretend to faint while Mary Lynne fans them, slapping their cheeks. They howl with laughter. The ladies all know Dev.

Ella leans in closer. Joel flushes red, almost messing up his pour into the row of low glasses. She holds his gaze until Ginny slides the sizzling burger before her. Hand-cut fries and a sliced pickle complete the meal. "This looks fantastic, thank you, Ginny." Ella pats her arm. The older woman wipes her hands on her apron, tucks a stray into her hairnet, and prays to all the saints, wishing she could live a single day in Ella's body. She goes back behind the partition separating the kitchen from the bar.

"Welcome, Miss." Ginny mumbles. She seldom speaks, and Joel warms at Ella's kindness.

"She's had it tough: comes from a bad family, abusive husband, criminals for kids, and nothing but misery. I depend on her, but I hate seeing her struggle. She's got nobody, so I try to look after her." Joel's voice is low. He loads the drinks onto a round tray and heads over to the table while Ella wolfs down the burger in several quick bites. She's tapping on the bar again when he returns, but he doesn't dare ask why.

The place is filling up, but when a tall guy with wavy brown hair wearing black jeans and a faded denim shirt that's seen better days strolled in, every female sat up straighter, brushing imaginary crumbs from their cleavages. Devin Tanner had that effect on women. Removing his mirrored sunglasses, he surveyed the room like an apex predator until his eyes locked on Ella.

"Hey, bro." With a one-handed swoop, Dev popped over the bar like a stuntman, punching his younger brother on the shoulder. He fixates on Ella, who has stopped tapping. She's enjoying her bourbon while surveying the room. Dev flipped the green John Deere ball cap he wore backward, his blue eyes sparkling with mischief.

"Hello, Beautiful. I'm Dev." Ignoring him, Ella pointed at Joel.

"Send another round over to the party. I'll join them." Dev shook his head. He wasn't used to striking out.

"Thanks for coming in, Dev. Looks like a full house, and the Black Swans are playing. You know they draw a crowd." Joel was glad to see him; they didn't hang out as much since he bought the bar. Dev attracted trouble and thrived on it, but it felt good to have him close tonight. Joel looked up to his older brother even though Dev always stole the show and got the girl.

"No problem. Do you know anything about the new girl?" Joel explained how Ella came into their orbit as he poured, watching to ensure the band didn't blow a fuse while testing equipment in the old building. The all-female classic rock group deserved their following, and lively women now filled most of the seats. Despite his brother's reputation, Joel appreciated that his place was a safe zone for them. A group of young men entered, scrambling back to the pool tables without acknowledging the girls. Some nights are for the guys, with no drama.

"I got 'em." Dev picked up the tray of shots and sauntered over to the loudest table, where more women now surrounded Ella. "Hope these go down easy, ladies."

"Get lost, Dev," Mary Lynne said. She knew the devil all too well, and tonight, he wore a denim shirt.

A petite redhead tipped over in her chair, covering her mouth with her hand to stifle a scream. She pointed at the floor. A large brown scorpion crawled over the toe of Dev's boot. Without hesitation, Ella pinched the offending beast dead between two fingers, then plopped it into her shot of tequila. Resourceful girls improvise when worms are scarce, and when Ella threw back the shot, it was Dev's cue to leave. *I'm not taking a chance with this one. She's too much for my taste!*

The band started playing, and when the first notes of a popular song sounded, ladies of all ages, shapes, and styles filled the dance floor. Joel, Dev, and the other guys watched with amusement, delighted at their antics.

"Kind of odd. Outnumber us for once, but who's complaining? Dev was in heaven. Joel noticed Ella remained seated and was again doing her fingernail tap-dance on the plastic tabletop.

"I don't think your Miss Thing enjoys our social scene. She's got a nervous twitch." Dev wipes down a bottle, then sets it back in the well. "There's a lot of crazy out there dancing, and trust me, I've had my share of it, but something tells me she'd be the one to beat! I'd stay clear of her, brother." He smacks Joel on the back, who nods in agreement, and then pours two more beers for the guys down at the end. *It's easy for him to say. Dev gets whatever and whoever he wants.*

More women enter through the door, causing the antique bell to ring nonstop. The mix of perfume, booze, and girl sweat filling the bar was intoxicating. Magnetic. Feral.

"Damn. Did I die and go to heaven? If I'm dreaming, don't wake me up!" Dev cuts through the gyrating female dancers, cornering three curvy brunettes, known as the "Sassy Sisters" and stars, grinding against one until all three are in his arms, whirling and dipping to the beat. A girl at Ella's table twists a braid into her hair, and another strokes lotion from a small tube into her hands. Joel watches. *Amazing. With enough drinks, chicks can transform any place into a spa day.* The music is louder, the voices shriller, and he's feeling the stab of a headache closing in. Women come and go at the table when Ella Martel holds court like a crowned queen, whispering and giggling with her. Some copy her tapping motions mimicking each other with an odd crescendo.

Glancing around, Joel's attention lands on Dev. He has his arms wrapped around a tall, willowy blonde wearing a skimpy white tank top. His head rests on her shoulder, the ball cap pushed to one side. She's nuzzling his neck. For a fleeting moment, his brother's happiness mattered. Owning a bar is a full-time job. There's no time for anything else. *I'm fine with casual one-night stands but I want to be with all the women. I want to be like Dev and have them all for myself! What I wouldn't give, but it's only a dream because he'd win every time.* Joel eventually gave up trying to have a serious relationship because every girl he cared for switched her interest to his brother. He tried not to hate his charismatic sibling, but he did. Life was too easy for Dev Tanner.

Joel spots Ella dancing in the center of the crowded space. Her back is to him, but her hips in the snug skirt are unmistakable. She dips and sways, resting her hands on her partner's shoulders. But as the beat intensifies, Ella twirls with Ginny in her arms; her hairnet and apron are gone, and the stout woman doesn't miss a beat. When the song ends, Ella guides Ginny back to her table, where the chatter and laughter continue. Joel slid down the partition, declaring the kitchen closed. By now, the regulars are gone, leaving only the rest of the males, still hoping to get lucky. And Dev, who's chatting with the blonde. Dozens of giddy females aren't ready to call it a night; they're all still drinking, dancing, and happy tapping, fingernails clicking while they rest between songs. Turning around, he's startled by Ella standing close to him.

"Nice thing you did for Ginny. Appreciate it." He flusters. She smells like a carnival midway: sweet, sticky, dusty, salty, and unpredictable. Dangerous. Rising on her bare toes, Ella Martel kisses Joel Tanner's cheek.

"Your spot isn't what I had in mind, but when car trouble kept me from meeting with the Council to inform them of the location for our new hive, serendipity took over, and here we are, Joel. I secretly informed my sisters that the Come Back Inn, though quaint, would suffice, and they came. We'll need to feed, but after that, only a single male will be necessary for ... mating purposes. Look on the bright side: you enjoy your bar a little longer. To the point of exhaustion, we will care for and maybe even love you. Downside? We will relentlessly pursue our goal until the species' future is secure, which could take a long time. Our breed doesn't have a human lifecycle, but it's better than the alternative, right? The alternative is your immediate and unpleasant demise."

Joel blinks, trying hard to understand. Ella runs a finger down Joel's cheek, then pops it into his mouth. She's moving it in and out, forcing him to suck on it. *She tastes like honey.* Ella moves her hands. He's oblivious to anything but how this strange woman's fantastic body feels tight against his, and when the bar explodes with screams and unhinged terror over the screeching guitars, Joel Tanner couldn't care less. He's immersed in Ella, tearing at her clothing, pulling her hair, and hoping like hell it's not a dream because it feels so fucking good. Sex with her is like drowning in a vat of hot syrup. When he finishes, Ella opens her bruised lips, sinking her needle-sharp black proboscis into his neck. His blood spurts, mixing with the rest of the red spray painting the walls, and once she's satisfied, it retracts back behind the rows of flawless white teeth.

"Just a taste, lover. You'll do nicely." Joel's senses return. The condition of his bar is unspeakable. Pools of blood cover the floor where several women still dance, sliding and pivoting, and the bodies of the unfortunate males caught in the hive's gathering are limp, empty husks, sucked dry of their delicious juices. *Dev. Where's Dev?*

Ginny's wearing Dev's John Deere cap, swaying solo on the dance floor with her arms wrapped around herself. Her red-stained teeth glow like an obscene holiday ornament below. Dev's body sprawls on a chair at the "Ladies Night" table, where a young girl wearing a flowered sundress is twisting his matted hair into tiny braids. Joel tries to wrestle away from Ella and get to his brother, but she's holding his arms behind his back in a vice grip.

Her strength is inhuman. Joel fights against a wave of desperation and madness, kicking out hard.

"Stop, or I'll break your limbs. Ginny's one of us now; we'll take good care of her. She'll experience what genuine happiness is, and Joel? She suggested I stay. The Black Swans, too. Joel glances at the girls in the band, and Amy, the drummer, twirls a stick in the air and then points it at him with a smile. You should lie down in the back. Get some rest. We'll clean up the mess and have everything looking fresh by morning. Word will spread about the terrible case of food poisoning that took out the others, but we've already got the details covered with our sisters at the hospital and in law enforcement. Under the circumstances, there will be no investigation, and I am confident people will respect a "Closed for Renovations" sign. Any future hours of operation will be contingent on our fertility cycles and, shall we say, *needs?*"

Ella runs her hands over Joel's backside, and he shivers in disgust and excitement. "I can't be greedy. You'll need to service us all in rotation, so hang onto your stamina." She pours two generous shots, forcing one into his clenched fist. Joel's trying not to vomit. His head spins with the gore, sour perfume, and booze in the air.

"Celebrate with me. Isn't this what you wanted? To be surrounded and loved by women all the time? Well, darling, your dream is about to come true. Until it becomes your worst nightmare, but I'll suggest they go easy on you. At first." Women surround them, giggling and pushing in close. They claw at his body, tapping and touching him. They reek of desperation and death.

Joel Tanner, the once proud owner of The Come Back Inn, clicks his glass to Ella's, forcing the bourbon down. Then he guzzles the burning liquor straight from the bottle until it's empty.

Epilogue:

Folks in Smithville look the other way when they pass by what used to be Joel Tanner's popular bar on the outskirts of town, The Come Back Inn. No one knows the actual story or isn't telling if they do. Shortly after many people died one night from food poisoning, eating Ginny Antler's tainted Honey Dew burgers, people began hearing strange noises coming from the boarded-up building. Women's voices. Screams. Laughter. Low-thumping music like in a bad porn movie and terrible wailing and crying. The town condemned the building when sticky yellow fluids seeped through the foundation, staining the concrete and surrounding dirt.

And the smell was another story. Rot and decay filled the air for miles.

The church ladies buried handsome Dev Tanner on Hillman Road. Several bring flowers to the site weekly. There's been only one sighting of his younger brother, Joel, in years. A kid delivering newspapers early one morning claims he saw the bar owner through a crack in the window. Skinny, filthy, and naked on his knees, his back covered in bruises and red scratch marks, caused by sharp fingernails. Many women surrounded him, also nude, dancing around him in a circle, tapping, stroking, and touching him non-stop. Joel Tanner was sobbing and begging for mercy.

The Fifty Yard Fox

DE McCluskey

T he bar was dark, busy, and noisy. The music was so loud, he couldn't hear himself think, and that's what he'd come here to do, to think. It sounded to James like nothing other than tribal drums banging insistently on and on. He couldn't tell when one song ended and the next one began.

It was giving him a thumping headache.

It wasn't just the music annoying him, the smoke was everywhere too. Dry Ice, they called it. It was hurting his throat and drying out his nose. He was dying to pick it, as he could feel a build-up up there, but he was far too self-conscious to do anything about it.

'Excuse me,' he shouted across the bar to the young man standing behind it who was cleaning a glass with an apron tied around his waist.

The barman ignored him.

'Excuse me,' he shouted again. 'Can I get a drink please?'

The barman looked up from his cleaning and nodded. 'What's it gonna be?' he asked, sounding bored.

'Spiced rum and ginger please.'

'Double?' he asked, turning away and plucking a large bottle from the shelf.

'Why not? It's not like I've got anywhere to be,' James replied, leaving the conversation open for the barman to ask him a question.

He didn't.

He poured the drink into the glass and opened a bottle of ginger beer from the fridge behind him. 'You want ice?' he asked, with his back to him.

'No thanks. Just as it is.'

He handed him the drink and James reached out to grab it. As he looked at the white band on his ring finger. For some reason it glowed brighter than any of his other fingers as if it were vying for his attention. His wry smile lingered as he stared at it.

'Did you hear me?' the barman said, holding his hand out towards him.

'Eh?'

'I said five pounds fifty, mate.'

'Oh, right, yeah. Here you go.' He delved his hands into his pocket and pulled out his wallet. As he did, something else came out with it. The small band of gold chinked as it hit the bar and rolled before falling on its side.

The barman's eyes followed its progress. A wry smile now filled his face as he regarded James. He hadn't noticed this and was taking his first, long swallow of his fresh drink.

'You dropped something there, buddy,' he said. His voice had more than a hint of humour to it.

James looked at him, his eyes hooded quizzically. 'What?' he shouted over the pulsating beat of the next, or maybe still the same song, he couldn't tell.

'I said you dropped something there,' the barman shouted back, pointing to the golden band lying on the bar.

James' eyes followed the barman's gesture. 'Oh, shit,' he said, reaching out and grabbing the wedding ring. 'I'd be in some serious trouble if I got home without this.' He laughed as he spoke, but the barman had seen more than his fair share of lonely men who'd removed their sacred symbols before walking into this den of iniquity.

'You want to be more careful,' he said, his voice telling the man that he was already bored of this conversation. He flashed a smile and walked off to serve someone else.

James looked at the ring, and then he looked around the club. *What the hell am I doing here?* he thought with a shake of his head. He went to put the ring back on his third finger, left hand, but as he did, a shrill, but not annoying laugh came from somewhere behind him. It was unmistakably female. He turned to see where it had come from, and what he saw standing behind him in the doorway to the bar made him rethink almost every life choice he'd ever made, with the exception of coming here tonight.

She was gorgeous. She was maybe the same age as him, maybe younger. She was in fantastic shape, and James couldn't help but allow his eyes to crawl up and down her curvaceous body. He knew he was being misogynistic and was apparently, in this day and age, *invading her personal space as a woman*, but he couldn't help it. She was tall. He liked them tall. She was brunette. He liked them brunette. She was alive. He definitely liked them alive. He smiled at this thought as his gaze passed from her toned legs wrapped tightly into her short skirt then to her breasts. She was obviously not wearing a bra, and it didn't look like she was having any problems with gravity. He then looked at her face. He blushed as he noticed her looking back at him. He cringed, waiting for her disgusted look at catching him spying into the toy-shop window, or maybe he would get the 'What are you looking at, perv?' remark he knew men of his age were want to get when ogling beautiful ladies.

But there was none of that. All he got for his troubles was a returned smile.

James's eyes narrowed as he saw a twinkle in her eye. Nothing like this had ever happened to him before. In a flash, the ring was gripped in his hand where it dug into his flesh.

He swigged the rest of the drink in one and signalled to the barman to pour him another.

He did.

James wasn't used to this. Even though he had been to this bar on at least four occasions before, it was not something he did lightly. It was just so unhappy at home. He'd turned forty-six two months earlier, and he could only ever remember being happy, truly happy, for maybe fifteen of those years.

He met *her* when he was seventeen years old, and they'd been together ever since.

They were married when he was twenty-two, and the four children came swiftly after that. Far too swiftly for his liking. He couldn't remember having any fun with his wife before life took over them. They'd been on a couple of holidays in Spain, mostly spent with her lying in the sun all day, drinking, and the nearest thing to any fun they'd have was when he had to smear the after-sun over her body when she'd caught too many rays.

Then the drinking started.

She would come home from work, tired and angry. He knew that was his cue to get out of the way. From the refuge of his man cave, where his computer and video games console were, he would hear the chink of the wine glass, the opening and slamming of drawers, followed by the glugging of the wine pouring into the glass.

He'd sit there, his adrenaline pumping, and anger rising in his throat. He knew he'd be getting sex tonight, but it would be rough, drunk, stinking sex, the kind he'd come to hate.

She'd become argumentative too. She would snap at the kids, then take a swipe at him for no reason other than the fact they were in the same room. She'd let herself go too. The fat hanging from her bingo-wings turned his stomach, and her arse had gotten so large that she'd started buying elasticated trousers. Whenever they were invited to parties, which was very rare, she'd complain all night about how fat she'd gotten, while scoffing two or three large plates of buffet food and drinking up half of the bar's wine collection.

Their relationship was in tatters, their life was in tatters, and if it wasn't for the children, he'd have left a long time ago.

So, that's why he found himself here, in this bar. A bar he knew he had no business being in. It was too young, too trendy, and too expensive for him; but he needed the escape.

... And by the look of the cheeky smile from the stunning woman in the doorway, he was staying. He looked at his wedding ring in his hand. The gold was almost glowing in the neon lights. He smiled and put the ring into the small pocket of his jeans, the one no-one ever used, so there was less chance of him dropping it again.

'Excuse me,' he shouted to the barman again, waving his hand to capture his attention, as he was further down the bar, serving other people. 'Can I get another spiced rum and ginger please?'

The barman tipped his head to acknowledge the request and commenced to pour the drink. With his fresh refreshment firmly in hand, he turned back towards the bar, and the mass of writhing people inside it. They were gyrating and moving to the pulsing rhythm of the music. His eyes were scanning the room for, what he thought was, the most gorgeous woman here. All the faces were young, happy, sweating, but none of them were who he was looking for. He stepped away from the bar, deeper into the throng of youngsters. He'd never felt more out of place in his entire life, but right now he didn't care. He knew what he wanted, and he knew she was in here somewhere.

The club wasn't that big, but there were many nooks and crannies where people might hide themselves away and conduct whatever business they were compelled to conduct in the relative privacy of the smoke and darkness.

However, no matter how hard he looked, he couldn't see her face anywhere, or her legs for that matter.

He took another swig of his drink, ready to make his way back to his stool, when he heard the shrill laugh again. Instantly, his heart began thrashing in-time with the pulsating music, and the palms of his hands sheened over with sweat. His eyes followed the laugh, and sure enough, there were the legs he'd seen before, stretched out at a booth. They were lovely, long, and muscular. He liked that in a woman. His eyes again travelled up her legs to her body and finally to her face. She was as gorgeous as the first time he'd seen her, with her long dark hair and bright red lips.

He gripped his drink tighter and began to make his way over. He didn't have a clue what he was going to say when he got there, but he felt compelled to go anyway.

As he got closer, he realised why she was laughing so loudly. Opposite her in the corner booth was the most handsome young man he'd ever seen.

James was far from gay, but this youth was an Adonis among men. His chiselled jawline was both rugged, with stubble, but smooth in profile. His jet-black hair was thick and long, and his frame made him look like he'd spent many a long session in an expensive gym.

James exhaled a long, mournful sigh from his nose, and his shoulders sank. He averted his eyes from this beautiful couple, took another swig of his drink, and moved away. As he did she caught his eye. A smile broke on her lips, and her deep dark eyes lingered on him for longer than would have been deemed normal. James' heart was thrashing again. She nodded at him in acknowledgement, and he thought he saw a small wink sent his way.

He swallowed hard, before turning away, making his way back to his stool at the bar.

The barman approached him with a smile on his face. 'What's up with you?' he asked friendly, more friendly than he'd been all night.

'Mate, I think I've just fallen in love,' he replied without even thinking who he was talking to.

'With your wife? The woman who gave you the ring from before?' the barman replied, with a condescending tone to his voice. James didn't notice it; he was far too busy thinking about those legs, and that wink.

'You want another drink?'

He looked at his empty glass and nodded.

'Same again?'

He nodded again, although this time his lips were tight, and he sighed through his nose again. 'Yeah man, same again.' A melancholy descended over him as he thought about the handsome young man sitting with the woman of his dreams, making her laugh.

The drink came, and he gripped, no longer knowing why he was still here at this bar. *This isn't the life for the likes of me,* he thought, sipping the amber liquid in the tall glass.

A young man bumped into him as he leaned over the bar. 'Oh, sorry mate,' he said. 'Mal,... Mal,' he shouted, trying to get the barman's attention. 'Here you go man,' he shouted waving a small slip of paper towards him. The barman grinned and took the paper. He opened it up and read it, his smile grew even larger. He looked at James whose head was down, concentrating on his drink, before he walked off towards the back of the bar.

James' glass was almost empty again, as was his spirit, and what was left of his dignity. He picked it up, drained it, crunching the last few remaining ice cubes between his teeth, and stood. He stretched, realising he was a little drunk. He tapped the bar as if to say *goodbye* before turning to leave.

'Excuse me!'

James heard the shout but ignored it; he didn't think it was aimed at him. He continued walking towards the exit.

'Excuse me, wedding ring guy!'

This time he knew it was for him. He turned back to the bar and saw the barman standing, holding a tray, grinning at him. 'This is for you.'

'For me?' James cocked his head in confusion. He looked at the contents on the tray and shook his head. 'I don't drink Champaign, mate, specially not expensive stuff like that. Sorry, I think you got the wrong fella.'

'I don't think so. It says here to give this to the man at the bar with the spiced rum. You're the only one who's been drinking that all night. This is for you, with this note.'

James' curiosity piqued, and he made his way back to the bar. 'Who's the note from?' he asked, hoping beyond hope it was from the woman with the legs. The barman shrugged, handed him the note, and put the tray with the bottle of expensive Champaign, and two glasses, on the counter. At that point, he lost interest as someone else was vying for his attention further up the bar.

James gave the room another scan, looking for the lovely, long legs, but couldn't see them anywhere. He opened the folded piece of paper in his hands and looked at it.

Hi.

Sorry I don't know your name, but I saw you at the bar earlier, and then at my table not long ago.

I saw you looking. I liked the mischievousness of that look.

I've never done this before, and I feel so brazen, but please accept my little gift to you. My nephew will be leaving soon, and I'll be alone. I don't like being in places like this on my own, so why don't you bring that bottle I sent you outside. Meet me by the exit in the parking lot.

I'm sure we can have some fun!

Legs Eleven!!

James' hands were shaking. He looked into the smoky room, scanning again for the lady who'd called herself Legs Eleven. *A fitting name,* he thought, folding the paper and putting it into his pocket. As he did, he noticed the tall, ruggedly handsome man she'd been with walking towards the exit. Suddenly, leaving the bar didn't seem in James' best interests.

He sat back down and re-read the message. He was not certain that it was for him. He waved the piece of paper at the barman, trying to get his attention, but several new customers had entered, and he was more than busy down the other end.

He looked at the bottle before him, marvelling at the drips of condensation racing down its neck. He'd heard of the brand name before, but had never tasted it, mostly due to the excessive price tag the label brought with it. Once again, he thought the drink probably wasn't for him, and there'd been a mix up. *Can I risk that though?* He thought. *What if it is for me?* He didn't know if he should take that gamble.

While he was pondering on this quandary, he saw her. All thoughts of not going out to the parking lot to meet her exited from his head. She was a pure vision. The way her hips swung as she glided through the smoke. The way her breasts, obviously not contained beneath her thin top, swayed with every step. The way her nipples rubbed against the fabric of her top.

What swayed it for him was the smile, and the tell-tale wink.

He turned to see if it was the barman she was winking at, but there was no-one behind him. The gestures *had* been for him.

He couldn't believe that this was happening.

At the closest point she got to him, she held out her hand, all her fingers spread wide, as if to indicate the number five; then, she pointed to the exit.

He looked at the indicated door, and then back to her, nodding excitedly like a child being informed that if he was good, he would get a great reward. He *was* going to be good, *very fucking good*, he thought.

She disappeared through the door, and he honestly didn't know what to do with himself. He looked at his watch and was horrified to see only ten seconds had passed between her leaving and right now. *How am I going to survive five minutes?*

'Are you going to open that, buddy?' a voice from behind him asked, and he turned, surprised to see the barman standing behind him, pointing to the bottle.

'Erm, no. No, I think I'm going to take it with me, if that's OK.'

'Fine by me,' the barman pulled a *I don't care what you do* kind of face. 'Can I get you another drink? Another ... erm, spiced rum and ginger, wasn't it?'

'No mate, I'm good to go here I think. Thanks.'

The barman pulled another *not bothered* face and moved on.

James looked at his watch. Three minutes had passed since she'd left. He thought that was long enough. He needed to get out of here and into that parking lot as soon as he could. He picked up the bottle, ignoring the glasses, and made his way towards the exit.

As he left the barman watched him go. He shook his head and smiled before someone else caught his attention, and he went over to ask what they wanted to drink.

Outside, the night was still warm, but then it had been a hot day. Despite the balmy breeze, James was shaking like a leaf. The adrenaline surging through his body was causing this quake. He stood beneath the single streetlamp in the almost deserted parking lot. He was holding the bottle of expensive sparkling wine in one hand as he checked his watch. It had been six and a half minutes since *Legs Eleven* had left the club.

There was no sign of her. Disappointment and disillusionment were creeping into his psyche. He looked at the bottle, and everything it might have signified for his life, and sighed.

Once more he looked around.

There was no one around.

'Well, at least I got a free bottle of booze.' He spoke these words aloud, into the night and everything it encompassed around him. He shrugged and began to make his way towards the main road, to see if could flag a taxi, or at least get a mobile signal to call one. That was when he heard the roar of an engine.

It sounded loud and expensive.

He looked back towards where he'd been standing to see an expensive looking, red sports car idling beneath his street lamp. As he watched, the window wound down in one smooth motion, and *she* was behind the wheel, looking at him, smiling.

He'd heard of the notion of someone's heart leaping but didn't think he'd ever experienced it before, not even when his kids were born. Right now, he could have sworn his most vital organ had leaped, for the very first time, and he rather enjoyed the feeling.

'Is that a bottle of Champaign you have there or are you just glad to see me?' she called, her voice was deep, throaty, and very sexy. Exactly how he'd imagined it would be.

He looked at the bottle of wine and laughed.

'Why don't you get in? We can go somewhere a little more...' She looked around the parking lot, and then back to him. As her eyes settled on him, he felt her stare smouldering into him. '... private?' she finished. There was a purring vibration to her voice that he liked very much. 'It's not every day I buy a man an expensive bottle of wine.'

He looked at the bottle again and shrugged, trying his best to look as nonchalant as he could, but was failing miserably. He rubbed his free hand through his hair, leaving it sticking up in odd angles, as his palms were sweating so much. The smile on his lips made him look like a lustful thirteen-year-old boy when confronted with his first, real live naked breast.

He looked around the parking lot, as if expecting a camera crew to jump out on him at any moment or maybe his wife and his kids, lurking around the corner, ready to catch him in this lewd act. When none of these scenarios played out, he began to make his way over to her.

She was smiling at him. Her long hair was blowing slightly in the breeze. The light of the single, yellow streetlamp above her gave her skin a bit of a sallow look to it, but given her fair complexion, he saw it as just a trick of the light.

He took a few steps closer, reducing the distance between them to maybe fifty yards. The light was not flattering to her at all. It was beginning to show off a few wrinkles here, and a bit of wear and tear there, on her otherwise stunning face. *What am I worrying about? I'm not exactly the best specimen for my age group, and she's still stunning!*

He continued his advance, non-perturbed.

Another few steps and he noticed that the blonde of her hair was mostly grey. Her eyes, that he could have sworn were a deep green, were really a washed out brown. The whites of them more yellow than white. James began to have second thoughts about this, and he gripped the bottle just a little tighter as, for some reason unbeknown to him, his legs continued to carry him closer to the woman in the car.

The door opened, and she turned her body, allowing her long legs to stretch out onto the asphalt. His eyes hungrily darted to them. He knew they were fantastic legs as they were the part of her that had initially attracted him to her. Long, silky, and smooth.

However, these legs must have belonged to someone else. Yes, they were long, but the skin was dry and cracked. Thick, purple veins ran through them that undulated and pulsed. They weren't smooth either. Coarse black hairs covered them, making him think more of wire wool than of silk.

He stopped. He pulled his gaze from the repulsive legs hanging out of the car and looked at the rest of her. Her long, flowing hair was now brittle and grey, her chin had grown in length, giving her a rather horsey look. The lips he'd thought of as lustful and full were nothing but cracked and bleeding scars across her face. Her nose looked like it had been fake, and the glue had worn off. It hung off her skeletal thin face, exposing a raw, dirty scab beneath.

James wanted to run. His body screamed at him to turn and bolt, far away, into any direction it wanted, just away from the hideous creature before him.

'What's the matter, lover?' her voice had changed too. Gone was the purring vibration of only moments ago. Moments that now felt like years—only to be replaced with a horrible scratching sound, like fingernails being dragged down a chalkboard. 'You haven't gotten cold feet, have you?'

James *had* gotten cold feet. In fact, he had gotten cold legs, a cold penis, a cold stomach, chest, neck, and head too. He needed to go. The sight of this thing before him was turning his stomach. How could he have judged it so badly? Were those drinks stronger than he thought they'd been?

Finally, his body released strength back to his limbs, and he turned from the hideous monster in the car. The instant he took the first step, he felt arms around him. Strong arms holding him in place, holding him hostage, preventing him getting the million miles away from this abhorrent degradation as he could.

He dropped the bottle of Champaign; his mind took a moment to realise it didn't smash. It made a strange noise as it bounced once, before rolling off in another direction. James envied the freedom the bottle had, freedom to roll just exactly wherever it wanted. He, unfortunately, no longer had that luxury.

The long fingers that were gripping him were gouging his skin. He could feel them piercing the material of his shirt, scratching and slicing him. A burning sensation in the fat on the overhang over his jeans told him something he didn't really want to know. He looked down at his midriff for clarification, and got it, instantly.

The long, bony hand that gripped him, ended in dirty yellow fingernails that looked more like talons than nails. These were digging into his pink flesh, and he could see long trails of his own dark, fresh blood escaping from the wounds.

He opened his mouth to scream, but just before his breath could catch, something entered his mouth. It was disgusting, and it tasted even worse, like the aftertaste when you had been vomiting, suffering from a hangover. There was another taste there too. This one, in his hyper-awareness of the situation, could only identify as decay, and degradation, and maybe blue cheese.

The taloned hand that was in his mouth worked his body around, so he was now facing the thing he had once thought was the sexiest woman in the world, which now was anything but. The long, lustrous golden hair was now gone, leaving behind it a bald and flaking scalp. Her eyes were deep black holes. Even the sickly yellow ones would have been preferable to the eternity he was faced with inside her skull.

Her teeth were gone too, leaving behind pink suckers, akin to that found on the tentacles of octopus.

Even though she was still vaguely humanoid, James could feel more than one arm pulling him towards whatever she had become, while her filthy hand was still inside his mouth.

'Do you want me to suck you off? Do you still want to fuck me?' she whispered. James didn't know what was worse: the smell of her breath, or the multiple voices he could hear inside the whisper, some of them even child-like.

He tried to struggle, to scream, but found out rather quickly he could do neither. All he could do was mumble and dribble as the obstruction in his mouth prevented him from anything more.

She continued dragging him, and the closer she got the more horrendous the vision became. 'It's ironic that you don't want to fuck me anymore, because you've never been so fucked in your whole life,' she, or rather, it, whispered in the same unnerving multi-voice.

James was pulled into the car, through the open door. His body helpless to resist the strong arms forcing him, crushing him. The grip had gotten tighter, and a small crunching sound, followed by a series of snaps, and eventually severe agony told him his ribs had now been broken, yet still the arm around him tightened. The hand in his mouth ventured further, deeper than any hand had any right to venture. He'd passed the need to gag, his terror had bypassed that feeling, but the hand in his throat was rummaging. It was a strange sensation, his internal organs being gripped and pulled and jostled.

More tightness followed by more snapping and bucket loads of pain came James' way. His bloodshot eyes rolled in his head as blessed blackness threatened to engulf him.

He found himself at home, in his favourite chair. He was wearing a shirt and tie, and his briefcase was at his feet. On his knees was a little girl and a little boy. They were both hugging and kissing him, excited to see him. His wife was in the doorway between the living room and the kitchen wearing a housecoat with her hair in a bun at the top of her head. She had a full face of make-up on and was looking sexier than he'd seen her in a long time. 'If you get the kids to bed, I'll put the dinner on the table,' she said, looking at him with a twinkle in her eye and a smile on her face. 'Then, we'll see about taking dessert upstairs, eh. What do you think about that?' She offered him an exaggerated wink and disappeared back into the kitchen. He looked at the children, kissed them, and stood up. 'Sorry kids, I love you and everything, but you gotta get to bed. Daddy has needs.' With that, the little girl's face changed, it contorted. Her hair fell out, and her features became that of a screaming skull. Horrified, he looked at the boy and his mouth was open wide, his teeth had turned into pink suckers.

He dropped both children and turned back towards the kitchen. He couldn't see his wife, but he could hear her. She was talking in a multi-voiced whisper. 'Come in here, James. Come and do to me what you wanted to do with that little slut in the bar. I'll let you ...'

Another, serious stab of pain snapped him from his reverie, and his eyes shot open.

'Don't you dare fall asleep on me,' the thing whispered again. 'You taste better alive.'

She opened her mouth wide. Much wider than any mouth had any business opening. The image of a snake dislocating its jaws to swallow a baby deer for lunch sprung into his mind. *That's exactly what I am,* he thought. That was his last thought in this world, as the darkness of this thing's mouth enveloped him, and the suckers of its gums stripped his body of flesh.

Within a few, hellish moments, it was all over.

The woman, back in her original form, stepped elegantly out of the low sports car. She pulled her short dress down over her shapely behind and long legs. She raised her arms into the air and stretched. As she did, she released a loud and long belch. Putting her hand to her mouth to hide her un-lady-like behaviour, she scanned the parking lot looking for possible witnesses to her feeding. Happy there was no-one around, she bent down and picked up the expensive bottle of Champagne. She sat back behind the wheel of her car and checked herself in the mirror. Her long, thick golden hair was immaculate, but her lipstick needed adjusting. Suddenly, she pulled a face, wiggled her lips, and frowned. A long finger with elegantly painted and expertly manicured nails entered her mouth and fished about. Something was lodged in the back of her mouth, caught between her teeth.

She fished about before eventually finding the offending object.

She looked at it on the end of her finger. It was covered in saliva and a little blood, but there was no mistaking what it was.

It was James' wedding ring.

She regarded it as if it were a piece of forgotten rotten meat, and without any regard for the holy sanctimony of what it symbolised, she tossed it into the back seat of her car.

It chinked as it landed on the seat. Clinking against one of the many, similar looking golden bands adorned the seats back there.

'Another one bites the dust,' she laughed, before gunning the engine and speeding out of the parking lot, and into the night.

The red sports car pulled into the dark street. It was almost four am, and the only illumination in the street was a few dull yellow lamps. The houses were dark, except for one, three-quarters of the way along the row of semi-detached properties.

The car made its way up the street, stopping outside the house with the light on in an upstairs room. The woman stepped out, once again fixing her skirt, covering her shapely bottom and equally shapely legs. The cold of the night made her nipples stand out from inside her flimsy top, all six of them rubbed like bullets against the thin fabric.

Flicking her hair, she made her way to the passenger side door and opened it.

The glow from inside illuminated her beautiful face, and she smiled. She reached in and clutched at the bag. It chimed musically as she hefted it out of the car and placed it on the floor. She closed the door and looked down at the contents of the bag. *Someone's going to be happy,* she thought as she hefted it over her shoulder with a grunt.

The front door opened into a nice, average looking hallway. There were a lot of candles, all of them were out on the sideboards and underneath the long mirror. A faint light was glowing from up the narrow staircase that ran parallel to the mirror.

'Hey,' she shouted, dragging the heavy bag through the door. 'Anyone home?'

'Up here.'

The voice that answered wasn't a strong one. It was masculine, but it sounded old, frail, and weak. 'Did you get them?'

'I did my love. I think I got enough. Although I don't think I'm going to need to eat for another month,' she laughed.

'Ah well, that will do you the world of good. You could do with losing a few pounds,' the voice laughed, cheekily. 'Hang on, I'm coming down.'

'No, don't tire yourself out. I'll bring them up. I'll set it all up for you.'

'You are far too kind, my dear. I knew there was a reason I loved you.'

The woman pulled her skirt down, over her bottom again and bent down to grab the heavy bag. With more chinks and chimes, she pulled it up the stairs, one at a time, counting all fifteen steps as she went.

By the time she'd struggled to the top, her breathing was deep, and a thin sheen of sweat covered her forehead. 'Do you want me to put them straight into the bath?' she shouted.

'Thank you, my love. I'd help you, but, I think tonight's activities have tired me out more than I knew,' came the sallow reply.

'I know, baby. You stay there. I'll call you when I'm done.'

The bag made a musical sound as it was heaved along the beige carpeted floor towards the small bathroom at the end. Finally, when the bag was inside the room she stood and rubbed her hands to the small of her back, wincing as she did. She looked at the bag and opened it. The glow from inside made her skin look fantastic. It complimented her long, flowing hair. She turned, taking a large plastic jug from the sink, and dug it deep into the bag.

As the jug came out of the bag it was filled to overflowing with different kinds of wedding rings. Some were gold, others were silver, each one of them could tell their own story. She emptied the jug into the bath. The noise of them hitting the Perspex coating of the large tub echoed around the house.

'Ah, that sounds delightful,' the feeble voice from outside the room spoke up. 'Did you get enough to fill it?'

'It took a while, my love, but these months have been worth it if we can get you back to your true form,' she shouted back, as she continued filling the tub with hundreds of wedding bands. Once it was half full, a shadow shuffled into the room. It was tall and old. It was also hideous. Yellowish, sickly flesh was sagging from its face. It looked like melted cheese dripping from his neck. Its eyes were sallow and pale. The mouth was drawn into a perpetual grimace and the lips were deep red lacerations on the old, drawn out face. 'Thank the Lord. It's getting harder and harder to keep my form these days,' the thing spoke, its voice tired.

'Well, get into this bath and the loss and despair from all this symbolism will bring you back to your former glory. They'll bring back the man I know and love.

The hideous creature reached out a claw and caressed her face. She revelled in the touch of this monster, coveting it in her own hand.

'I do feel I put on you too much sometimes,' he said, attempting to smile.

'It's not your fault you must revel in human sorrow to gain strength, my love.'

'I just wish I could ingest their essence to survive, like you. I need you so much, my Queen.'

He removed his robe, exposing the rest of his body that was similar to his face. The sickly colour continued over the rest of him, and the melted cheese effect was consistent as it looked like his skin was attempting to escape from the rest of him.

'You will never lose me, my love. We're to be together for all eternity.'

She held out her hand, and the old, frail thing accepted it. He stepped gingerly into the tub. His ancient legs shifted the rings so he could fit in. He did the same with his other leg, and then finally he was able to sit down. Once he was steady, she resumed filling the tub with the rest of the wedding rings.

The monster in the tub relaxed with a long sigh and sat back.

'Do you want a cup of tea?' the woman asked, once the final jug full of rings had been emptied.

The ancient man's hand reached out and held hers. His old face was smiling, making him look more repulsive than he had earlier. 'Why don't we have something stronger, eh? This is a celebration.'

'Should I open the bottle of Champagne?'

The man smiled and winked.

'Coming right up,' she purred, and left the room to get the bottle from the car.

She poured the fizzy amber liquid into two tall glasses and made her way back up the stairs. She could hear singing coming from the bathroom. It was a tuneless ditty, but it made her smile; it meant he was getting stronger. *He'll be back to his normal self soon,* she thought as she opened the door to the bathroom.

She handed over one of the glasses. 'Here you go, it's a bit warm, but it should be OK.'

The barman from the club was naked in the tub of rings. He beamed a smile at her as he accepted the glass. His handsome face looked younger than he'd done earlier that night. 'That's fine,' he replied with a wolfish grin and a twinkle in his eye. 'Now, how do you feel about jumping in here with me and giving me all the gory details of your night?'

Rolling her eyes, she allowed herself to be pulled into the tub, with a salacious smile of her own. As he kissed her on her lips, she revelled in the delights of his fully restored body, and his full appetite.

Death Walks Into a Bar

Paul Avery Tindol

I t was two o'clock on a Wednesday afternoon, and, other than the bartender and a couple of roughnecks playing pool in the back, The Goat was dead. He'd driven past the place enough times to know that it would soon be crawling with folks once five came around. Cade planned to make sure he was far away from The Goat before that happened, though. Other than the bartender, he didn't wish to engage or converse with any other patron.

But he couldn't be caught drinking back at home. The Goat would have to do.

Cade walked down to the other end of the bar, the darker corner of the room, closest to the wall with the least amount of neon beer signs, pulled out a barstool, and took a seat. Despite being four years sober, he was going to attempt to drink his pain away.

The gorgeous woman behind the bar must have been in her late twenties, if that. She had dark caramel-colored skin covered in tattoos and thick curly hair that hung halfway down her back. She was drying glasses and stacking them under the bar when Cade sat down.

"Whatcha drinkin' today, hun?" she asked.

Standing right in front of him, she was even cuter than Cade had first thought when he'd spotted her from the door; however, she did nothing to remove the image of the crash site from his head.

Nor the closed mahogany casket.

"Just a whiskey and Coke, please. Well is fine."

"Right on it," she said with a smile. Cade watched her scoop the ice into the cup and fill it about two-thirds full of Benchmark Old No. 8. Then, she topped it off with a quick spray of Coke from the tap.

Just how he remembered them being made at dive bars.

Cade was about halfway through his drink when the room lit up in a blinding white light.

He looked across the bar to the open door that was bleeding sunlight. Cade squinted his eyes, but the man in the doorway looked like nothing more than a silhouette until he stepped in and shut the door behind him.

"You're early today," the bartender said. She was already bending down to grab the man a Lone Star from the beer fridge.

"Thanks, Sam," the man said as he took his beer from the bartender. Cade could see now that he was an older Black man with a snow white beard in Wranglers, boots, and a black Stetson hat. The man turned around to wave at the folks in the back. "Who's winning?"

One of the men in the back answered, "Mike is gettin' his ass whooped today. This about to be three-and-zero."

The older patron got a good laugh out of it. "That boy sure does like to talk some shit, don't he?"

"Yeah, well, I'm about to get another beer and show him who's boss here in a minute," the losing player responded.

"That's what I like to hear. You'll get him next time, playa."

He took a seat down at the bar to the left of Cade, leaving one stool open between them. Despite staring at his phone to avoid engaging, Cade could feel the man's eyes on him.

Cade looked up from his phone to meet the man's gaze. He smiled and gave a friendly nod to Cade, but Cade could see something else behind his eyes that he knew well.

Sorrow.

It had been the same look in everyone's eyes today it seemed.

Then the old man said something that rocked Cade to his core.

"I'm sorry for your loss, brother. Let me get the next one," he said, gesturing to Cade's almost empty drink.

Cade stared blankly back at the man, unsure how to respond.

"What?" Cade shook his head, as if that would get the gears in his head turning enough to make sense of the man's words. "How did you know that I ..." Cade trailed off. "Do I know you?"

"I don't believe so. I don't think I've seen ya in here before now. Name's Willie Cartwright. You can just call me Willie, though. Unless you know someone else named that. In that case, Black Willie is fine too."

Cade almost spit out his drink.

"Now that's a nickname. I don't know any White Willies—other than my own—so Willie should be fine. I'm Cade ... How did you know?" Cade couldn't even bring himself to admit that he had lost someone. He didn't want it to be real. He was here to pretend it wasn't.

"I didn't mean to startle you, Cade. I just have a sense about these things. Ya see—I can smell him on ya."

"Him?" Cade finished the rest of his drink.

Willie turned to the bartender. "Get Cade here another ... whatever he's drinking."

"Sure," Sam responded.

Willie turned back around to face Cade. The old man was no longer wearing his playful smile. Instead, his face was relaxed, the unwanted empathy having resurfaced.

"What was that supposed to mean?" Cade asked. "Did you say you could smell him on me?"

"Yes, sir," Willie answered. "Death."

Cades's skin must have gone three shades lighter.

"It has a smell, you know?" Willie continued. "It ain't the same for everyone, but to me, it smells like fine pipe tobacco. Just like my granddaddy used to smoke."

Cade, still shocked silent, considered throwing down a twenty and getting the hell up out of The Goat, right then and there, but then Willie laughed to break the tension.

"I mean it's that and the suit, son. Ain't nobody coming in here dressed like that. Be for real now."

Cade threw his head back and joined in with the laughter, which he immediately felt guilty for. He hadn't laughed in over a week now. But *of course!* Cade hadn't even changed clothes since leaving the funeral.

Of course everyone at a shitty dive bar would be giving him all sorts of crazy looks.

"You scared me there for a little bit," Cade said. "It's been a long day."

The bartender returned with another whiskey and Coke and traded it out for Cade's empty glass.

"Sorry, man. I like to fuck with people a little bit. I didn't mean no harm by it."

"None taken." Cade took the first sip of his second drink.

"I mean—I'm not entirely joking," Willie said. He took a sip from his Lone Star. "I saw him back maybe twenty years ago now ... Now I know how crazy that sounds, but you don't get to be my age without getting to see some strange shit, ya hear?"

"Right," Cade chuckled nervously. He was unsure what the man's intentions were. He couldn't tell if he was fucking with him again or if he was just some loon off his rocker.

"It was right here in this bar, back when it was called Rusty Ray's. Believe it or not, the blues scene was on fire back then. Had all kinds of blues musicians coming through and playing every weekend. Sup-posedly, even B.B. King scheduled to headline a show at one time or another, but his bus broke down on the way. It turned out to be a load of BS. King was never gonna play here. The show promoter just put him on the bill to sell tickets."

The front door of The Goat opened, bringing the intense light of the glaring sun in with it. Cade leaned back so that he could see past Willie and to the front door. Again, there was no use. The sun behind the man in the doorway was much too bright, blacking out the man's features.

"Goddamn that's bright," Willie said, trying to blink his eyes back into focus. "Now what was I saying?"

"B.B. King."

"Sure as hell weren't no B.B. King ever step in this place unless one of the Bs were for Brandon or something. We did have good music playing here every weekend, though. Mostly local acts. One Saturday night, we had a blues act by the name of Skinny Bones Jones. Fantastic musician that was blowin' up in Deep Ellum at the time. That was gonna be the headliner. Well, the first act goes up and it's this kid from Tyler—I forget his name now—but he was playing for a small crowd of early birds. Most of the folks didn't show up until the headliner would go on and not leave until the afterparty was wrapped up. Well, the kid is basically background music to the early crowd. Ain't nothing wrong with that, but he wasn't the main focus, you know? Everybody is chatting and cuttin' up with their friends, not paying the musician any mind. Then, in walks this man who—"

"I'm sorry to interrupt story time, Willie."

Both of the men looked up to see Sam the bartender standing across from them with a drink in her hand. She looked as confused as they did. "Want a free Jack and Coke? Dude at the end of the bar said he wanted a whiskey and Coke and that it didn't matter which liquor I used. Except when I said here's your Jack and Coke, he said he doesn't like sour mash. He apologized and said he'd still pay for it and to send it down to see if one of you wanted it."

Willie shook his head. "Not me. I done told you my whiskey days are long behind me. That shit'll put me in a grave."

"Well, I was thinking more for the guy who's already drinking the same thing." Sam placed the drink in front of Cade.

"Well, hell. I appreciate it," Cade said. The door opened, and a group of three entered.

Sam waved and shielded her eyes from the harsh sunlight that poured in behind them. "Welcome in, guys!"

Cade could see someone sitting at the far end of the bar closest to the door, but he couldn't get a good look without blinding himself. Still, he leaned forward and toasted the man who'd sent the drink from across the bar, before shifting his attention back to his new acquaintance.

Cade apologized and prompted Willie to continue from where he'd left off. "Sorry. The musician is playing ..."

"And he's pretty good, but folks are going on about their business and not payin' him no mind ... Then the front door swings open and I heard a woman gasp. She was loud enough that we all heard her over the sound of the boy going to town on the piano in the corner over there. We all turn to look at the woman and she's scrunched over like this. With both her hands over her eyes, like she'd walked in on her granddad naked or something." Willie leaned over the edge of the bar with his hands cupped one over the other tight across his eyes for a second before looking back up to Cade.

"And she's screaming at everyone to not look at the man who'd just walked in. Well, that's the first thing I try to do. I wanted to see what this sonofabitch looked like, but when I looked up, everyone was covering their eyes and turning away from the front door. I didn't know what the hell was going on. Now this was back when you could smoke in bars, so I was already accustomed to the smell of the place, but all of the sudden, all I could smell was my grandad's pipe tobacco.

"And that made me think about the night he died, and I watched my dad and uncle hold and light his pipe for him so that he could smoke one last time. Then I was all of the sudden scared to die.

"I don't know no other way to put it. It was an overwhelming sensation of existential dread. Then, other people are shoutin' and hollerin' the same thing. *Don't look at him! Don't look at his face!* Shit like that ... Then, I saw who they were talking about. He was the only person besides me not shielding their eyes or looking away from anything—other than the boy on the piano, that is. But I only saw the man's face for a split second before a pain in my gut like nothing I'd ever felt before had me hunched over and I damn near collapsed.

"But the blues act was still going strong. He was in his own world playing his set and he didn't even see the man approaching him until he was right in front of the piano standing over him. I looked long enough to see the pianist raise his head and see the face of the man standing over him.

"The young cat on the piano looked like he'd seen a ghost. Hell, whatever he saw must've been worse than a ghost because he stopped playing and stood up and tried to run but collapsed there in place. His head hit the piano and the keys and it made a jarring sound. The poor boy laid there on the ground behind his piano with a pool of blood forming around his head.

"Then, the man began to turn around and so did I. I covered my eyes and I heard everyone murmuring to help the musician who'd just fell out. When I looked again, no one was covering their eyes anymore. A lot of the folks were trying to help the boy on the floor who turned out to be as dead as a doornail. The rest of the folks were watching in concern but going back to drinking at the same time.

"As far as I know, there was no trace of the man in the joint after that. I no longer smelled my grandad's pipe tobacco. The bar smelled like cigarette smoke again ..." Willie trailed off, then tilted his beer to his lips and finished the bottle. "You know what's always bothered me about all of it, Cade?"

"What's that?"

"I don't know why I was able to look at *it* and walk away. Because I saw him too, ya know? Hell, maybe it's because I didn't look him directly in the eyes. Maybe it's not really about *you* looking at him, but rather when *he* looks on you. Maybe he just wasn't after me—at least not that night. Just a matter of time, though... And that goes for all of us. Just a matter of time."

Cade was still trying to make sense of this man, but at the same time, he knew he needed to get something to eat and get back home to his family. Back to the real world.

Still, Cade was curious, so he played along.

"Well, based on what you did see of him that night, what would you say he looked like?" Cade thought he smelled smoke right when he asked the question.

Willie looked down at Cade's half-empty Jack and Coke, then he threw his thumb back over his shoulder, gesturing behind him.

"He looked a lot like the fella down there at the end of the bar that sent you that drink."

True Believers

CS Jones

"**I**s this really the stage?" asked Kel as she pulled her bass from its case and climbed up.

Crash, already behind his drum kit, made his usual "whatever" shrug and tightened his hi-hat.

It was the size of a pool table, but Kel had played smaller, her bass practically upright to fit. In truth, she'd play in a toilet cubicle if it meant she could tell everyone she'd played at the infamous Jizzy's.

It was dank, it was dingy, it smelt of sweat and puke, and to the band Death By Lasagne, it was perfect. An underground bar in their hometown, rooted deep in the heart of the Welsh Valleys, it had built a formidable reputation amongst the hardcore clientele for its infamous punk rock shows and even rowdier after-parties, and it was a legacy Kel couldn't wait to become ingrained in.

Unfortunately, the building itself was in a state of total ruin—its gritty punk appearance more than quirky aesthetics. The original stage had caved in after excavations months ago, and the venue changed hands not long after, leaving a lot of work for its new owners, much of which was already underway, and this left the four-piece to perform their rambunctious set on a makeshift wooden platform haphazardly propped up in the corner.

The previous owners, Posh Charlie and his wife, Vanessa, vanished in the dead of night, leaving behind a mountain of debt and a whole host of health code violations. Many theorised they'd set up another club over in the States, others that they'd owed a local gangster money and were six feet under the foundations. Crash even claimed it to be the work of aliens, though when pressed on the matter, he quickly shot holes in his own story.

Regardless of the reason, it hadn't stood in the new owners' way and, though mysterious, they welcomed the droves of punk rockers who ventured out every Saturday night, their multi-coloured mohawks and cherry red Doc Martens on full display as they skanked along to the rowdy music in a place that could collapse at any moment. Perhaps the thrill was just another quirk to its rough and ready patrons. Punk rock hadn't been this dangerous in such a long time, after all.

The club had been open barely an hour, and it was already heaving. Outside, darkness had descended on the chilly Autumn night—not that anyone could tell down here—and under the artificial lights, the floor was already awash with bodies that stank of BO and stale beer.

"No pressure Kel, but we best get it right tonight. We're on last," said Tomo, sat tuning his guitar despite having no actual way to hear the notes he picked. Not that it mattered; he had the playing ability of a fingerless coma patient, but damn did he look good doing it. With such a talent-to-sex-appeal ratio, Sid Vicious would have been proud.

Kel gasped. "Last? We're last? What about Solid State? They're the elder statesmen. Wait, what about Nobby Harris? The man's a psycho. Please tell me he knows he's not headlining?"

"It was Nob what told me. He weren't happy, I can tell you that. Fucking fuming, more like, so I didn't stick around. I dunno about you lot, but I'll be giving him a wide berth tonight." Tomo moved on to the next string, keeping up the pretence.

Some groupies must be watching, thought Kel and shook her head.

"Good call," said Crash as he twirled a drumstick. "Best avoid the old fart, I've heard he's got a right temper. Story is, he burned down his house one night with his missus still inside. Police couldn't prove nothing, so he walked."

Kel nodded and ran her fingers along the shaved side of her head. "I heard that, too. That's where all the burn scars on his scalp came from."

Crash carried on. "Besides, imagine fronting a band that's played with the big dogs, UK82 and all that, only to get told some young no-names are on after you. Fuck that, man, I'd be livid, too."

"Point taken, Crash."

"I'd go on a right rampage, tear up the joint—"

"*Crash*! Let's just get this sound check done and get out the way. Hang on, where's Neck?"

"That's why we're on last," said Tomo. "His shift at his dad's creepy book shop ran over."

"Fuck sake, late again? He's been pretty flaky lately. He'd better be here, though, I'm not singing "True Believers" again."

"Trust me, Kel, *no one* wants you singing 'True Believers' again. It was abysmal. You're right, though, he'd better be here, he's the only one that can carry a tune, even if he would rather play Genesis or whatever troglodyte bollocks he goes on about these days. Personally, I'm perfectly happy behind this thing," Tomo said and held up his guitar. He then glanced over at two girls smirking to one another between longing gazes.

"Ah, that'll be why."

"What's that?"

"Nothing, you carry on. Can't be out of time *and* out of tune." Kel turned to the crowd and did a double-take.

Behind the masses, through the glaring lights, someone in a white hooded robe stared at her. It was difficult to make out their features, and after a lingering moment, they shuffled on and disappeared into a room marked *Staff Only*.

Kel shook her head. "Huh, all the crazy get-ups and *that's* the one that sticks out."

"What's that?" asked Crash.

"Doesn't matter. Right, I'm heading to the bar while Crash finishes up, then we'll rush through sound check."

"Wait, Kel, we were given a case of drink when we got here," said Tomo.

"Yup, but it was just some shitty out-of-date cider. Besides, I'm driving, so you lot can dig in."

Tomo winced. "Urgh, no thanks, I can't stand the stuff, not after Rebellion fest. All yours, Crash, just remember we're playing later."

"I do my best work drunk," said Crash and necked a bottle before wincing. "Eww, fuck sake, they're flatter than Tomo's nan's tits."

"Classy, Crash. Just pace yourself, OK?"

Kel nodded her agreement, but Crash had already popped open another. "Tomo, maybe hide the crate until I get back, I don't want another Wrexham incident." And with that, Kel hopped down and made her way across the bustling dancefloor.

As she neared the bar, she spotted Nobby Harris, or more specifically, his scarred head and pink mohawk, sans gaping bald spot in the middle. Loud and obnoxious, he whistled and clicked his fingers at Big Sally, the barmaid. Curiously, Kel noticed she wore a white hoodie, tucked into her jeans, not dissimilar to the robe she'd seen moments ago, but was quick to dismiss it.

Unwilling to risk setting Nobby off, Kel curved her route and headed for the bathroom, convincing herself she needed to go anyway.

She sat on the toilet for a full two minutes without so much as a trickle. Seeking a distraction, she stared at her phone, annoyed by the lack of signal. Despite how much she willed herself, she couldn't go. "Bollocks," she eventually muttered and hitched up her jeans.

Kel swung the cubicle door open to see Nobby swaying in the entranceway.

"You took your time, Little Miss Headliner," he slurred. An empty bottle of cider dropped from his grip, and he kicked it aside before it could bounce. With his elbows out and fists pumped, he marched right up to Kel, stopping mere inches from her face. "You think you got it all, don't you? You bunch of young'uns, fucking us over like that, going behind our backs."

"Fucking you over? Nob, come on."

Nobby's face flared crimson. "*Nob*?! Did you just call me a fucking *nob*?"

"Oh, shi—"

Nobby gripped Kel by the front of her t-shirt, snapping a strap on her bra. Before she could collect herself, he spun her and slammed her against the wall.

Through gritted teeth, Nobby hissed, "Think you little bastards can waltz in and fuck me over? Think I'll lie down and take it? I've earned this. You haven't done shit. Was your idea, wasn't it? You birds are all the bloody same! You planned this!"

In a daze, Kel felt her body peel off the wall, only to once again slam back against it, the back of her skull bouncing off the cream-painted brick that may have once been white.

The impact caused the world to waver, the sound to distort. Kel anticipated another blow and tensed up, but it never came. After a moment, she realised he'd let go.

She regained focus in time to see Nobby wild-eyed and staring at something above them as he nervously backed away.

"Christ, no! Oh, Christ! Not you!" he pleaded.

In her confusion, Kel dropped to all fours, the heel of her palms sticky against the dingy bathroom floor, and peered up, worried at what she might see, but to her surprise, nothing was there.

Nobby wept as his craggy face boiled and grew red, then blackened before her very eyes. He was burning. Soot spread across his brow, and blisters formed—angry, wet pockets that sizzled and burst. "I'm sorry, Liz!" he cried to empty air. "Please, I'm—no—"

Nobby's final, blood-curdling wail was cut short as his body burned and shrivelled, engulfed in flames Kel could not see.

Still smouldering, his body lifeless, he dropped to the floor, now no more than a blackened, crispy husk.

Kel's heart was racing, and with heat radiating from Nobby's crackling body, she scrambled for the doorway, her head darting back and forth, in desperate search of this unseen threat. But, again, nothing was there.

Before she could pull the door open, a series of rattling screams rang out from behind it, quickly becoming a cacophony.

Shaken, Kel took a deep breath and tried to regain her composure. Determined to make her way back to Tomo and Crash, she muttered, "Fuck it," and yanked the door wide.

The dance floor was a massacre, but it was impossible to pinpoint why. Closest to her lay the lower half of a body, its intestines long and slick, like a ball of eels that had wormed their way out, but the top half was nowhere to be seen.

Beside its twitching legs, another person lay, convulsing and frothing foamy blood from their mouth. Though difficult to make out, Kel could see a series of dual punctures spread across the man's swollen hands and face. They looked like snake bites, but again, nothing was around.

Behind the bar, Big Sally flicked her hood up and skulked towards the *Staff Only* door, a vicious grin plastered across her face.

Before Kel could call after her, someone barged past—one of the girls eying up Tomo. She batted at her big curly hair, screaming, "No, not the bees! Please, I'm allergic! Get them away!"

Kel went to run after her, but she was already lost in the crowd.

"Kel! Where are you?" came Tomo's voice through the PA.

Kel peeked over the thrashing bodies to see him waving from the stage. She yelled back, but there was no way for him to hear her over the carnage.

She went to make her way to him when another punk flailed in front of her, shaking his body in some form of deranged jitterbug. All over, chunks of flesh split and tore away. Dozens of tiny, little things appeared to be chomping into him, turning his torso into a gory pulp.

Petrified, Kel pushed through bloody body after bloody body, the final one with the nauseating appearance of someone dissolving in acid, until she finally reached the front.

Streaked with gore, she was met by Tomo's hand, and he hauled her up onto the stage. "What the hell's going on?" he said, his mouth agape at the sea of awful events unfolding around him.

"It's carnage, everyone's seeing something different. Maybe it's their biggest fears, I dunno? It's mad, it's like whatever they're seeing, it's killing them. What about you? What have you seen?"

"Me? I haven't seen a thing. I don't understand any of it. Crash, you seen anything? *Crash*?"

They turned, expecting to see Crash wielding two drumsticks, ready with another boneheaded quip, but to their shock, he wasn't there.

Kel scanned the room, unable to see their drummer through the bloodshed.

"Shit, we have to get out," said Tomo and took her hand.

"We need to get Crash first. He's here, somewhere. We need to find him before—"

Tomo yanked Kel back just as Crash leapt back onto the stage, missing her by inches. Fidgety and on edge, he snapped his head back and forth. "He's after me! I've got to hide, he'll kill me if he gets me!"

"Crash, settle down," said Tomo, his arms outstretched in placation. "Who's after you? We'll help, but you need to talk to us first."

Crash's eyes fixed on the side of the stage. Tomo looked around, but Kel knew there wouldn't be anything there.

"He's grinning at me. Oh god. He wants me to run. The sick bastard's enjoying this. I've got to go."

Before Tomo could steady him, Crash leapt back off the stage. "Wait, Crash, who's after you?"

Before he disappeared into the mangled crowd, Crash called over his shoulder, "Phil Collins!"

"Phil Collins? The fuck?" said Tomo and looked to the empty space.

Kel grasped Tomo's shoulder. "Come on, there's no signal down here. If we get upstairs, we can call for help." She studied an empty cider bottle that spun to a stop at her feet. "I've got a feeling we might be OK, but tell me if you see anything trying to kill you."

The two wrestled their way through the mass of bodies, each experiencing their own personal hell until they reached the bar. Stretched across it were rows of bottles, some smashed, some unopened. Beside them, multiple signs read *Free beer– out of date.*

"It has to be the drinks," said Kel. "We've not had any. They're laced with something."

"What with? LSD?" said Tomo.

"LSD wouldn't cause this. I saw Big Sally earlier. She disappeared through the *Staff Only* door."

"So?"

"Well, she didn't exactly look terrified. Whatever this is, I think she's involved. Maybe don't drink anything in here."

They passed by the door without a second thought and made their way to the stairs.

"I don't see Crash," said Tomo.

"Keep moving. Quicker we're out, quicker we help him."

They climbed the stairs, relieved to be away from the carnage. Alongside such awful sights, the smells and sounds were just as intense.

At the top, Kel let out a gasp. The doors were padlocked shut.

Tomo rattled the chain, but it wouldn't budge.

"Oh my God," came a teary squeak behind them.

The other girl who had eyed up Tomo stared at the sealed door, her features slack. But it was the fact that she was coated head to toe in gore that drew their attention.

Still, she stared at the door. "There's no way out. We're trapped. Fran, she's dead. Her face, it's inflated like a balloon."

Kel hushed the girl. "Hey, hey, deep breath. We'll be OK. It's only a lock, all we need is the key."

"Or there'll be a fire exit," interjected Tomo.

"Right, or that. OK, I need you to focus. What's your name?"

She still didn't take her eyes from the door. "My name's Anya."

"OK, Anya. Can you take a deep breath for me? We're in a bit of trouble here, but if we work together, we can get out of it."

Slowly, Anya nodded. As she calmed, she shifted her focus to Kel. "OK, I can help. I can do this."

"That's it. Now, we need to head back down there. Fire exit or key, whichever we find first."

Tomo squeezed Kel's shoulder. "Kel, back up a little."

"Huh?"

"She was drinking from the same bottle as her friend. Look ..."

Kel's brow furrowed. She studied the petrified girl. She hadn't noticed it at first, but beneath the gore, her skin was cracked.

"What–what do you mean?" said Anya. She tried to wipe away a tear, and part of her cheek crumbled beneath her fingertips.

She studied the dust that came away, and her voice hitched.

More skin crumbled when she wrinkled her forehead, the skull beneath just as dry and brittle.

Panicked, she rubbed at her face, but it only sped up the process. Her features and fingers disintegrated. Still, she rubbed and wiped until, bit by bit, her face fell away completely to reveal the brittle brain within.

Reluctantly, Kel and Tomo circled round and made their way back downstairs as Anya's legs buckled, and she fell in a messy heap with a final whimper.

Back in the club, the massacre raged on. The room filled with the exclamations of fears all too familiar. "*Spiders!*" screamed one crust punk and batted at his leather jacket. "*Maggie Thatcher with a knuckle duster,*" cried another before his jaw exploded.

Though he was wounded, both were relieved to see Crash still on the run, his face black and blue as he held his bloodied side.

"He hasn't got much time," said Kel and rifled round the bar in search of the key. With no sign of it, she pulled Tomo towards the *Staff Only* door.

"Woah, hang on, do we really want to go in there?"

"You rather stay here? Besides, where else can we go? I don't see any other doors. The fire exit must be this way."

"Good point."

Kel twisted the handle and ran into the door. "*Locked*. Of course the bastard thing's locked."

"Step aside," said Tomo and pulled a fire extinguisher off the wall. "It may not make a dent in that padlock upstairs, but—"

He slammed the extinguisher against the door handle. There was a snap, and it crashed to the floor.

Through the door, the two were shocked to discover a makeshift scaffolding staircase that spiralled down.

"What the hell is this? We need to go up," Tomo said as his heart sank.

"Looks like the only way is down. How deep is this place? A basement in a basement? Seriously?" said Kel, and without a chance to rethink her decision, she descended the rickety stairway.

As they made their way down, a series of large, grisly paintings adorned the granite wall, their majesty out of place, given how slapdash the rest of the area had been thrown together.

The first painting, set within a grand, golden frame depicted a battlefield centuries old. Celtic warriors, their blue-painted faces etched in feral fury fought an army of Roman legionnaires. The brutal scenes depicted were vicious, visceral, familiar. In the centre of the Celtic army, a figure stood tall, far taller than the rest. Clad in black armour and a white overcoat, he wore a mask fashioned from a deer skull, its antlers huge against the backdrop of battle. All around him, Roman soldiers were on their knees in the throes of agony.

Further down, the next painting displayed what appeared to be a medieval festival, but when studied closer, it revealed the festival-goers were in the process of being massacred. Limbs flew as bodies fell, each grisly brushstroke revealing another awful end. Blood marred the canvas, all while that familiar figure watched on from a parapet above, arms outstretched.

The final painting presented that same hulking presence, this time, in a great hall, sat upon a throne of skulls. He still wore the armour and overcoat, only now his deer helmet rested upon his lap. Beneath a thick, black beard, his face was taught, sunken, and angular, a chilling, skeletal visage of death itself.

Kel instantly detested the piece, convinced the presence within was more than just a series of delicate brush strokes. She had the overwhelming sensation that it stared right into her, something she had experienced before, though she struggled to place it.

"You seeing a pattern, here?" Tomo said, causing her to jump. She wouldn't admit it, but she was desperate to get away, her vague familiarity for the figure causing a full-body shiver.

"I think I know these," she said. "I've seen them somewhere before. It's Celtic mythology. I can't remember his name, but the big, creepy dude, he's the king of the underworld."

"Christ, Kel. If that's the case, maybe calling him *the big, creepy dude* isn't the wisest thing to do. You know, they're horrible, but you're right, they're familiar. I'm sure I've seen them. Recently, too."

At the bottom, where the encroaching shadows were chased away by a couple of feeble lanterns, a large, wooden door blocked their way, its bolt undone.

"Kel, are you sure we—"

Before Tomo could finish, Kel barged the door open.

They found themselves in the mouth of a dank, empty cavern. Workman tools lay abandoned, left to gather dust. Stifled and grimy, with the reek of stagnation and copper so thick, they could taste it on the air. Undeterred, they quietly skulked on, soft music disguising their movement.

Further inside, hidden by crags and rock mounds, five figures, clad in white, hooded robes, knelt around a rock pool, though the water was far darker than it should have been. It was from there, the coppery scent emitted.

Unable to hold herself back, Kel lunged from the shadows and shouted, "What the hell is this?"

Three of the figures turned, while the other two shied away.

Determined to find answers, Kel stopped dead in her tracks. "Oh, shit, it's you two."

Beside Big Sally and her piercing death stare, the previous owners, Posh Charlie and Vanessa, gawped back.

"You ain't supposed to be down here," spat Vanessa. "You grotty little punks should be up there, taking your medicine with the rest of 'em."

Kel ignored her. "Hang on, we thought you'd both gone missing?"

Posh Charlie snorted. "You was meant to. Police will look for the new owners, they won't suspect it's really us what killed you lot."

"But, why all this? What have we ever done to you?"

"You dirty little bastards have run my place into the ground. You come in here, drink the cheap shit, wreck the joint. I put in a new hand dryer last week, and it's already knackered. You're a cancerous tumour on this society. *Parasites*, the lot of you."

"We wanted to open a wine bar," interjected Vanessa, her teeth bared. "But that'd never happen with you lot here, driving the posh crowd away. That's why we turned to Arawn. When we started renovations last year, we found his resting place. Of all the luck, eh? His blood flows through this land. We just needed to tap the right vein."

"You're all mad," said Tomo. "How the hell would you even know about this?"

One of the other worshippers stepped forward and revealed himself as Bill—Neck's dad. "Because I've followed the old gods since before you were born. I know all the practices, the rituals, and I knew with some patience, we'd eventually find Arawn's resting place. All it'll take is a few offerings to entice him from his slumber, and I must say, this banquet will do nicely."

"Your bookshop," said Kel. "That's where I've seen those creepy pictures before. I knew I recognised them. That's why you had Neck work late, was it? So you ..." Then the penny dropped. "Fuck sake. Neck, come on out."

Sheepishly, the fifth member stepped forward and pulled back his hood. "Sorry, guys. It's just, y'know, we can't be doing this punk thing forever, what with it being just a phase and all. Besides, I wanted to sing Genesis, but you wouldn't let me. Crash said he couldn't work out the timing. He didn't even try. Anyway, way I see it, we gotta grow up sometime, right?"

"Seriously? Are you listening to yourself? People are dying in here, and that *stuff*," she pointed to the pool and a bunch of bottles beside it. "It's messed up. Surely you can see that?"

"I know. I know it is, but it's to curry Arawn's favour. Like it or not, he's coming, and this way, we can show him we're worthy."

"Neck—"

"His name's *Nick*," interjected Bill. "Honestly, you punks are so ridiculous with your stupid fucking nicknames."

"We're ridiculous?" This time, Tomo spoke. "You seen yourselves, all dressed up like some mad cult?"

"We are the true believers."

Kel and Tomo snorted. Even Neck let out a giggle.

"What?"

Kel stepped forward. "Nothing, you wouldn't get it. But you let me tell you what *I* believe in. All through the week, I slave, I 'yes sir,' I 'no sir,' all with a dopey smile on my face. But come the weekend, that's when I get to live. *Really* live. I'm with my friends, my music, I get to have my life just how I want it. Why vilify me over a few bad apples, that I might add, you get *everywhere*. As for me, I don't hurt no one. If anything, if I saw you fall, I'd help you back up. But no, you look down and you don't want to know. You've got your own ideals, fuck what anyone else does." She grabbed for a bottle next to the pool, but Big Sally kicked her back.

"Oh, boo-fucking-hoo," chided Posh Charlie and picked it up. "I'd get you a violin, but I doubt you could string more than three chords together."

He uncapped it, ready to douse the two of them, when Crash burst into the room, followed by the few remaining punks. "The hell is all this? Hang on, *Neck*?"

"He's fucked us, Crash," said Kel. "He said he'd rather play Genesis."

"Fuck that right off!" Crash roared and threw himself through the air. He cross-bodied both Neck and Bill, and they all fell backwards into the pool.

The backsplash drenched the three remaining worshippers, who cried out and tried to run for the door, but lost their balance as a booming crash rang out and the ground began to shake and split apart.

Fissures formed, the floor giving way to a hellish, red glow that roared as it got brighter and brighter.

"Bill, what's happening? What is this?" cried Vanessa, her voice barely audible.

"He's here!" declared Bill as he flailed maniacally in the pool.

"What the bloody hell you mean *He's here?* He's ruining our pub!"

Boils and pustules formed on Bill's skin, oozing blood and puss as sickness took hold and his laughter drowned. With his last ounce of strength, he cried, "There won't be a pub! This is his grave, his birthing ground! The sacrifices! They worked! He has power!"

Beside him, in the pool, Neck thrashed as he aged decades in seconds, his screams slowing to a horse rasp that dried out as he mummified and disintegrated in seconds.

Below, a rumbling voice let out an ear-piercing roar that quickly descended into a deep-rooted chuckle as the pool, the remaining worshippers, and a whole host of terrified punks fell through the forming chasms.

Understanding there was no way out, and with their end fast approaching, Kel dragged Tomo from the slaughter, avoiding the numerous obstacles as they made their way to the door.

At the foot of the stairs, they heard someone behind them. "Wait!" They spun, elated to see a blood-drenched Crash catch up to them. "That fucker ain't got me yet!"

As they passed the paintings, they noticed Arawn had disappeared from each one.

"Where we going, Kel? There's no way out," said Tomo.

Through bittersweet words, Kel said, "To the stage; the show's about to start and there's nowhere else I'd rather be."

Even with the venue collapsing all around them, the moment Kel saw that tiny platform, she couldn't help but smile.

It was gonna be a hell of a set.

The Red Thirst

Steven Pajak

Wooden door creaks open to the dimly-lit bar,
Three desperate thieves with guns, we've gone too far.
The Red Thirst tavern seemed an easy score—
A deadly mistake we'd pay for in flesh and gore.

The patrons sit with whiskeys clutched in hands,
Unmoved by threats and all our harsh demands.
The bartender points us to the ancient owner's chair,
Where in the shadows, obsidian eyes silently stare.

"Empty the safe," we shouted, waving steel,
Not knowing our own entrails we'd soon feel.
Bullets merely tickled his unholy skin,
As black veins pulsed with hunger from within.

My first friend's wrist snapped like brittle chalk,
His screams cut short as teeth tore through soft jaw.
His ribs pried open with inhuman strength,
Heart still beating as it's devoured at arm's length.

My second friend split open throat to spine,
His organs harvested while still alive.
The creature fed with savage, raw delight,
As gore-soaked floorboards glistened crimson bright.

"This bar is mine," the monster calmly said,
As he crawled across the ceiling, dripping red.
Centuries of watching thieves like us come and go,
Each one rendered meat for his unholy show.

I alone was spared, trembling, slick with piss,
My soul laid bare beneath his endless abyss.
Claws against my throat, he made it clear—
Speak of this night and suffer worse than fear.

Centuries of hunting taught him ways to flay,
To keep a victim conscious for days and days.
Should I speak of what I saw or break his claim,
He'd peel my face and wear it like a game.

No distance far enough, no name I change will hide
From the ancient one who marked me deep inside.
For someday he will find me, of this I have no doubt,

When The Red Thirst rises, and his hunger seeks me out.

Mulligan

Andrew Najberg

J ojo wiped at the scuffed lacquer of the bar top, thinking for the thousandth time that someone had left a streak of sauce or snot or something. Really, she was just grateful she only had to polish the counters. The whole interior of Mulligan's was wood. Wood floors. Wood booths. Wood walls. Wood benches. A fire hazard, Jojo always figured. No way all that lacquer wouldn't just blow into a blaze.

Above her, the row of wine glasses hung upside down by their stems, and Jojo continued to pluck more from the dishwasher and wipe away the water spots. She hung the last of them in their line where they reflected the dim lights and glistened like a chandelier.

A murmur came from the end of the row of stools. Her brother Garret perched there, unwrapping a pack of cigarettes. He beat the pack-top against his palms three times, and then he transferred the cigarettes one by one into an old box of Marlboros so worn that the print had almost entirely worn away and the edges were all soft and rounded. His fingers moved the cigarettes deftly, almost unconsciously, and he twirled the final one before bringing it to his lips.

Jojo's eyes flicked to the silver Zippo that stood by his palm. "Don't even think about lighting that in here."

Garret rolled his eyes. "Ain't gonna."

Jojo lifted her chin in a vague gesture at the pack in Garret's hand. "One day that pack's gonna fall apart in your pocket."

Garret shrugged. "What you care if it does?

Jojo slapped the bar rag over her shoulder. Its light dampness against her skin gave her a shiver. "I reckon I don't, but I know you holdin' onto it because it was Pappy's." Then, she bent over and pulled up the dishwasher door. It groaned before it clicked into place. When she rose back up, she pointed to the front door. "Why don't you lock the door and turn off the sign?"

Garret grunted. "Do I look like I'm working?"

"Do me a favor, you ass. Faster I close up, faster we get you your damn six pack."

Garret's eyes flicked to the line of taps. "Would be easier if you just carried normal beer instead of all that fancy shit.

But, then Garret set down his cigarette by the lighter, straightened the pack beside it, and then slid off the stool. His weight seemed to settle on his frame, his belly a bit larger than the rest of his build should support. He adjusted the collar of his jean jacket and clomped his boots along the wood planked floor. Jojo ran her eyes over the bottles behind her, licking her lips. Even if she wanted to spend some of her tips on a drink, she'd given it up six hundred and ninety-seven days ago, that day marking the day she'd realized that she'd cost herself custody of her daughter. When her mom had died, her world had come apart–but she just hadn't been able to force herself to realize that didn't mean she stopped being a wife or a mother herself. Now, her ex and Rachel lived on the other side of the country.

She reached into the cabinet under the bottles to grab a box of cocktail napkins.

"Oh shit," Garret said sharply.

Jojo rose like a prairie dog and spun on her heel to her brother. Then, she saw the front door.

The woman stood on the other side of the glass, clutching a purse, picking at the strap with her fingers. Her eyes looked down and to the left. Her face was smudged with dirt and her hair hung in filthy clumps.

She reached forward and began to push open the door, but Garret caught the frame.

"We're closed," he said gruffly.

The woman whimpered. She wore a knee length dress, but it was torn under one underarm, the rip hanging open, exposing the side of her rib cage. Her knees shook, badly.

Jojo held up a finger.

"Hang on," she told her brother. Garret furrowed his brow, his face wrought with annoyance. The woman glanced over her shoulder, and as she did so, her hair fell away from her neck, and Jojo could see that it was heavily bruised. Had she been attacked in the parking lot? Was someone after her? Forgetting about the napkins, about closing, Jojo tossed the rag down and jogged around the counter. "Let her in."

Garret groaned, but he pulled the door open. The woman stood there still trembling, her hands now clutching at her elbows. Her eyes flitted left and right. Behind her, the night was deep, the overcast blocking out the moon and starlight.

The wood sounded hollow and Jojo's steps deep as her soles crossed the space between her and this woman. She reached out and took the woman gently by the bicep. Her skin was cold, like she'd been outside for way too long. Was she homeless? Jojo frowned as she recognized the designer logo on the dress; if she was homeless, she'd fallen far.

With a gentle pull, she eased the woman forward. The woman complied, stepping into the bar. Garret closed the door and locked it behind her, then he walked back toward the bar. *His cigarettes*, Jojo knew. No doubt he wanted to grab his cigarettes, the unaware dolt.

"Are you okay?" Jojo asked. Her eyes flicked back to the door glass. The parking lot looked empty. A mist hung over the spaces. Her own battered SUV was at the far end in the dim light. Was that someone moving in the shadows? Or was it just one of the saplings the owners had planted just the week before?

She looked back and realized Garret had stopped halfway to his old seat. He now stared back and forth between the woman and the door over his shoulder.

"Has someone hurt you, mam?"

The woman's face twitched. She drew in half a sharp breath. Her neck twisted slightly left and then right.

"H-h-have," she said, half-whisper, half-rasp, "have you seen a little girl? Is my daughter okay?"

A cold feeling welled in Jojo that something terrible had happened. The woman seemed dazed. An accident maybe? Or an attack?

"What happened?" Jojo asked. The woman's mouth quivered. Her knuckles whitened as she clenched at her own ribs. The tendons in her neck stood out, and Jojo could see her pulse in her temple. What to do? What to do? She needed to call the police, Jojo knew, but the woman seemed so skittish. She was like a thin pane of glass waiting for a rock that had just been thrown. Could she try to run? Jojo took her by the bicep again. "I'm going to take you to the back office. We'll get you cleaned up."

She caught Garret's eye and raised her eyebrows. She mouthed the word 'call' and hoped he understood. Then, she led the woman across the bar and through the door into the back. The kitchen shut down at nine so it was totally dark, but the single desk lamp in the office/storeroom was still on. The room itself was cluttered, stacked with boxes of napkins, packs of paper towels, and cleaners. An old utility sink stood in one corner, and after Jojo sat the woman down in the swivel computer chair, she grabbed a clean rag and wet it under the tap.

The woman said nothing as Jojo crossed back.

"I'm going to wipe your face and neck, okay?" Jojo asked.

The woman nodded slightly. Jojo pressed her lips together and leaned forward. A smell like old fruit mixed with that of a musty basement came off the woman. As the towel dragged a clear streak on her forehead, Jojo realized the woman was far dirtier than she'd initially looked. Her whole face was coated in a thin layer of grime that she hadn't noticed because there were darker streaks of bruise and mud or grease that were so much bolder. Her skin beneath all the dirt was dry and cracked, and there were tiny scars all over her cheeks and around her eyes.

"You've seen better days," Jojo said, attempting to make it sound good natured, but she cringed at her own insensitivity as she said it.

The woman said nothing.

"My name's Jojo, what's yours?"

The woman's lips parted as if she might answer, but before she could, a sharp rap sounded in the other room, and her mouth snapped shut. The rap came again, and Jojo knew the sound she'd heard many times over the years. Someone was knocking on the glass of the front door.

Just then, Garret called from the main space.

"Uh, hey Jojo?"

Had he gotten a hold of the police? Jojo's brow knit. Were they here already? It wasn't the best part of town, so patrol cars were often practically around the corner, but still …

"What is it?"

"I think you should come out here," Garret said.

The tone in his voice was guarded. Anxious. *Uh oh*, Jojo thought. Had whoever hurt this woman shown up?

Jojo snatched a can of mace from a shelf over the desk.

"I'll be right back," she said to the woman. "Everything's going to be okay."

Then, she strode back to the serving room, her hand clenched around the caustic weapon. There stood Garret in the middle of the floor, his hands held out from his sides in a helpless gesture. He gave a half-ass waft towards the door, his eyes wide with confusion.

Jojo followed his lead and gasped.

There in the window of the door stood the woman, again clutching at her arms, picking at her purse.

W. T. A. F. Jojo thought. Could this be a twin? But no–she wore the exact same tattered dress. Clutched the exact same purse. Her face was smeared in all the same places. Jojo looked back over her shoulder towards the office. The door was still open, but she couldn't see the desk inside. Couldn't see the woman sitting at it.

She looked at Garret.

He mouthed, "what the fuck?"

Jojo shook her head and shrugged.

"I'll get the door," Jojo said. "You stay with her in the office."

"That's not safe," Garret said. "What if—"

"I've got mace," Jojo said, holding up the can. "I'll be fine. You're usually not here to protect little old helpless me."

Garret opened his mouth but then he didn't argue. Instead, he just headed to the back. *Good little brother*, Jojo thought as she herself crossed to the door.

She was just reaching for the lock when Garret called out, his voice full of panic. "Stop."

Jojo turned. Garret stood there in the office door, his face pale as bleached briefs.

"She's gone," Garret said.

Jojo's eyes widened, and she sought out the corners of the bar. Was the woman in the booths? Had she slipped into the little hall to the bathrooms? Could she be crawling behind the bar?

She practically leapt out of her skin as the woman outside rapped on the glass again. Jojo spun to the door, her breath coming in fast gasps, her heart pounding.

The woman pressed her palm to the glass.

"Have you seen my daughter? A little girl?" she called out.

Ice ran through Jojo's veins. The mace in her hand felt like a hollow thing, and it almost fell from her grasp. A knot dropped down Jojo's throat as she tried to swallow down the fear rising up her gullet.

Behind the woman, the night had darkened further; all the parking lot lights seemed to have gone out, the only lights now coming from the windows of the hotel a little ways past the edge of the parking lot. The mist gathering over the lot had thickened, so even those bright lights felt dim and distant. Within the mist, however, it looked as if dark shapes moved back and forth. Like tall men were stalking from one end of the lot to another.

Suddenly, the glass between her and the outside seemed too thin. There'd been a mugging once in the parking lot where a man had been set upon by a group of local thugs from the bad part of town, but this was a decent stretch. The hotel mostly served corporate folk. Jojo had never felt uncomfortable; everyone in the neighborhood knew her.

But this—this was different.

This looked like something demonic. This looked evil. She wasn't one to believe in evil, but her bones knew something was wrong.

The woman stood there waiting. Trembling. She glanced side to side and back over her shoulder. What would she do if Jojo just didn't open the door?

She startled again as a floorboard groaned behind her. She jumped and spun, only to find Garret standing right there. She punched Garret in the chest.

"You scared the shit out of me, you asshole," she said.

She tried to punch him again, but he caught her wrist. He gestured with a half-nod to the door.

"What are we going to do?"

Jojo frowned. She didn't want to look back at the woman. She hated leaving her out there, even if she knew something was wrong.

In the woman's bathroom, on every stall and every door, hung a list of drinks women could order to let her know if they were in danger. Could she live with herself turning her away if there was even the slightest chance she'd been abused? What about her daughter?

"I don't know, I don't know," Jojo whispered.

"I don't like this. But I'll tell you one thing," Garret said. Then, he stuck a cigarette between his lips and flicked the wheel of his Zippo. "I'm smoking a fucking cigarette and there ain't shit you can do to stop me."

As Garret lit his cigarette and took a drag, he set the lighter on the booth table beside him. He'd set it next to a bottle of Jack Daniels he must have grabbed from behind the counter. She wanted to be mad, but Jojo smirked and let out a chuckle. It felt so good to chuckle, like some spring wound up inside her released a little of its tension. The anxiety that had been clawing inside her backed away. *Thank God for her brother*, she thought, *always the asshole*. Somehow, that thought grounded her, and the rest of her thoughts felt a little clearer, and she realized that whatever this was, it was not normal. It was not something that a little can of mace would help with, not even the handgun behind the bar under the register.

"I don't know what this is," Jojo whispered, "But I think we should get out of here."

Even as she said it though, she winced inwardly. Her car was at the far end of the lot. Through the mist. Past all those dark shapes. She'd have to open the front door or go all the way out the back and around—

Or, she thought, they could just go out the back. They could go straight out and run through the little green belt between Mulligan's and the row of fast-food restaurants. They wouldn't have a car, but that was fine. They could just keep running until they found somewhere safe where they could use a phone and call an uber. The car would be there the next day. The next week. Whenever they felt safe enough to get them back.

She pointed discreetly towards the back, hoping Garret would understand without her having to spell it out. He did, raising a single eyebrow in confirmation. They started towards the back door together in stride with each other. Jojo peered about as they did, still hoping that somehow the woman she let in was crouched or sat somewhere inside, that it was some bizarre coincidence that an identical woman had come to the door.

The door itself though ... Jojo didn't dare look back. Couldn't bear to see that woman standing there, if she still was, looking petrified and helpless. She couldn't bear to see those dark shapes in the mist, the darkness of the world outside from which that woman had come. That ghost.

That had to be it, of course, Jojo knew. Who's to say what had happened to spawn her, but it was the simplest and most obvious explanation, as impossible as it was.

They reached the back door, and Jojo turned the deadbolt. As she pressed her palms to the bar, she hesitated, convinced that when she pushed it open, there she'd find that same woman waiting in the back alley. To assure herself, she chanced a single look to the front of the bar.

The woman still stood in the window, except that now she was just a dark shape. Her arms had grown long, her fingers hanging all the way to the ground. Her eyes glowed a pale yellow.

With a yelp, Jojo shoved the back door open and spilled herself out, Garret right behind her. The cool night air barreled over her, the evening damp and heavy. A crumpled wrapper skittered across the pavement with a rustle. The open dumpster stank of rotting chicken and milk. The old fence behind it ran the length of half the property, but Jojo's eyes went straight to the gate that she knew was there.

She pointed to it.

"That way," she told Garret, and they both broke into a run, their shoes scraping the grit of the pavement. Though Jojo was out of shape and even a short run immediately raised her heart rate, she already felt better. Safer. Her and her brother were running unfettered through the outside. Just moments until they'd be off Mulligan's property. Until they were simply out in the night looking for somewhere they could find help.

When they reached the gate, her fingers found the latch with ease, and she lifted it and flung the door open.

A huge, black figure stood there, blocking the path.

It reached out a thick, black arm, and its huge black hand passed straight through Garret's shirt and into his left breast. Its muscles flexed as its hand clenched, and it crushed his heart with a sickly squelch. Garret's legs instantly buckled, and he thudded straight to the ground.

His eyes were wide open, dead in their moment of shock.

Jojo backpedaled frantically, her arms pinwheeling to keep her balance, even as the black figure stepped through the gate toward her. She turned to run out the side exit of the alley, the one that would take her right to the street. There, in the mouth, stood three more hulking black figures.

With a gasp, she skidded to a stop and launched her momentum back towards the back door of the bar. She slammed against the wall beside it even as she grabbed the handle and flung it open. She practically poured herself into the back hallway, jerking the door shut behind her. Frantically, her fingers found the deadbolt and threw the latch home. Her breath came in ragged gasps as she staggered back into the bar.

She leaned against the counter as her raging heart sent pulses through her vision.

Movement out of the corner of her eye drew her gaze to the office.

The woman shuffled out. She still clutched at herself, but her arms were four feet long now, her elbows angled outward like spider legs, and her mouth was a mess of fangs that jutted out like hedgehog quills. Her breath rasped in and out of her nose, and foamy spit dripped down her chin.

Despite the malformation of her mouth, she managed to hack out the words, "My daughter."

"I don't even know who you are. Who your daughter is."

"Then. I'll. Take. You."

The woman's massive arms launched out and grabbed Jojo by the face. They were icy cold, and that frigid chill instantly spread into Jojo's bones. She felt something grinding through her skull that spread down her neck and into her shoulders. Her ribs seemed to crunch in on themselves, and she could feel her spine twitching and bucking against itself. Agony filled her being, but even as it did, she found herself aware that she seemed to be collapsing in on herself.

No, not collapsing. Shrinking.

She staggered backwards across the main floor, every joint jerking and twisting. Her mind flashed with images. Of rancid whiskey breath. Of swinging fists. Of cracking bones. She could remember being beaten savagely, pummeled off her feet, even as she managed to catch herself as she fell on the edge of a booth.

Something fell over with a sharp clank and something wet and stinking splashed down her face. Her fumbling fingers found the bottle of Jack that her brother had left on the booth. Her knees snapped and reformed, her body continuing to transform. Her feet were now too small for her shoes, and her heels slipped right on out. The ghost woman approached her with slow steps, those hideously long arms outstretched like they hoped to scoop her right up.

Jojo slapped around on the table until her palm landed over the lighter.

The whole place was wood and she was whiskey drenched.

She didn't know what exactly this was, only that this creature was making her something she could not accept.

She flicked the Zippo wheel until a flame danced on the metal housing.

Then, she tipped it onto the whiskey coating her hand and gave a snarling grin as the blue flame burst down her skin.

Original Artwork by Alexandrea Christianson

The Special on Tap

Jay Bower

B ill Clark's ass stung, so he took another drink of his beer to numb the pain. The vinyl barstool was cracked and the cushion exposed, making for an uncomfortable seat, but he didn't dare move. The bar was nearly full with college kids doing stupid shit like drinking shots of Jager or pounding down endless glasses of cheap margaritas. He already had to fend off one girl that tried to claim his seat. It was a dumb idea to come here on a Wednesday $5 pitcher night, but that's what the girl he was texting with wanted to do. Who was he to say no when a chance to get into her pants was on the line?

Bill chugged the rest of his Blue Moon and ordered another. If Tanya didn't show up soon, he'd be as sloppy drunk as most of the kids in the bar. Good luck getting it up then.

It had been four months since he last enjoyed the pleasures of a woman. Since then it had been a nightly ritual of Pornhub and lube. Not that he was too upset about it, but it was nothing like the real thing.

When he and Tanya found each other on Tinder, the possibility of a casual relationship seemed imminent. It had taken four attempts at going out before Tanya finally agreed to meet. It was her that chose The Cove, one of the few remaining bars in Brownsville. Though not a college town, it was close enough to the university that many students would crowd into their cars and make the fifteen-minute drive to swarm the place, especially on discount nights like tonight.

The bartender, a kid barely old enough to drink himself, dropped off the beer with a sickly looking slice of orange clinging to the brown lip.

Bill glanced at it, then up at the kid. "Thanks," he said, trying to sound like he meant it. The constant thump of Kendrick Lamar followed by Drake and back again was a wild dichotomy of sound. The kids playing the music through the jukebox giggled every time it switched between the two artists as though their real life feud was playing out in The Cove.

Ten years removed from his college days, Bill hoped he wasn't like them when he was their age. Most likely he was, though instead of margaritas, he was all about the cheap beer nights.

Bill pushed the orange into the bottle and prayed that he wouldn't regret using the sad looking slice, and then took a long drag of the cold beer.

A cool rush of citrusy wheat hit his tongue, washing away the bitter thoughts starting to crowd his mind. He checked his phone again. 9:48 p.m. Still no text. Tanya was twenty-three, according to her profile. Twenty-three-year-olds were always late. Still, unease had started to set in.

A chair screeched behind him, metal legs scraping concrete. Bill turned his head just enough to spot a guy in a backward hat, eyes glassy, collapsing into a booth with a pitcher in each hand. His friends howled with laughter, one of them slapping the table hard enough to knock over a salt shaker.

He shifted his weight, instantly regretting it as a spring jabbed his thigh through the exposed foam. Bill grimaced and took another drink. The bar smelled like cheap tequila, Axe body spray, and sweat. But underneath it all was something else...something metallic. He wrinkled his nose and looked around.

The bar was long, lined with half-empty liquor bottles with color-ful plastic toppers as though a rainbow puked all over them. Behind them flashed neon beer signs surrounding a mirror that reflected the crowd in warped, watery shapes. At first, he thought it was just the beer messing with his vision, but when he blinked, the reflection didn't match what was behind him.

In the mirror, he saw himself in the same seat and same posture, but Tanya sat next to him, leaning in close, lips moving like she was whispering something in his ear. Except, she wasn't there.

He turned to the seat beside him. Empty.

"What the hell?" he muttered. Was he getting to be that much of a lightweight that two beers was already sending his head into a tailspin?

The kid behind the bar caught his eye and gave a goofy smile. "You good, man?"

"Yeah." Bill looked back at the mirror. No, Tanya. Just his tired, slightly flushed face and the flickering neon framing the mirror.

Maybe he really was getting too drunk. He set the beer down.

That's when he noticed it.

Everyone in the mirror was frozen.

The frat boys mid-laugh, the bartender mid-pour, the blonde girl at the end of the bar mid-sip. All perfectly still. Only his reflection moved, confused and slowly turning toward him with a bottle of Blue Moon in hand and a slowly widening grin.

Bill stumbled backward, knocking over his stool. The clatter startled a few of the college kids, but most just laughed and turned back to their conversations. The mirror, when he looked again, was back to normal.

What the hell was in that beer? He thought about the orange slice, the slightly rotten look of it. Had someone tampered with it and given him some kind of hallucinogen? Was he roofied?

He picked the stool back up and sat, eyes glancing toward the door. Maybe he'd just leave. Tanya wasn't worth this. Pornhub was looking like a better option by the second.

Then his phone buzzed. It was a text from Tanya.

I'm here. In the bathroom. Be right out.

He exhaled. She had been there all along and was probably nervous about hooking up with an older guy. He shot a look toward the mirror and everything was normal. He smiled. *Ok. Maybe it was just the beer. Or the orange. Or both.*

Bill stared into the mirror toward the bathrooms. They were tucked in a shadowy hallway near the back, behind an old pool table no one seemed to be using. A pair of neon beer signs flickered like candles about to die. That metallic scent drifted again, stronger this time. Like iron. Like blood.

He told himself it was nothing. Just nerves.

Tanya emerged a moment later, wearing the same dark blue dress she'd posted in her last selfie. She was even prettier in person, though her eyes looked darker somehow. Not in color. Just their depth. Like you could fall into them if you weren't careful.

"Sorry," she said. Her voice was light, but her smile didn't quite reach her eyes. "Had to get ready. You know how it is."

"No problem," Bill said, standing, unsure whether to hug her or just sit back down. She slid into the seat beside him before he could decide.

"I like this place," she said, drumming her fingers on the bar. "Feels old. Like the walls remember things."

Bill laughed nervously. "That's one way to put it."

They ordered more drinks. The nervousness Bill felt slowly dissipated. They talked over their drinks and the loud music. Most of the conversation was Tanya asking him questions. Where he worked. What he liked. If he believed in ghosts.

That one caught him off guard.

"I mean, not really," he said. "But I did have a weird moment earlier. Probably nothing, though."

"Nothing's ever just nothing," she said, swirling her margarita with a straw. She could have fit right in with the rest of the kids in the bar, though there was an air of mystery around her that Bill found intriguing and slightly unnerving. "Some places remember. And some things don't like to be forgotten."

Before he could respond, the lights flickered. He wrinkled his brow. Then it happened again. Then everything went dark for three seconds.

When they came back, the bar was empty.

No drunk college kids. No music. No bartender. Just him and Tanya, sitting in the eerie stillness.

Bill's eyes bulged. He stood, but the room felt wrong. The air was heavy, like walking underwater. The bottles behind the bar were coated in dust. The jukebox was unplugged. The floor was damp and streaked with what looked like old blood smears.

"What the hell is this?" he whispered.

"This is what it really looks like," Tanya said. "Not the illusion. Not the sugar-coated version the drunk ones see."

"I...I don't understand."

Tanya stood, her expression dark, with deep shadows beneath her eyes and on her cheeks. "The Cove was built over something. A long time ago. When the town was smaller. They buried it, like they always do. Built over it. Covered it in laughter and drinks. But it's still here. And it needs to feed."

She stepped close. Her breath was ice. Her eyes were bottomless pits, black from corner to corner.

"And you, Bill, are the lucky one tonight."

The floor trembled. The bar rippled, like a mirage seen through heat.

Behind the counter, something moved. Something huge. A shape writhing under the cracked tile. Pale arms began to emerge, too long, too many joints, slapping blindly at the floor and dragging a slick, glistening mass of an abdomen behind them. It was like a spider fused with a giant squid and as large as a man and seemingly growing larger as it pushed through the floor. Long fangs descended from its mouth that snapped open and shut. It hissed a terrible sound that sent shockwaves of fear through Bill's body.

Bill backed away, but his legs were sluggish. He turned toward the door. It had vanished, just a blank wall now. The windows were gone. He was trapped.

"No one will remember you," Tanya whispered. "Tomorrow night, your seat will be full again. And the next. And the next."

She smiled, her mouth widening until it split her cheeks, her flesh ripping, revealing rows of teeth like jagged splinters of bone.

"And if they do remember, they'll call it a ghost story."

The last thing Bill saw was his own reflection in the mirror, frozen with a horrified open mouth scream etched on his face, watching without moving as the spider thing pulled him screaming into the floorboards.

The Special

Elizabeth Devecchi

B ob sauntered into the diner and let his gaze wander. The top left portion of his lips crawled into a sneer, and his nose scrunched up as if attempting to escape the thick cloud of greasy smoke that greeted his flaring nostrils.

A shit hole, of course, he thought, not surprised in the least. His colleagues had no sense of class. No clue about how to navigate—or even locate—the path to success. No worries. Soon they would no longer be his colleagues, just skid marks in the depths of his memories. Bob had no intention of lingering any longer than absolutely necessary on this subpar rung of his ladder to success.

"Whoa. This place is *authentic*," said Ken, cuffing Bob on the shoulder.

Bob tilted his head, focusing in on the dark blue fabric of his fine wool suit jacket. Was that a grease print? Maybe it was just the oily feeling of the air in the bar creating an illusion. Ken did have sweaty palms, though. A sign of his inferiority, as far as Bob was concerned. Mindy, the office secretary, found Ken's insecurity endearing. It made Bob nauseous. He would be getting this suit dry-cleaned as soon as he arrived home.

"Damn, yeah. Feels like we've been whisked back to the 50s! ... or were the 60s the heyday of family establishments?" asked Big Randy.

Bob side-stepped to avoid a nudge from Big Randy while wishing there was a way to avoid his gritty, needy voice and fetid breath. If only he hadn't left his earbuds at the hotel. He could have at least bested the first of those assaults. A mistake he would not be making again. He sighed and forced his mouth into what he hoped resembled a smile. His *salesman smile*. Was it convincing? He really didn't care. After his performance at the conference this weekend, he was certain he would soon be moving up a floor to management, where his resting scowl-face could be put to good use.

"Bi ...," Bob cleared his throat, secretly chuckling at his averted slip. "Umm, Randy?" *Big* Randy was *his* name for his oversized coworker. His *secret* name. He gave his throat one more clearing, his hand fisted in front of his mouth as if to politely stifle a cough. Then he extended the other hand, index finger raised to let his audience know he would be right with them. "Ahem. Randy, my man." Randy stared, patience in his wide eyes and sweat beading on his forehead, oblivious to the smile behind the fist. "Weren't there any nicer places nearby?"

Big Randy was the one who suggested the little bar and grill, claiming it had fabulous reviews online. Now, looking around, Bob was certain those reviews must have been written by the owner and his friends and family.

"Nope. None that were open and close enough to walk to."

Close enough for you *to walk to*, Bob thought, his head swaying in an almost imperceptible shake.

"Yeah, I looked, too," said Ken, planting a claw-shaped palm on Bob's shoulder, thereby cementing his plans to have the suit professionally cleaned as soon as possible. "But, this will be fine. I mean, the nostalgia alone is worth the trip." He lifted a hand and swept it through the air in a grandiose gesture recalling that of a giddy tour guide.

"The bar at the hotel is open, but you said you wanted to get out of there, to take a walk and get some fresh air," Big Randy added, shooting Bob a knowing look. "We could go back there if you want."

Bob sighed. He had, in fact, told them he wanted to go somewhere outside of the hotel. He had actually wanted to go somewhere outside of the hotel to eat *alone*, but his *team* had seen him heading for the door and decided they should all eat together, maybe do some strategizing for their return to work the next day. Bob didn't want to strategize, but he also did not want to jeopardize his *teamwork* score. He needed it to implement his advancement strategy, the one that would leave the other two teammates in the dust.

He was about to suggest that maybe the hotel bar wasn't such a bad idea when a voice interrupted the thought.

"Party of three?"

There was something hesitant about the silky voice, like it belonged to someone who was afraid she might be intruding. Someone insecure. Young and insecure. Bob turned his head to find its source. A shapely young waitress stood beside the group. Her large doe-like eyes flitted to and fro, briefly locking her gaze on each member of the small group, then away.

"I'm so sorry if I startled y'all," she said, a slight blush animating her cheeks. "Would you like a booth or would you like to sit at the bar?"

"I think we might actually head back to the hotel," said Ken, side-eying Bob.

"Nonsense. We'd love a booth," Bob said, taking a step toward the young waitress. He was smiling his widest smile. The toothy one he used to close a deal. The one Charlene—his third and current wife—said made him look like a shark.

It's a shark's world out there, babe, was his got-to comeback. Charlene would giggle and hold her hand out, wiggling it as if it were a little fish. *Does my big strong shark want some dinner?* she'd taunt. And it always made him hungry for her.

At least, that's what used to happen. Now, the hint of a wrinkle or two marred his wife's otherwise unblemished face. *Laugh lines*, she called them. *Crow's feet*, he thought. But he wasn't about to walk away. Charlene was good at chatting up the wives of the higher-ups. They liked her silly stories and her childish laugh. And, he knew that another divorce might upset the image he was going for. The one that would land him an office next to their husbands. Get him invited to the club. Besides, he was sure that at least a couple of those guys had girls on the side. That's the kind of thing you could do in C-suite.

"Follow me, gentlemen," the waitress said, turning to lead them into the heart of the old bar.

Ken smiled, obviously thrilled at Bob's change of heart. Big Randy shrugged, his mountainous shoulders pushing up his neck until it looked like it would swallow his head. Bob shuddered—on the inside.

He was wearing his confident-but-loveable-trustworthy-guy costume on the outside. It never failed him.

Bob made sure to be the first to follow their waitress. He didn't want to be caught focusing in on the firm young ass that swayed in front of him. He ran his tongue along the inside of his bottom lip, hypnotized by her hips and the way they tugged the fabric of her short pink dress, sliding it up and down the backs of her thighs with each step. He already knew where his imagination would take him the next time he had sex with Charlene.

His gaze shifted to scan the room. Business was slow. This did not surprise him. The hotel where the convention was located was in the middle of fucking nowhere, an eyesore among cornfields. The bar in the hotel was one of those big chains with a grill and a menu that covered just about anyone's taste. As generic as the suits most of the conference-goers wore.

An older woman sat by herself in a booth on the far side of the bar, near a little hallway that led to the restrooms on one side, and the entrance to the back of the kitchen on the other. On the table in front of her, a large mug of something and a wedge of some kind of pie wearing a tall pile of meringue like a top hat. The waitress directed the men to the other side of the room, next to a window. She stepped aside, laying out menus and motioning for the trio to sit.

When her hand drifted down to the pocket sewn into the front of her uniform, Bob felt his pants tighten and hurried to slip into his seat, where his appreciation for what lay beneath that pocket would go unnoticed. She pulled out a small pad of paper and a tiny pencil that barely had enough length to it to fit between her index finger and thumb.

"Can I get you boys something to drink while you look over the menu?" she asked, positioning the pencil so that the lead hovered just over the pad, then shifting her weight to one side, causing her hip to bump out in what Bob saw as a very provocative movement.

He looked across the scratches on the chipped wooden table to his companions. They were already scanning the menu. How could they not notice the aura the young woman exuded? Were they dead inside? Bob leaned forward to look at the name tag pinned to the waitress's uniform. Well, that and the breast beneath it, young and perky. He imagined it cupped beneath his palm. Imagined pushing her gently against the bedroom wall of the small studio apartment he could rent for her near his office.

"I'll have a Blue Moon," said Ken, snapping Bob from his own mind, where he had already undressed his future lover and was preparing to further explore her innocent, yearning body.

"I'd love the special on tap," Big Randy added with a smile, shifting all the attention to Bob.

"Well, Jen," he said, curling his lips back into an impish grin, "I'm feeling stout. Why don't you pick one for me, if it's not too much trouble?"

Another blush from the girl. Was she blushing because she knew where he'd had to look to know her name? Or had she noticed exactly *where* he was *stout?* He thought he saw buttons appear, pushing up the fabric at the tips of her breasts.

"I'll get those in and be back for the rest of your order," she said, jotting the information down on the pad. "Oh, and I'm Jen, and I'll be taking care of you tonight." She tossed a nervous glance around the room, then at Bob. She grinned. He nodded. She obviously didn't want to get into trouble for not introducing herself sooner.

Bob watched Jen walk away, letting his gaze wander from her dark, curly hair—which was gathered into a loose bun at the nape of her pale, sensuous neck—down to the backs of her worn white tennis shoes. His eyes drank in each and every curve on the way, bringing water to his mouth. She headed to the bar in front of the open portion of the kitchen, where a short, burly man dressed in greased-stained white sauntered back and forth tending to whatever he had cooking. It couldn't have been much. They were the only customers besides the old woman in the back, and she was already eating pie.

The cook adjusted the dirty white beanie hiding what Bob imagined was a balding—if not completely bald—head and grumbled something at Jen. Well, he couldn't actually hear, but it must have been a grumble by the sullen look on the man's face. Bob felt a pang of sympathy for the young waitress. She looked tired as she grabbed a full carafe off the warmer atop an ancient Bunn coffee maker, then rushed toward the old woman.

"Eh, Bob? You in there?" Ken snapped his fingers and laughed.

Bob did his best to mask the fact that he wanted to punch his colleague in the mouth and watch his teeth rain down onto the dark stained floor with an amicable smile.

"Sorry," he said, the imagined sounds of canines, cuspids, and molars clattering against the floorboards inspiring a much more genuine smile. "I'm thinking about that last lecture. It really spoke to me." He had a million primed work responses like that ready to go. This one seemed to fit the occasion.

Big Randy nodded, the rolls of his neck shifting forward then back. "Yeah. It was brilliant."

"Absolutely," Ken agreed. "But we should probably decide what we want to eat before the waitress comes back."

Jen, thought Bob. *She's a person. She has a name, you troglodyte.* Indignation broiled inside him.

"Damn! These prices are great," Ken said, focusing back on his menu. "And, there's so much to choose from." He tapped his index finger against the lamination. "I could go for some catfish. I wonder if they fish it from the river we passed on the way to the hotel?"

"Could be," said Bob, scanning the choices before him. "That would explain how they can sell it that cheap."

He wasn't a fan of anything that came from the water, himself. He was a red meat kind of guy. A meat-and-potatoes man. He held up his menu and glanced at the list of burgers. Those prices were also phenomenally low. Of course, the homes they had seen in the area were pretty decrepit-looking. If their prices were any higher, the locals most likely would not be able to afford to eat or drink at all.

And Bob didn't imagine many people wandered over from the hotel with a big named bar/grill located right there on the property. People liked convenience, and they preferred to eat at places they knew, with a recognizable name that inspired memories of past get-togethers and family meals. People did not like to risk dining at an unknown little joint like this, especially with all those reality shows about failing bars and restaurants and what went on in the kitchens.

"Do y'all know what you want?" Jen asked, setting their beers down in front of them. Her sweet, velvety voice pulled Bob's attention up from the list of possible hamburger combos with kitschy names, like the *Hungry Trucker* and *Officer Beef.*

Do I ever, he thought, unable to contain a grin. It took every ounce of his self-control to keep his gaze locked on her deep brown eyes. Not to let it wander down her curves to the dark triangular shadow just below her hemline that had caught his attention as his eyes had rolled up from the long list of burgers. Yeah, he knew exactly what he wanted.

"I'll have the catfish," said Ken, though Jen was not looking at him. Jerk didn't even say please.

She turned to smile at Ken and jotted down his order. Then she asked if he wanted fries or something else as a side, which, of course, led to a back and forth about what else was available. Like he couldn't read the fucking menu and leave the poor girl alone.

Once Ken had finished pestering Jen, Big Randy cleared his throat, then let out a *hmmm* like he was still making up his mind. "What's the soup of the day?" he asked, putting a hand to his almost nonexistent chin and rubbing at the patchy stubble that would never make a decent beard.

"Potato and bacon soup. Would you like some?"

He squinted his eyes and cinched his mouth as if gearing up to make a life-altering decision.

Jesus. Do you want the damn soup or not? Bob thought, desperate to have those fathomless brown eyes back on him where they belonged. He could see, no, *feel*, her desperation to get away, her need for assistance.

"That does sound good, buddy," he said, offering Big Randy a toothy smile, in hopes of moving things along.

Big Randy nodded. "Yes, it does. I'd like a bowl of the potato soup and a plate of fried chicken, please. Oh, and a side of French fries—the ones with chili on top." He raised the menu and pointed to something as she looked on. At least the big guy had said please, unlike the asshole sitting next to him.

While Jen jotted down the order, Bob watched her roll her top lip between her teeth in concentration. She shifted her weight from one foot to the other, erased something, then wrote again. He thought she must have to deal with customers like Ken and Big Randy all the time. Men who simply saw her as an object. Someone whose sole purpose in life was to bring them food. A simple avatar. Invisible.

Well, *he* could see her. Bob could almost smell the aura of mildew from the tiny, rundown house, or maybe trailer—he'd seen a couple trailer parks driving to the hotel— where she inevitably made her home nearby. She had a cheap gold ring on her pinky finger and a heart pendant lay cradled in her cleavage. Gifts from an abusive boyfriend? Husband? He knew desperate girls sometimes married young to escape their families. He didn't see a wedding ring, though, so it was probably a brutish boyfriend.

She turned her eyes to Bob, her smile sending warm, pleasant ripples through him. He felt his chest swell outward and his stomach pull in as he straightened in his seat, gripping his menu a little tighter. The deep resulting breath pulling in a miasma of the tantalizing scents of whatever soaps and shampoos she used, mixed with the salty sweat of a hard day's work.

"I was wondering if you have any specials," he said. "Or, maybe you can recommend something for a meat-eater like me. A very hungry meat-eater." He winked, donning a paternal smile. Something to put her at ease and to let her know that he was there for her. That he would be there for her if she came with him. He blinked a few times to refocus his mind to the present.

"Well, actually." She tapped her lips with the pencil eraser.

Oh, to be that eraser, he thought. He leaned in a little closer.

"We do have an off-menu item that might interest you," she said.

From the corner of his eye, Bob saw his work companions straighten. The quiet discussion they had begun after ordering fell silent.

Oh no you don't, Bob thought, shooting them each a side-eye. *You already ordered.*

"We have a new burger that the chef is trying out, with a special sauce. It isn't quite ready for the menu, but I think it's delicious." She ran her tongue over her lips to emphasize. Bob thought he might explode, envisioning that tongue against his skin. "We might be calling it The Flyboy Special. But the owner hasn't decided yet. I could ask the cook to make one up for you, if you're interested?"

Bob really didn't care too much about what was on The Flyboy Special and wasn't really listening when Jen described it to him. He was too busy watching her lips, her soulful eyes, her body language while she spoke. Imagining how difficult life in this backwards town must be for such a beautiful, innocent creature. Envisioning the grateful look in her eyes when he would tell her that he could get her out of here, help her escape. Picturing those eyes, attached to that body, when he let her express her gratitude to him over and over.

"Would you like that?"

The question was obviously referring to the Flyboy Special. But Bob knew that it would extend to a number of different situations in the near future and found it difficult to contain his fervor.

"That would be wonderful," he answered.

When Jen left to turn in their order, Bob excused himself from the table.

"Gotta hit the John," he said, throwing his team a knowing look. "Hold down the fort, will ya? Oh, and you guys go ahead and get the ball rolling on our return strategy. I'll jump in when I get back."

"Will do, team leader!"

Big Randy's enthusiasm elicited a twinge of guilt about what Bob was planning to do when they returned to work the next day. But it was just a twinge, and he was able to stifle it before it took hold. He gave a thumbs up and headed toward the restrooms.

On his way by, he cast what he hoped looked like a nonchalant glance at the sign hanging on the entrance to the bar. It closed at 10 that night, the early closing he was hoping for given it was a Sunday. He looked at his watch. It was 7 o'clock. His brain set to work on the math as he continued on his path to the bathroom. They would definitely be finished eating by 8. There was no one else in the joint, so he imagined the food would arrive quickly enough. That would leave plenty of time to get back to the hotel, tell his companions he was hitting the hay early so he could get an early start driving home (because he missed his wife so darned much), and get back to the diner in time to see Jen when she got off work. Thank God he had turned down the offer to carpool to the conference, an offer he had only ever entertained to save some money.

His mouth slid up into a wide smile, his shark smile. One side faltered when he noticed the old woman staring at him. She, too, was smiling. Shit. Maybe she thought his smile was meant for her. The other side of his mouth dropped, resulting in a more neutral, polite "stranger" smile. She winked and ran her gaze the length of him, then went back to eating her pie, as if she hadn't just assaulted him with her eyes.

Bob entered the bathroom and splashed some water on his face to help shake off the heebie jeebies. I mean, really? Did it look like *he* would be interested in someone that old and wrinkly? She reminded Bob of his first wife, for Christ's sake. He relieved himself at the first of the two stain-streaked urinals, then washed his hands, adding one more splash of water to his cheeks for good measure.

On his way back to the table, Bob made a point of not looking in the direction of the table where the old woman sat. He could feel her stare, though, like tentacles reaching for him, trying to turn his head.

Nope, he thought, stepping up his pace to rejoin his group.

The rumblings of a disagreement reached his ears. It was coming from the kitchen. He looked over at the pass, where Jen stood leaning on the base of the large opening, talking to the cook. He was pacing back and forth between the window and whatever was sizzling, throwing up steam and or smoke behind him, sliding his beanie back and forth on his head whenever he spoke with her. A scowl distorted his weathered face.

Shoot. Bob hoped he hadn't gotten Jen into trouble by asking for the special. Poor kid. That fat, greasy bastard was probably berating her, maybe even threatening to fire her, to take away her only source of income. Well, he could go to hell. After tonight, Jen would be okay. Bob would make sure of that. Maybe he wasn't an executive yet, but he would be soon. And, he was sure enough of that to put a deposit on the little rental he'd seen when he was flipping through the paper last week. It would be perfect. Only a few blocks from work. In the meantime, he could put her up at one of the motels he passed every day on his way to and from the office.

When their meal arrived, Bob made sure to pay extra compliments about the speed of the service. And when they were paying the check, he thanked Jen for selecting a tasty stout and telling him about such a delicious burger (which he really did enjoy). She gazed at him with abject appreciation, with such a sincere and innocent smile. He wondered whether this poor girl had ever received a proper compliment in her life. That would soon change. Bob would appreciate her. He would make sure she knew what she meant to him. He would worship her. And man, that body. He would worship every inch of that body any time he could get to the apartment to be with her.

At around 9:45, Bob snuck down the stairwell outside his hotel room and out the back door. He hopped into the car, completed his early checkout online. He had decided he could help Jen escape that very night. If they left right away—after a quick stop to gather up anything she might need— they could spend the night together in a motel. Charlene did not expect him back until the next day. And, the yearning he felt, the incredible pull of his desire, would deny him any sleep that night anyway. No. He needed her, and he needed her now. Needed to save her from this desolate, hopeless town.

He parked just down the street from the bar and turned off the engine and lights. Shapes hurried to and fro beyond the shades of the windows, which were now down. Chairs were being stacked. Good thing he had come a little early. They had probably decided to go ahead and close. given the lack of clientele.

Bob exited his car, making sure to smooth out his suit as he stood. He had taken a quick shower and shaved. His body shivered with excitement as the night air greeted him, feeling like a cold, wet kiss against the thin, fresh layer of after-shave he'd applied. He slid through the darkness toward the diner. A large oak tree stood a mere ten feet or so from the back of the joint, offering the perfect place to wait for Jen. She'd most likely be emptying the day's garbage into the dumpster in the back soon. Then he could get her alone, spirit her away to her new life.

A door opened, the spring of an old rusty screen door squealed, followed by the sound of the door slapping against its frame. Bob peeked around the trunk of the tree, and there she was. Jen walked to the open dumpster and tossed in the two garbage bags she was lugging one by one.

She stopped and cocked her head. Had she heard him? He scanned the area around her to make sure that she was alone. Then he stepped out into the pale, flickering light of a nearby streetlamp, his hands extended palms out to show he meant no harm.

"Don't worry, Jen," he said just above a whisper. "It's me, Bob." He couldn't remember if he had told her his name, but knew she would recognize him. And, he knew by the longing in her eyes when he'd left the diner earlier that she would be happy to see him.

She startled at his appearance, but immediately calmed when she saw it was him. A sweet, hopeful smile crept across her soft, full lips.

The light from the lamp cast shadows across her face, making her eyes appear even darker, deeper, more inviting. Bob motioned for her to join him, unable to resist any longer. And, when she hurried over to him, he barely had the time to say hello before she threw herself into his arms, pressed her warm and willing body against his.

"Come away with me, Jen," he said, shocked by her fervent acceptance of him. She nuzzled her face into the crook of his neck, lighting flames inside him that burned with an almost painful intensity. "Come with me. I will rent you a place in the city where we can be together. I am in for a promotion and will soon be an executive in my company. I'll be making more than enough to take care of you. To treat you the way you deserved to be treated."

As he held her, let his hands fall and rise, exploring every curve of her, Bob confessed his desire. He told her how happy she would be. How she would be his. How he would save her. He held her out in front of him, drinking in the relief shimmering in her beautiful brown eyes. And   Bob was the happiest he had ever been.

Right up to the moment the hatchet buried itself into the nape of his neck, relieving him of his head and his life.

"Jesus, Hal, it took you long enough," said Jen, pushing the bloody, headless businessman away from her. "You almost hit me, too. You need to be more careful." She pushed past the man holding the ax, the one who had so recently been flipping burgers and deep frying strips of potato.

"At least you were able to keep this one occupied," said Hal, tossing the ax to the side. "When that pilot guy spotted me coming, I thought he was going to get away!"

"We're ready, Mother," Jen called toward the shadows cast by the dumpster.

The elderly woman who had been enjoying her coffee and pie earlier sauntered out of the dark to join them. She pulled out a measuring tape and did some quick calculations in her head. Then, leaned down to prod the meaty portions of the dead man's arms and legs before reaching into his pocket and retrieving his car keys.

"Take care of clean-up," she said, tossing the keys to Hal. "Your sister and I have some work to do prepping the ingredients for the Executive Special."

The Band Played On

Lance Dale

The fretboard of my bass is stained with red streaks and smears. Blood seeps from my fingertips with every note, but I have to keep playing. If I don't, we all die. I grit my teeth and play on, trying not to make eye contact with anyone for fear that I might break. They are watching me like rabid dogs ready to pounce. I must keep playing.

Our drummer, Matt, was the one who found out about the gig.

"Dude, they are going to pay us $1000 to play a show," he said with a loud voice that distorted my phone's speaker. Matt had the same temperament as a child who wouldn't stop jumping on the bed. "$1000," he repeated, just in case I didn't catch it the first time.

"Where is the show?" I replied.

"Some shithole out in the middle of nowhere. It's called The Boondock Junction. Seriously, who cares, though? Let's fucking do this, man. Jerry is onboard," he replied.

Jerry was our singer and guitar player. He had aspirations of being a rock star and loved being in the spotlight. It worked well because it took some of the heat off of me. I could sit back and play the bass in the shadows. I liked the bass because I didn't have to put myself out there. The thought of being at the front of a stage, singing to a mob of people, was about as appealing as getting kicked in the ass with a cowboy boot.

In the rare event that our band was invited to play a show, we always went with a band vote. If two of the three of us wanted to do something, we did it, no questions asked. It was smoother if we were all on the same page. Something about this show felt off, but I chalked that up to the usual nerves. Plus, one thousand bucks was double what we usually got paid to play. We could replace our shitty mixer with that.

"Alex? You still there?" Matt asked.

"Just let me know the date and when I need to be there," I said.

"Fuck yeah, dude," he replied.

I followed Matt and Jerry through a labyrinth of gravel roads lined with tall pines. They shot off in tendrils that seemed to twist and turn in every direction. I was happy I was following the guys, or I would have been lost, driving around in eternal circles like a motorized reenactment of the *Blair Witch Project*. Where the fuck was this place, and did anyone actually live out here? There wasn't another car on the road.

We rounded another corner and saw the flickering sign that read Boondock Junction. The building would have fit in perfectly with one of those 1800s replica towns we went to on school field trips. The warped boards were coated in flaky white paint. It didn't seem very big, but we had definitely played in smaller venues. There were a couple of guys in leather vests smoking cigarettes out front. We parked our cars and started unloading our equipment.

"You guys the band?" the biker with the mustache asked as we lugged our amps up the stairs and through the door.

"No, we're here with pest control. We heard there was an infestation here," Jerry said.

The man grabbed Jerry by the shirt and lifted him off the ground with one hand.

"We don't like smart asses around here," he said. Spit flew from his mouth with each word.

"Easy, man, I was just joking," Jerry said.

The man held him for a second, and a grin spread across his face. The other biker and he both started laughing.

"I'm just fucking with ya'. You looked like you were going to shit your pants," he said. "Here, let me help you out with that." He opened the door and grabbed a side of the amp, helping Jerry carry it inside. Jerry looked back at me and gave me an awkward smile. There was a lead weight in my stomach.

The inside of the place looked like every other small-town dive. There was a long wooden bar, tables, and a few TVs that flashed sports highlights. The pool table was shoved into the corner to make room for us to put our stuff. The lights had a yellow tint to them and shone off the bald head of the man behind the bar.

"Levator Scapulae?" he shouted, sounding out of breath.

"That's us," I replied, not giving Jerry a chance to be a smart ass again.

"Thank you guys for coming out. I'm Jimmy. I run this place. We only do the band thing once a year and everyone goes nuts for it. What the hell does Levator Scapulae mean anyway?" he asked.

"It's a muscle in your neck. You use it when you make a fist in the air," Jerry said. He and the biker set his amp down.

"That true?" Jimmy said, squinting.

"I think so," Jerry replied. We all looked at each other and shrugged. None of us fact-checked that. We just thought it sounded cool.

"Alright. Learn something new every day. Well, I'll stay out of your way. Let me know if you need me for something. Just remember what we talked about on the phone," he said.

"The 1000 bucks?" Matt added as he stumbled in carrying his bass drum. "Also, can I get a beer?"

"You're getting paid to play all night. No stopping," Jimmy said, ignoring Matt.

"Look, we're professionals. We got this," Matt replied, setting down the drum. "Now, about that beer ..."

"Coming right up," Jimmy sighed. Beads of sweat were running down his forehead.

"Dude, must be an alcoholic," Matt said to me.

"Why do you say that?" I replied.

"He's got the shakes. My old man used to get those," Matt said.

Jimmy came back with two beers. I noticed his arm shaking as he handed one to Matt. He extended the other one to me.

"No thanks. It's too early for me," I said.

"Don't mind if I do," Matt said and grabbed the second beer out of his hand.

Jimmy looked at me with a furrowed brow and leaned in. "Look. Some guys are going to be showing up, and they call themselves the Hell City Devils. They're a rough bunch, but they'll be fine. Just keep playing your music."

"We've played some rough places in the past. I'm not too worried about it," I said, which was a lie. My heart was racing like it was in the Olympics. I forced a smile.

Jimmy forced a smile back, and we stood there with that stupid look on our faces until Jerry interrupted us.

"Come on, Alex. We gotta get our sound dialed in," he said.

"I'm coming," I said, carrying my amp over while Jimmy returned to his perch behind the bar.

We spent about an hour setting up and then did a sound check. A few people shuffled in, mostly bikers. I wondered if any of them were the dreaded Hell City Devils Jimmy had warned us about. Whenever I looked at the bar, someone was staring at me. They would look away quickly when I made eye contact.

"You getting some bad vibes about this, or is it just me?" I asked Jerry.

"Yeah, things seem a little off, but I have the medicine for it," he replied. He pulled a flask out of his coat pocket and took a drink.

"I don't know what the fuck you guys are talking about. We're going to melt some faces tonight," Matt said, cracking open another beer. "Let's do a shot!"

Sometimes I wished I had Matt's ability to not give a fuck and be oblivious to what's around me. It must be pure bliss.

We went up to the bar, and Matt ordered us all a shot of tequila. It was a tradition we followed whenever we finished a setup. I looked at the clock, and it was 9:45. We were set to go on in about fifteen minutes.

"To a great show," Jerry said, and we all downed our shots. It burned a path down to my stomach, and I did my best to control what my face was doing. I hated tequila.

I ordered a beer to wash the taste out of my mouth, hoping it would also mute the feeling of dread I had in my guts. It seemed to work for the other guys.

By the time the clock struck ten, the place was packed. We were all set up in our corner and ready to play "Hair of the Dog" by Nazareth. We figured this was the kind of place where 70s rock would be our best way to win over the crowd before slipping in a couple of our original songs. Jerry had brought his acoustic guitar, too, just in case, but this didn't seem like the crowd for it.

Suddenly, the doors opened, and a group of bikers walked in. All of the air left the room, and people parted like the Red Sea to let them through. Their jackets read Hell City Devils on them. Their faces oozed with a miasma of malevolence. I stood as far back in the corner as I could.

"I want to thank you all for coming out. We're Levator Scapulae, and we're gonna play some tunes for you," Jerry said.

We broke into the song, and the crowd began to bob their heads. Some sang along, but not the Devils. I saw them hanging out in my periphery like a mob of sleep-paralysis demons. One of them was right in front, staring directly at me. I looked down at my bass and did my best to pretend he wasn't there. It didn't work.

We finished the song and broke into the next one, a cover of "Roadhouse Blues" by The Doors. The Devils didn't move or applaud. They just continued to stare. Jerry looked over to me as we neared the song's end and nodded. He wanted to slip in one of our original songs. We finished Roadhouse Blues and Jerry started talking into the microphone.

"This next song is one of ours. It's about ..."

"Shut the fuck up and keep playing!" Jimmy shouted from behind the bar. His voice was filled with panic.

"Fuck you, man. The message of this song is important," Jerry said back.

"Jerry, you're going to get us all killed. We're a little outnumbered here. Let's just play," I said.

"Can someone get me another beer?" Matt said from behind his drums.

Some of the Devils were beginning to snap out of their trance. The one standing in front of me started shaking his head back and forth like he was being attacked by invisible bees.

"Hurry up!" Jimmy shrieked, his voice raw.

I started playing the intro before Jerry had a chance to respond. He shot me a look of displeasure and started in on the guitar. The Devil in front of me snapped back into the trance and stared at me with mackerel eyes. His mouth was agape. We played through that song, which seemed to have a warm reception from the crowd, and then broke into a few more covers. After about eight songs, Jerry addressed the crowd.

"We're gonna take a smoke break," he said.

"No. No breaks," Jimmy shouted from behind the bar.

"Is this guy fucking serious?" Jerry said to me.

"Yeah, I need a smoke, and I gotta piss like a baby," Matt standing up.

"What does that even mean? In a diaper?" Jerry replied.

"No breaks. Keep playing!" Jimmy shouted as he was running towards the stage. He was in a state of panic.

Some people in the crowd joined in, shouting to keep playing.

"Look, we need to be able to take a break, or the show is off. I don't give a shit how much you pay us," Jerry said.

A woman's scream cut through the air. I looked just in time to see one of the Devil's heads jerk away from her neck. A stream of red shot into the air, and he shoved her to the ground. His mouth resembled a shark's, lined with razor-sharp teeth that jutted out in all directions, and his eyes glowed red. More screams rang out. The Devils began transforming, their faces distorted. Despite the chaos, no one ran for the exit.

"Start fucking playing!" Jimmy screamed, his gruff voice changed to falsetto.

Without thinking, I began playing the bass. The Devils stopped and faced me. They were snarling, and their razor-sharp teeth were barred.

Matt and Jerry were both frozen.

"Come on, guys," I shouted, and they joined in. The Devils returned to their trance state.

Jimmy mouthed the words "Thank you."

We played for what felt like forever. The Devils continued to stare while the rest of the bar patrons watched anxiously. Jimmy held up a piece of paper.

I can't explain everything, but it doesn't matter anyway. We have to be here and can't leave until the sun rises. It's the only way to break the curse. Keep playing or we all die.

I looked at the clock. We had at least four more hours until the sun came up. Jerry kept playing, and sweat was rolling off of him. He looked like he was going to keel over. There was no way we were going to make it. I started yelling, trying to get Jimmy's attention.

Maybe they had a jukebox or something. They could just stream the music, and we could wait it out.

Jimmy approached and put his ear up to me. I asked him about the music, and he shook his head back and forth. He went to the bar and began scribbling and held up another note:

Do ya' think I'm a fuckin idiot who didn't think of that? They don't respond to it. It needs to be live music. I don't make these rules.

I looked back at the crowd. We couldn't keep playing like this. We had run out of songs and returned to playing "Hair of the Dog" again. The Devils were still staring, frozen like statues. I thought about jumping down and smashing my bass over one of their heads but was scared that it would just wake them up. I heard Matt shouting behind me and leaned back to listen to him. Maybe he had an idea.

"Can you have them get me another beer?" he said and then passed out face-first into his drum kit. The music stopped. Jerry jumped off the stage and ran through the crowd. He went through the door before anyone could stop him. There was a wet-sounding explosion, and gore shot back into the bar. Then the lights went out.

Red eyes began to light up through the bar. There was a moment of silence, and then the room erupted with screams and inhuman growling.

"Matt, wake up!" I screamed, but he didn't move.

I saw the moonlight peering through the open door, and sickening, wet, explosive noises came from outside as people tried to flee.

I ran towards our equipment to try and hide. It was the only thing I could think to do. It was just a matter of time before they would find me and rip me to shreds. Then I saw it. Jerry's acoustic guitar. I unlatched the case and pulled it out. I had to do it. The only way I was getting out of this alive was if I played and sang. Then something ripped at my leg. I felt claws burrowing into me, and a flash of pain surged through me. I resisted the urge to scream and began to sing.

I felt the creature's grip loosen as I strummed a chord. They grew weaker. I kept strumming and singing, and they released. The bar went silent. There were no more screams, and I could see the silhouettes of the Hell City Devils standing still, staring. I wondered if anyone else was alive. I silenced those thoughts and kept playing. I was making up the words as I went, and it was all nonsense, but it was working. I kept going and going, my vocal cords getting increasingly raw. It had to have been hours. Then I saw a hint of sunlight peer through the windows, and relief fell over me. Just ten more minutes, and this would all be over. I strummed again, and there was a pop. I broke a fucking string. I saw red eyes light up around the room.

The last thing I heard was Matt shouting, "Can one of you get me another beer?"

Vintage

Elizabeth J. Brown

L iam Hoglund had worked in more London bars over the past couple of years than he cared to admit, but none of them had ever had an entrance like this one.

It wasn't numbered or marked. Just a matte black panel halfway down a side alley off Covent Garden, with a brass knob at its centre and a burnished lion's head knocker mounted above—like something pulled straight from a Dickens novel. There were no windows to speak of, no signage, no drinks list. Nothing to suggest what lay beyond, only the faint glow of a gaslight attached to the weathered brickwork to its right, casting flickering shadows over the cobblestones.

With a frown, Liam reached for the knocker. No sooner had he released it than the door swung inward, revealing a man in a sharply tailored suit—deep black with a subtle sheen that seemed to catch the light spilling from the hallway. His sharp features were framed by dark, neatly styled hair, his amber eyes sweeping over Liam with a calculating, almost predatory gaze.

The hint of a smirk played at the corner of his lips as he said, 'Mr Hoglund.'

Liam felt an unexpected heat rise in his cheeks: part embarrassment, part something harder to name. It wasn't just the man's appearance, but his poised, self-assured stature that made it hard to look away.

'Call me Liam.'

The man smiled and gestured for him to enter, closing the door firmly behind him. 'Liam, if you'd like to follow me.'

The air in the narrow hallway was thick, spiced with sandalwood, citrus, and something like burnt sugar. Liam let his eyes wander as they walked. Dark oak panels lined the lower half of the walls, their polished surfaces gleaming beneath the soft, golden glow of ornate sconces. Above the panels, deep plum wallpaper—decorated with intricate curling black patterns that seemed to writhe and shift with every step—stretched upwards, meeting the elaborate moulding of the ceiling.

The place felt like a goth's wet dream.

'This is the servants' entrance,' the man said over the sound of their echoing footsteps. 'Guests, of course, are received upstairs.'

Liam glanced at the back of the man's tailored waistcoat. Neat, expensive, and about as far from Liam's worn jeans as it was possible to get. 'Are you ... the owner?'

'Heavens, no. My name is Matthias. I am the head sommelier. It is most unlikely you will encounter Mr Ravenshaw during your tenure with us.'

'Oh. Um. Okay.'

Jeez, talk about airs and graces.

Liam couldn't remember the last time he'd heard such a perfectly clipped, upper-crust accent. It made him painfully aware of his own rough-edged east-end drawl. Compared to this bloke, he sounded like a street thug. Maybe this was a mistake. But God, he needed the money. Rent wasn't going to pay itself.

'I trust you have an appreciation for wine, Liam?'

'Uh, yeah. I do,' Liam said quickly. *Sort of.* It wasn't exactly his go-to drink of choice, but he could tell a Cabernet from a Merlot.

Matthias paused, glancing back with an expression of delicate amusement, as if he'd caught Liam's unspoken thoughts.

'How reassuring. Here at Ravenshaw's, a refined palate is not simply preferred; it is requisite. Our patrons have cultivated tastes, most ... particular. Naturally, we aim never to disappoint.'

Liam nodded, swallowing the impulse to say something that might make him sound stupid.

They turned a corner and began to descend a narrow staircase, the temperature dipping noticeably with each step. At the bottom,

Matthias drew an iron key from his pocket and unlocked a heavy oak door. It swung open with a low creak, revealing a vast shadowed cellar beyond.

Liam stepped through and stopped short, his breath catching in his throat.

The room stretched out before him like some ancient catacomb, its cool, dry air wrapping around him like a second skin. Stone walls rose into graceful arches overhead, sweeping curves more suited to a cathedral than a cellar. Rows upon rows of finely crafted wooden racks lined the chamber, each cradling dark glass bottles that caught the dim light and threw it back like polished obsidian. A subtle, layered scent threaded through the space: the earthiness of old stone, the faint musk of aged cork, and something sweeter—almost coppery.

'Impressive, is it not?' Matthias said, his voice soft. He moved with a dancer's grace to one of the racks, selecting a bottle with a gloved hand. He turned it carefully, presenting it to Liam as if unveiling a priceless artefact.

The label read: *First Summer Love. A bright, expressive vintage with top notes of sun-warmed skin and breathless laughter. The palate opens softly with fleeting touches and lingers on the ache of promises never kept. Finishes light, with a trace of something lost.*

Liam frowned, reading the words again, slower this time.

They didn't make any more sense the second time round.

Matthias smiled knowingly. 'Here at Ravenshaw's,' he said, each word precisely enunciated, 'we do not merely serve wine. We curate experience. Each vintage has been crafted with exquisite care to distill a memory, a feeling, captured at its purest and preserved for the discerning. Thus, you will find no mundane descriptions of region or grape upon our labels. Instead, each bottle offers a sentiment, a recollection … a fragment of a life once lived.'

He replaced the bottle with almost surgical precision, his gloved fingers ghosting over the rack.

'Now that you're joining us, it will be your responsibility to ensure that our patrons savour not merely the taste … but the memory.'

'The memory?' Liam echoed, trying—and failing—to keep the scepticism out of his voice.

'Indeed. Our clientele pay a premium for our service. It is not an experience they can obtain elsewhere. Mr Ravenshaw prides himself on what he has created here. Quality. Authenticity. Exclusivity. These are the pillars upon which Ravenshaw's reputation is built.' He tilted his head slightly, that calculating expression returning. 'Do not fret, Liam. It will become second nature in no time.'

Sure.

'Plus, all gratuities are shared amongst the staff.'

There was no way to conceal the smile that tugged at the corners of Liam's mouth. Based on everything he'd seen so far, these hoity-toity eccentrics probably had deep pockets. And if all he had to do was spout some bullshit about a bottle of red having the full-bodied warmth of a first kiss, then so be it.

A soft chime echoed from the far side of the cellar.

'Ah, excellent. Liam, do come and observe.'

Liam followed Matthias across the room to where three large oak doors stood. Set between the two on the left was a polished wooden panel, fitted with a row of small, age-worn brass bells, each neatly labelled: *Tasting Room, Stock Room, Staff Room.*

'This is our butler's bell system. Should any member of staff require assistance, they simply pull the cord in their designated room, and the corresponding bell alerts us here. It dates back to the nineteenth century, when efficiency and discretion were paramount. Mr Ravenshaw had it meticulously restored; he has a certain fondness for tradition.'

'Uh. Yeah. It's cool.'

The bell marked *Stock Room* chimed again.

'I'm afraid you'll have to excuse me for a moment. Please, acquaint yourself with the space. But do be careful, each bottle you see here is irreplaceable. To damage even one would be a grave disservice to our patrons ... and to history itself.'

'No worries.'

Liam watched as Matthias withdrew another key from his pocket and disappeared through the door to the stock room.

Left alone with nothing but racks upon racks of bottles for company, Liam let out a slow breath.

This was definitely weird. He'd be having words with his cousin for setting him up with a job like this ... when he actually managed to get hold of him, that was.

It had been a couple of days since he'd replied to one of Liam's messages. Maybe he knew Liam would have something to say and was avoiding him on purpose. He hadn't even read the last few texts.

Arsehole.

He stepped forward and gently plucked a bottle at random from the rack.

Quiet Resentment. A tightly wound vintage, sharp on the nose with hints of strained smiles and held tongues. Mid-palate offers undercurrents of brooding antipathy, rounded off with bitter notes of mutual disdain.

'Jesus.' Liam shook his head and returned the bottle to its place. 'The tips better be worth it.'

Within a few minutes of his departure, Matthias returned, this time with another man who looked to be around Liam's age, just shy of his mid-twenties. Like Matthias, he wore a tailored black suit, but his hair was dyed a vibrant red, and his expression remained impassive. In one hand, he carried a neatly folded stack of clothes.

'Liam,' Matthias said, 'this is Felix. You'll be shadowing him for your shift tonight. He'll show you to the staff room, where you can change into your uniform'—he nodded towards the bundle in Felix's hands—'and sign all the relevant paperwork.'

'Oh, okay. Nice to meet you, Felix.' Liam offered his hand.

Felix stared at it without emotion until Matthias cleared his throat. Then, without a word, he shook it.

'Excellent. I shall leave you in Felix's capable hands.' Matthias flashed a smile, turning towards the door to the tasting room. Just as he placed his palm upon it, he glanced back at Felix. 'Don't forget to get Liam to sign the non-disclosure agreement.'

Liam's eyebrows rose. 'Non-disclosure agreement?'

'But of course. Absolute discretion is part of the service we provide here.'

'... Right.' Tugging at the collar of his T-shirt, Liam glanced at Felix, who was still watching him, unblinking.

Just think of the pay cheque.

Three months into working at Ravenshaw's, Liam had to admit the exclusive wine bar had grown on him. Sure, the clientele were every bit as peculiar as he'd expected, but he found he didn't mind—not when his share of the tip pool on his very first shift alone had come to six hundred pounds in cash. He'd grown used to Matthias' regimented rules and obsession with perfection, and despite his unwavering demeanour, the man was always willing to offer guidance and the occasional word of praise. Even Felix was beginning to warm to him. All in all, it was turning out to be the best job that Liam had ever had.

'Liam, sweetheart,' one of the women called as he approached. She was immaculately dressed, her silver-grey hair swept up in a tidy twist. Her companion, equally elegant, gave him a small, expectant smile.

'Evening, ladies,' Liam said with a polite nod. He presented the bottle with both gloved hands, the label facing them. 'Your selection—*Moonlight Tryst*. A rare vintage. Delicate nose of forbidden affection and secrecy, with a haunting finish of what-could-have-been.'

The women gave a delighted murmur, and Liam stepped back half a pace to uncork the bottle. With practiced ease, he cut the foil below the lip, ensuring a clean line, then used the corkscrew with steady pressure, keeping the cork intact. No twisting of the bottle, just the worm into the centre, pulled slowly with control.

He presented the cork briefly for inspection, then wiped the lip of the bottle with a clean cloth. He poured a modest measure for each woman, careful to avoid dripping or over-pouring. The bottle remained cradled in one hand, label still visible.

Both women lifted their glasses with reverence. One inhaled deeply, then took a sip; the other followed suit. A beat of silence, then their expressions transformed: eyes half-lidded, mouths parting in something between awe and arousal.

'Oh my,' said the first woman. 'It's exactly as I remember it.'

'We'll take the bottle, darling,' her friend said, already pushing her glass forward.

With a smile, Liam inclined his head. 'Very good.' He poured carefully, filling each glass to just under a third—enough to allow the deep, rich liquid to breathe, as he'd been taught. Then he stepped back, leaving the bottle on the table. 'Enjoy.'

A glance around the room told him that, for now, all the guests were being well attended. Felix was returning with another bottle, and Amy, the newest addition to the team, was mid-pour at a corner table, serving an elderly gentleman. Matthias was nowhere in sight, though he had a talent for materialising exactly when required.

A sudden gasp snapped Liam's attention back to Amy. The glass she'd been pouring tipped, sloshing its contents across the table before tumbling over the edge and shattering on the hardwood floor. She froze, wide-eyed, the colour draining from her face.

Liam was at her side in seconds.

'I'm terribly sorry. Please don't move. I'll take care of that straight away,' he said to the guest, then turned to Amy, his voice low and steady. 'Go and get a new tablecloth. I've got this.'

Amy gave a shaky nod and hurried off, Felix close behind.

'Ah, don't worry, Liam,' the elderly man said, watching her retreat. 'These things happen. She's new, after all. Though I don't recall you ever making such mistakes when you first started.' He chuckled, a low, gravelly sound that petered out into a cough.

Liam crouched and began collecting the larger shards of glass.

'Place them in here,' came Matthias' voice beside him, sudden and close enough to make him flinch. He turned to find him holding out a dustpan and brush.

'Oh. Uh, thank you.' Liam dropped the shards in carefully, but as he reached for the final piece, a jagged edge sliced clean through his glove. Blood welled instantly, spreading across the white fabric in a vivid, red bloom.

The room fell silent.

Every eye turned towards him.

Matthias seized his hand with startling speed, enclosing it in his own and covering the wound.

'Liam, go to the staff room. Clean that properly and change your gloves. Then fetch Mr Hadlow a bottle of *Bitter Devotion*. You'll find it on the third rack from the left, bottom row.' There was an urgency in his voice Liam had never heard before: sharp, commanding, and edged with something colder. It chilled him to his core.

'Do *not* run,' Matthias added, low enough that only Liam could hear, his amber eyes intense. 'It is unbecoming of a Ravenshaw's employee.'

Without another word, Liam straightened and walked briskly from the tasting room. Only once the door swung shut behind him did he dare to breathe.

What the hell? Why had it felt like every person in the room had been transfixed on him? Their eyes, the weight of them, it was like a tangible pressure, squeezing down on his chest.

Shuddering, he peeled off his ruined glove, his bleeding finger instinctively finding its way to his mouth, and made his way towards the staff room.

After putting a plaster on his cut and pulling on a fresh pair of gloves, Liam straightened his tie. The feeling of disquiet he'd experienced earlier had ebbed, leaving him to wonder if he'd let his imagination run away with him.

Exhaling, he smoothed the lapels of his tailored suit jacket and stepped back out into the wine cellar. He'd expected to cross paths with Amy at some point, but neither she nor Felix had passed him. Not that it mattered, he had more pressing issues, like finding that bottle of *Bitter Devotion*.

Third rack from the left. Liam's brow furrowed as he scanned the bottom row. Of the twelve cavities, only three contained bottles, and from his earlier selections that evening, he knew none of them was what Matthias had requested. Even so, he gently pulled each one out far enough to double-check the label.

'Shit.' Had he misheard? He must have. Matthias never got anything wrong. He couldn't go back empty-handed and asking Matthias to repeat himself would definitely land him in the bad books.

No. He'd just have to keep looking.

A dull *thud* made him jump. He shot up, half-expecting to see the head sommelier marching towards him. But besides himself, the cellar remained empty.

Clearly, he'd forgotten to close the staff room door properly. It wouldn't be the first time. Chuckling to himself, he made his way over to it. To his surprise, it was shut tight ... unlike the door to the stock room.

In all his time working at Ravenshaw's, the stock room had always been locked. Always. Any questions he'd asked about it had been dismissed so smoothly that, somehow, he'd always accepted the vague answers without pressing for more. But now, the door was ajar and no one was around.

He raised his hand towards it, then hesitated. No. Matthias trusted him. If he got caught, at best he'd get an earful; at worst ... he really couldn't afford to lose this job. He let his arm drop.

Then, the soft chime of the butler's bell rang beside him, subtle but unmistakable. *The stock room.* If he'd needed any more encouragement to satisfy his curiosity, this was it. Somebody clearly required assistance, and it would be irresponsible not to see what they needed. Surely?

Carefully, he pushed the heavy oak door. It opened onto a set of steps that descended deeper than the cellar. The air was cooler here too, enough to raise goosebumps on his arms despite his uniform. Unlike the cellar, the lighting was almost non-existent, though a faint glow from somewhere in the stock room cast just enough illumination to see where to place his feet. The last thing he needed was for Matthias to come running if he tripped over himself.

Liam reached the last step.

Felix stood with his back to him, motionless, in the centre of the room. For a split second, Liam considered tiptoeing back the way he'd come. But the thought was obliterated the moment his brain caught up with his eyes.

Three reclining medical chairs stood in a neat row beneath the flickering fluorescent lights. Each was occupied by a motionless figure, strapped in place with restraints—chest, wrists, ankles, all bound with what looked like black leather. Dark tubes snaked from the crooks of their elbows to white machines with blinking LEDs, the quiet, rhythmic *whirr-chuck* of blood being drawn filling the room.

They weren't dead—*thank God*—but they certainly weren't conscious either. Clear plastic tubes protruded from their mouths, held in place with white medical tape. Their chests rose and fell in perfect synchronicity with the soft *hiss-click* of the ventilators beside them.

Something about the uniformity made the scene profoundly more disturbing.

Then he saw the fourth chair.

Felix stood over it, one hand steadying a transparent mask pressed to the occupant's face.

Amy.

Liam froze, his breath catching sharply in his throat.

She shifted weakly, a muffled sound escaping the mask, something faint, something almost like his name.

'Li …'

Her eyes rolled back. Her eyelids fluttered. Then, her body went slack.

Liam took a stumbling step back, his heel scraping loudly against the concrete.

Felix turned slowly, the mask still in his hand, his expression unreadable.

What the fuck? What the actual fuck is happening here?

A rush of air was his only warning before a firm hand clamped down on his shoulder.

'Ah, Liam,' Matthias murmured, warm breath brushing his ear. 'I hadn't planned on you seeing the decanting process quite so soon.'

Liam jerked in surprise, but with Matthias directly behind him and Felix in front, he had nowhere to go. He swallowed hard, his heart rabbiting inside his chest.

This was it.

This was the day he was going to die.

'Come,'—Matthias guided him forward with unsettling composure—'let's take a closer look.'

I don't want to. That's what he meant to say, but his legs moved anyway, dragging him forward mechanically, as if responding to something beyond his will. His eyes flicked constantly to Amy, even as Matthias steered him away from her and towards the nearest of the medical chairs.

Up close, Liam could see the blood siphoning machines were etched with strange little symbols. Delicate otherworldly markings that pulsed with an ethereal glow.

Matthias' hand shifted from Liam's back to his wrist. A feather-light touch that sent a deeper chill through him than anything he'd ever felt. If he ran now, how far would he get? To the cellar? To the stairs beyond the stock room? Would he even make it a step before—

'Within their lifetime,' Matthias said smoothly, 'every person amasses core memories. Those defining moments that shape who they are. These are the essence of their being. Their soul, if you will. You remember, I trust, that here at Ravenshaw's we curate an experience?'

Liam nodded weakly, throat dry, tongue like sandpaper.

'This,'—Matthias said, gesturing faintly to the scene around them—'is how. Every individual is hand-picked, either by myself or by one of my staff. We seek only the finest for our clientele.'

'B-but ... what about Amy? She works here.'

Matthias sighed, his head dipping with regret. 'Indeed. Unfortunately, Amy has repeatedly failed to meet the exacting standards Mr Ravenshaw expects. Tonight was her final misstep. I'm afraid her tenure with us has reached its end.'

Yanking his wrist free of Matthias' grasp, Liam backed away.

'So, what—you're just going to kill her? Drain her dry like some fucking vampire?'

The weight of his own words hit like a blow to the chest. Jesus Christ. *Vampires*. All those bottles ... they were blood? His knees buckled. He staggered, barely staying upright.

A slow smile curled across Matthias' face. 'Vampires? Oh, Liam,' he said, voice laced with amusement, 'I realise this has come as something of a shock but do try not to let your imagination run wild. This is simply a wine bar. A very exclusive wine bar.'

Felix, apparently dismissing Liam as any kind of threat now that Matthias had arrived, turned back to the machine beside Amy and began tapping at the controls.

'You're hurting her ...' Liam's voice rasped, barely audible.

'No. We're *preserving* her. Elevating her.'

Liam felt the bile rise in his throat.

'Why do you seem so shocked? She agreed to this. You both did.'

'W-what?'

'Oh, Liam.' Matthias gave a soft, chiding *tsk*. 'Don't tell me you didn't read the entirety of the contract before signing?'

'The contract?' *Fuck*.

'Indeed.'

Liam couldn't think. Couldn't form a single coherent thought over the pounding in his ears. His eyes flicked to Amy. Blood drained steadily from the tube in her arm. She was so pale.

He gulped. Jaw clenched. Hands trembling.

Matthias moved closer, his face just inches from Liam's. 'You have potential, Liam. Not just skill, but talent. You've seen beneath the surface of Ravenshaw's. There's no going back now. I want to offer you a promotion. Stay with us. Become a true connoisseur, an artist of taste.'

'Or ...?'

The silence stretched, taut and fragile.

The *whirr-chuck* of the machines filled the void.

Matthias' smile thinned. 'Take a moment to consider it.'

Matthias eased the heavy oak door shut with quiet precision. He did so enjoy his work.

Shifting the bottle in his grip, he made his way towards the table, letting the low hum of conversation wash over him.

'Apologies for the delay, Mr Hadlow.' He presented the bottle with a practised flourish. 'I'm afraid we were out of *Bitter Devotion*. May I instead offer *Unfulfilled Potential*? A little sharper on the palate, but wonderfully vibrant in the finish.'

Matthias uncorked the bottle and poured a generous measure into Mr Hadlow's glass.

Hadlow lifted it, inhaled deeply, then took a measured sip. A low hum of satisfaction escaped him.

'Ah,' Hadlow murmured. 'Now that is exquisite.'

'I thought you'd find it to your liking.' Matthias smiled, smooth as silk. 'It's a recent addition to our collection.'

The Wood-Man's Tavern

William Gray

The building materializes out of the rainy gloom like a picture in a darkroom, its features slowly taking shape as I grow closer to it. The drops hitting the roof of the car sounds are deafening, makes my anxiety even worse.

An open road map lies in the passenger seat of my Nissan Altima among days of fast-food trash. I know my doctor would have a fucking fit if he knew how I'd been eating, but desperate times. There are more important things than pre-diabetes and high BMI sometimes.

Things like a missing family member. A brother.

Shawn.

His picture is in my sun visor, held there by a large paperclip, and I pull it down as I creep closer to the business I've been looking for. I see our smiling faces, identical except for the fifty pounds between us, and feel a pang of grief.

He's not dead. He's missing, I tell myself. It feels like denial. Ever since July 5th—one day *before* Shawn's roommate reported he hadn't returned home after leaving our parents' house for the Fourth celebrations—I've felt like a piece of me is missing that should be there. A phantom limb.

The police couldn't find anything, so here I am. One would think that a person cannot simply disappear in the digital age, but apparently, it's still a thing. The cops say they've done all they can but aren't giving up.

So, I'll try my hand.

The route between our parents' home and Shawn's takes about six hours, but the evening he left had been just as nasty as it is now. I've got it marked in red Sharpie, a brilliant crimson line cutting through the roadmap I'd ordered from Amazon just for this purpose.

Kurt, come on, my father's voice says in my head. A memory of the conversation we had just before I left two days ago. *Let the police do their thing.*

Like he's already given up. Mom didn't even say anything. Just stared.

The building now has details. A gravel parking lot sits in front of an old, worn-down-looking single level, its name high on the roof in giant, wooden letters.

The Woodsman's Tavern, I read, but then realize that isn't quite right. The *S* is long gone, splintered chunks hanging to the board used for mounting them.

So, the Wood Man's Tavern now. Like Arget or Walmar. When we were little, Shawn and I would laugh about those missing letters. It was so *goddamned funny*.

I pull into a spot near the front and put my car in park. The rain continues its onslaught outside, never ceasing. Just the sound of it chills me to my bone. I check my phone to look at the forecast, but the weather app refuses to update. A quick glance at my service reveals three letters: SOS.

Ominous. I let out a chuckle, but there's an edge to it.

Stop being stupid. It's the middle of nowhere, and you know there isn't anything to be afraid of, don't you? You already know the truth. It's why Mom and Dad have already given up.

I throw my phone into the seat next to me and take a few shaky breaths.

Shawn wouldn't do it. Not like that.

Every time before, every *attempt*, he'd made sure that somebody would know if he succeeded.

Because the only thing more cruel than leaving someone is not telling them why or not telling them anything at all. Especially that last one. The not knowing.

He told me that after three quarters of a bottle of Jack Daniel's once. Drunk as can be, and suddenly his voice took on this somber, sober quality. Not a hint of a slur. We'd only been twenty at the time, and I was too young and dumb to stand up to him about the drinking. Too naïve to realize it was all a symptom of the same problem.

Shawn was six months sober when he left on July 5th. I can't imagine him throwing all of that away to stop at some shitty roadside bar, but it also wouldn't be the first time. Depression has a knack for finding its way in.

I pull the photo of us from the sun visor down and look at it for another moment. It was taken right after we got our matching tattoos on our arms: a simple logo from our shared favorite band. A flower with three arrows through it.

Before I can dwell too much on the two men in the picture, I shove it in my jacket pocket and climb out of the car into the pouring rain. My left foot is immediately submerged in a cold puddle, and I curse as I jog to the stairs and into the shelter of the rickety porch where the entrance awaits. A flickering red and blue open sign hangs in the only window that doesn't sport a closed curtain. Beyond it, a vacant bar sits in warm lighting.

I look back at the empty parking lot and feel a chill work its way up my spine. After a few moments, I turn back to the door and pull it open. A small bell above the door chimes, announcing my entrance.

"Hello?" I call out as I take my first few tentative steps into the establishment. The tavern is warm and dry compared to the damp air outside. Now that I'm inside, I can see that all of the furniture is made of carefully crafted wood. The bar itself is a huge slab of oak that is pockmarked with holes small and large. Dark rings where spilled liquid has stained it compliment the gnarled knots in the wood itself. "Anyone here?"

There's a clatter from behind a door set at the back of the room, and then a man pulls it open. The first thing I notice is that he's tall, the second is that he's very skinny. The two features together give him an otherworldly appearance when he raises his hand in greeting.

"Howdy, partner!" The phrase is so goddamn cheesy that I can't help but smile a little. The anxiety I was feeling alleviates some. "You look like you've been swimming."

"Might as well have. It's pouring out there," I say. I take a step closer to him, and a strong pine scent fills my nostrils. My nose wrinkles at the severity of the smell. "You the owner?"

"That I am," he says as he makes his way behind the bar and extends a hand over the scarred wood there. "John's the name."

The odd way the man speaks leaves me feeling unmoored for a moment before I hurriedly cross the distance and shake John's hand. His grip is stiff, his skin strangely clammy and the bones underneath too hard somehow.

"Kurt."

"So, what can I do for you, Kurt. You look like you could use a drink!"

I chuckle uncomfortably. "You're right on that count. Can I just get whatever you recommend on tap?"

"Tap's down at the moment. I've got bottles, though. You want a Coors or a Miller?"

Neither, really. "Miller will be fine. Lite?"

"Comin' right up."

I watch as John walks down the bar a few feet and drops to one knee. His bones crack audibly, and I narrow my eyes as I look at him. He doesn't look all that old, but he moves like he's ancient. When I look closely, I see scars along his hairline where stitches had healed unevenly. The pale skin of the healed skin stands out in stark contrast to the mop of black hair pushed back from his forehead.

Relax. You're being paranoid, I tell myself, but something about this place is making the hairs on the back of my neck stand at attention. It's almost like I can feel Shawn here, some lingering aspect of him.

I think he was here.

"Fridge doesn't run too cold," John says as he stands back up, his words underscored by the *pop pop pop* of his joints. "Hope that's alright."

"It's fine." Knowing full well I wasn't going to drink it anyway. "I have to admit, I didn't drop in for the drink."

"Oh?"

"I'm looking for my brother."

John makes a show of looking around the bar. When he turns his attention back to me, his lips stretch into a smile that makes my toes curl with fear. His teeth are brown, and the grin doesn't reach his eyes—which I now see are two different colors. Fuck, even the size of the irises isn't the same.

"Doesn't look like anyone else is here, does it?"

I reach into my pocket with a trembling hand and take out the picture. Place it on the bar between us. "His name is Shawn. He went missing a couple of weeks ago."

"Couple of weeks? That's a long while, partner. What makes you think he'd be here after all that time."

"I'm just wondering if he stopped in. Would you mind taking a look?"

John's mismatched eyes never leave mine when he responds, "I don't recall. Don't get a lot of strangers in these parts."

I break his gaze and look at his hands. See the same kind of scars there, and a fresh wound that is held together by...

Are those... staples? *Office staples?*

The red line circles his forearm just above the wrist. The cuff of his long-sleeved shirt is pushed up just enough to reveal it.

I need to leave. There's something very wrong here.

"Please," I say, my voice cracking. "Just take a look. If it isn't too much trouble."

John looks down at the bar and reaches out for the photo. His fingers are too long, the skin there stretched taut. I hadn't noticed it when he handed me my drink, but now I do. A pit opens in my stomach, and bile rises out of it.

"Twins. How... *peculiar,*" John mutters, mulling over that last word for a moment. "So much the same..."

His thumb moves over Shawn's face in the image, and I snatch the photo from his grasp. John recoils in surprise as I push back from the bar, my hand already shoving the picture into my pocket. Without missing a beat, I retrieve my wallet from my back pocket and toss a twenty on the bar.

"Thanks for your time..."

(get outside, call the cops, something is very very very wrong)

"... but I've got to get going."

John's face twists into an expression that I can't quite pin down. It looks like rage, but there's something else in it, too. Envy, maybe. Desire.

"You don't want your drink?"

"I told you, I wasn't really here for it anyway," I call out as I make a beeline for the door. I'm almost there when I hear his voice.

"I remember him quite well."

I freeze, shock fighting for dominance between anger and fear. My mouth is suddenly bone dry, and I wish I did have that Miller Lite on the counter. "What?"

When John doesn't respond, I turn back to the bar.

It's empty. There's no sign of the man.

"John?"

The warm light suddenly feels ominous. I notice there are too many shadows in the corners and above my head that it doesn't reach.

Mustering all the false bravado I can manage, I ask, "What did you do to my brother?"

From above my head, I hear a laugh filled with menace and evil. It makes my skin crawl as I retreat from the door. A form drops out of the shadows, so inhuman that it takes me a second to recognize the gangly shape of John.

How was he... how was he on the fucking ceiling?

"I repurposed him. Just like I will you, *Kurt.*" He hisses my name. "A piece of you will become part of the Whole."

I've heard enough. Whatever the fuck 'John' is, he's standing between me and the safety of my car, but I'm not without options. When I turn away from him and grab the nearest barstool, I catch him entirely off guard. I take in his slack-jawed surprise as I hurl the piece of furniture at him with as much strength as I can muster.

The fucker is *fast.* Even though I've caught him unaware, he manages to move entirely out of the way before it can hit him. His body contorts with a series of dry pops that make my skin crawl.

I continue to throw everything in my reach at him, which amounts to two more stools and an empty bowl sitting on the counter. John avoids all of them, twisting his limbs in impossible ways, but it slows his advance.

Because he *is* advancing. He's only six feet away from me now, and I can make out the murderous intent in his eyes. I'm not sure what he meant by *parts* and *wholes* and *repurposing*, but I don't really care to find out. My hand finds the neck of the still-full Miller Lite and I swing it in a wide arc, spraying amber liquid across me and the floor around us.

The bottom of the bottle connects with John's lower jaw, soliciting a pained roar that sounds anything but human. I see the glass shatter, watch the sharp edge of the bottle slice across the skin under his lip and then the right side of his face, but there's no blood. The flesh there simply splits and then slips away from his face as he collapses into a heap onto the floor before me.

What. The. Fuck.

For once, I wish my family had raised me around guns. If they had, maybe I would be carrying one right now. And I *really* think I need one.

"My... my FACE!" John howls, his voice slurring badly. His hand comes up to his jaw, and I feel nauseous as he snaps it back in place. *"My beautiful face!"*

He turns to me then, and I see him for what lies under the surface. The dark grain of the wood that hides just beneath his skin.

His teeth... they aren't just brown. They're wood.

Everything is wood.

John slowly pulls himself to his feet and grins like a maniac. The damage done to the human mask he wears makes it even more sinister. When he begins to laugh, I almost lunge at him with the bottle. The only thing that stops me is the knowledge that I can't really hurt. All I can do is cut away his disguise.

"You want to know what happened to your brother, Kurt?"

John moves, and I take a quick step back as he slowly pulls up the sleeve of his shirt. The skin above the fresh sutures slowly reveals itself—but it's the black ink there that causes my grip to loosen on the bottle.

I know that tattoo. I have the same on my own arm.

Shawn.

"Part of the Whole," John repeats, slowly sliding his sleeve back into place. "He begged me to stop, but it didn't matter. He died bloody.

"As will you."

When he lunges, I don't move fast enough. All I can do is scream as he makes good on the threat. It turns out, I bleed enough for the both of us.

Last Night at Dead Moose

D.W. Hitz

There was a hand around his mother's throat, but all Darryl could do was watch the screen and tremble. The biker raised her over the bar, and Mom's rules echoed in Darryl's mind: no customers behind the bar, no going into the cabinets, no slipping any alcohol to his friends, even as a joke. The years of growing up in Mom's bar led him to hate the place more and more over time, and as he watched the security feed on Mom's iPad, his disgust was at its peak.

No one knew about the hidden crawlspace except Darryl, his sister Mona, and Mom, and that was why she told them to hide there when the bikers crashed through the door. It wasn't a regular thing, having to hide, but it happened more often than any of them would have liked. Whenever there was a fight, whenever it got too crazy, or when the cops raided the place looking for meth every six months or so, they would slip in there to be safe.

Mom just thought these guys were regular bikers—bloody, angry bikers—and Darryl was trying to tell her it was worse than that, but she didn't give him time to explain.

"Go! Hide!" she had commanded, and he took the hand of the thing that looked like Mona, and they rushed into the office and slipped into the crawlspace.

Now, he had to watch.

He would have been embarrassed by the fear in his chest, the cold clamminess of his fingers as they gripped the tablet, but it wasn't Mona beside him. Other than the fear, what he felt was shame, because he should have known better.

The biker slammed Mom flat on the top of the bar. Darryl felt the floor shake when it happened. He heard Mom whimper through the wall.

There had been three customers in the place when this started. One went out the back, wanting nothing to do with whatever was about to go down. Spencer Hewitt, who practically lived at the Dead Moose was in the corner, passed out with his head on the table. Jeremy Withers, who had tried to pick Mom up more times than he could count, sat at the end of the bar with his eyes bulging.

Two bikers stood by the door, watching the big one lean over Mom. They were dirty, all three of them. They had beards down to their chests and bulged like they lived in a gym, not on the road or selling crystal from gas stations. None of that was what scared Darryl, though. What made him shake inside his crawlspace was what he was sure was inside them, what he saw enter his sister. There was blood, hidden by their colors and the leathers they had donned, and it was still tacky.

"Where is it?" The biker's face hovered over Mom's. Its voice sounded somehow too *wet*. "I can smell it. I want it."

Mom was crying. Darryl didn't think he had ever seen Mom cry—not since Dad left, anyway, and that was so many years ago, he wasn't even sure that was a real memory.

"What are you talking about?" She tried to yell back at him, but her voice was shaking, and it came out a broken howl. She had to have been cut by the shattered glass crushed between her back and the bar top. Her fingers were tight on the biker's hand as it squeezed her throat.

"It ran." The biker growled. "It came in here."

Darryl didn't know if the bikers caught his mother's change in expression, but he did. She flashed with realization. She knew they were after her kids. She may not have known why, but she knew they wanted her children.

"Out the back," Mom gurgled. The biker's hand was tight around her throat and getting tighter. "They ran out the back."

The biker looked around the bar, examining, contemplating this.

He sniffed the air. "No."

Darryl didn't know what he could be smelling. The only thing Darryl ever smelled in there was dried-up stale beer and a light stench of vomit that never seemed to leave no matter how many times Mom had him and Mona sweep and mop the building.

He remembered arguing with Mona about who would sweep and who would mop. He remembered her playing in the last booth with her dolls, blocking out the rest of the world, the drunks, the music, the chatter, and living through her princesses in some make-believe land that was far away from the stained tables and peeling wallpaper.

He felt the thing next to him breathing softly and watching the tablet over his shoulder, and he wanted to cry. The fear wouldn't let him. Not yet.

The sniffing biker stilled. He nodded with decision. He looked at Mom, leaned down toward her face, and his mouth dropped like a snake separating its jaw to swallow a meal three sizes too big.

Darryl wanted to look away. He feared what was coming. But something inside him told him that he owed it to Mom to witness what was about to happen.

There was a crunching sound that Darryl could hear through the walls. At first, he only saw the back of the biker's head hovering over hers. Then, the biker rose and stepped back, releasing Mom.

But Mom wasn't Mom anymore.

Her face—the entire top of her head was gone. A crater of blood and crushed bone, a small crescent of brain; that was all that was left. Blood pumped from exposed arteries and gushed from the open chasm onto the counter, streaming to the floor. That stopped as her heart stopped.

Darryl wanted to scream. He watched the screen and wanted to shout. That was his mother, now a corpse. That was the most terrifying thing he had ever seen, and it was just on the other side of a thin, plank wall. But he couldn't move, or they would hear him. All he could do was tremble as his bladder let go.

Jeremy Withers fell off his bar stool and thudded on the floor. All three bikers turned and examined him. The biggest one, the one that had eaten Mom's head, dripped slivers of skin and blood down his front, down the bar, down to the floor. He just made a grunting sound, and the other two walked toward the patron.

Darryl looked away now. He didn't see what happened to Mr. Withers. He heard him scream through the wall, though. When that stopped, and he opened his eyes, there was a pool of blood, spatters on the wall the size of a man, and limbs that couldn't possibly have belonged to Mr. Withers—they seemed so small without a body attached to them.

The biggest biker grunted again, and the three of them spread out. They were obviously searching for Darryl and Mona. They knew they were in there somewhere.

Darryl and Mona laughed as they raced through the woods. Tommy and his sister Bella may have had to be in at six, but that didn't mean Darryl and his sister had to stop playing.

Darryl appreciated his freedom. It wasn't something that a lot of eleven-year-olds had. His mom talked about how she grew up, playing outside every day until the streetlights came on and how kids today were over-parented and overly controlled. He didn't quite get what she meant that she was a "latchkey kid," but he knew that even though she was always working at the bar, she wanted him and his sister to have a fulfilling childhood. He guessed he did. He just wished it wasn't always his responsibility to keep an eye on Mona.

Today was a good day, though. It was only the third day of school, so there wasn't much homework, and every class just seemed like a review of last year's lessons. The warmth from summer days lingered in the air, so there was still plenty to do outside. Add to that, Mona was in a good mood and not complaining every five minutes like so many other eight-year-old girls did.

After school, they had met Tommy and Bella at the fort Darryl and Tommy built over the summer in the woods between Tommy's house and the bar. The thing was only made out of dead branches and pine needles, following the shelter building lessons Tommy had learned in

Cub Scouts, and it probably wouldn't last through the winter, but it was big enough for the four of them to play card games and act as home base when they shot foam rubber dart guns at each other or hung out reading comics.

Today, they played freeze tag, talked about the new kid named Theo who was in Darryl and Tommy's class, and ate candy they had picked up at the Wesker Pump as they walked there from school. It was fun, but it seemed like no time at all had passed when Tommy's phone buzzed with his *time-to-go-home* alarm.

Darryl hated that alarm. He hated that all his friends had phones. Part of that might have been because he didn't have one as well, but part of it was because it seemed like his friends were getting more and more boring the more time they spent with their faces down instead of having fun together. Regardless, he definitely hated the nightly buzz that meant his time with his friends was over. The sound was an unrelenting nag, a slavedriver that Tommy couldn't resist.

When Tommy and Bella left, Darryl and Mona agreed to a race back to the Wesker pump. The loser would have to buy the winner an ice cream cookie sandwich.

Mona squealed. She was two steps ahead of Darryl. They still had a ways to go, but she might be able to do it! She didn't think she had ever beaten Darryl in a race through the woods, but she tried her hardest every time. This time, it looked like she could do it.

"Get back here!" He was laughing, and it made her laugh. "You're the little one! You can't win!"

She pushed harder, putting her legs into overdrive. She imagined she was some kind of machine, a little robot girl, and she just had to reroute her power to get more speed.

She dodged a tree and ducked under a branch. She jumped over a boulder and turned left onto the worn-down trail that everyone from

Tommy's neighborhood used to cut through the woods and get to the store.

Mona glanced back. She had a ten-foot lead. It wasn't a lot, and it would have meant more if they were still in the trees where there were obstacles. On the trail, she wasn't sure if she could keep that lead. Darryl was fast, and with nothing in his way, he might get past her.

"I'm coming!" he shouted. He was gaining.

Mona tried not to focus on that. She could see down the trail to the back of the store. They were close, and she just had to hold onto that space between them. She just had to keep pushing as hard as she could, and she could make this the time she won.

"I'm right behind you!"

He was! She could tell by his voice and his stomping footfalls in the dirt.

She thought of the times they had run through the house, racing Darryl to the Christmas tree to see who got to open the first present. Racing to Mom's car to claim shotgun. Racing to this same store a week ago for the very same bet.

She knew some people would call her dumb for racing Darryl because she never won, but she didn't care. It wasn't about winning—not really. It was her brother. It was about a moment in time where they were having fun together, her and her big brother. It seemed like they didn't do as much together as they used to: different games, different TV shows, and now with school back in, different schedules all day long.

This was just her and him. It was dumb, but it was something they shared, and she loved it.

Almost side by side, they burst through the trees and into the rear parking lot of the Wesker Pump. She just had to round the corner before him—she was more nimble; she could do it.

Mona jumped onto the sidewalk. She was almost to the turn, and that new kid, Theo, turned the corner right in front of her.

She skidded to stop, almost slamming into him, face to face, and Darryl flew past them both, then past the corner, then he grabbed the handle of the front door.

"First!" Darryl shouted and walked back, panting.

That was when the bikers pulled up.

Mona didn't understand how Theo was strong enough to pick her up and carry her into the woods. She was glad Darryl followed, screaming for Theo to put her down.

She didn't understand how Theo melted into some kind of red ooze and shot himself down her throat as if she was some kind of cave he could hide inside.

She didn't understand the pain and burning as she died from being melted and devoured from within.

The things that looked like bikers tossed furniture around and banged on the walls of the bar. They knew Darryl was there, hiding. They knew Mona/Theo/whatever-it-was was there, and part of Darryl wanted them to find them. Tears were streaming, and though he had previously hoped there was a way to get the thing out of his sister and fix her, as he gazed at the tablet, seeing those bikers, seeing his dead mother on the counter, head erased, he knew he was deluding himself. Mom was gone. Mona was gone. He had to wonder if it would have been best to let them find him, and he could join his family in Heaven.

They pushed Spencer Hewitt from his seat as they checked around his table. The drunk rolled on his side and snored, oblivious to the commotion.

The smaller of the bikers wandered out of the main bar, into the hallway that led to the back door and the manager's office. At the back door, he sniffed around and came back, and he went into the office.

Darryl couldn't stop himself from shaking. The tablet jumped with his hands as the biker lifted the chair in front of Mom's desk and tossed it into the hall. He grabbed hold of the desk and flipped it over, and Darryl was sure the biker would hear him, either from his teeth chattering or his bones banging together in fear.

The biker grunted and sniffed the air. His eyes bulged. He picked up Mom's desk chair and threw it against the opposite wall, shattering the chair and leaving a series of gashes in the sheetrock.

He sniffed and moved closer to Darryl's wall.

He sniffed and started feeling the wall, running his fingers over the wood paneling that separated him from the secret crawlspace between the office and the main bar.

Darryl imagined the biker pressing into the lower right portion of the board and having it pop open. He saw himself face to face with the biker, and the monster biting half his head off right there.

There was a boom and a crunch from the other side. A hand crashed into the crawlspace, ripping a hole into the main bar's wall and tearing away a five-foot section of sheetrock.

Darryl screamed. He didn't mean to, but it just kind of exploded from his mouth.

Another pair of hands burst into the crawlspace from the office. The tiny hideout was flooded with light from both sides. Hands tore into the sheeting and ripped the once secret room into little more than a studded skeletal crevice.

Darryl screamed again, and the biggest biker grabbed him by the left arm and yanked him from the wall. He felt a hot tearing inside his shoulder and heard a popping sound from his arm.

The biker raised Darryl up to eye level and inhaled through his nose. Then he tossed Darryl across the room and seized Mona.

Mona screamed this time, but it wasn't a human sound. The noise was somewhere between a fox's howl and the shriek of a circular saw ripping through wood.

The biker carried Mona to the center of the room. The other two joined him, making a circle around the girl.

Darryl watched. He knew what they wanted. They were going to eat her, chew off her face the way they had Mom's. He didn't know if he should be happy or if he should cry. The thing inside her—he was pretty sure it killed his sister, and she couldn't be saved—he wanted it dead, but it still looked like her, and he didn't think he could bear to watch them eat her.

And what if he was wrong? What if there was still a way to save Mona? If that was true, could he just sit there and do nothing?

The bikers ignored Mona's screams. They each stared at her as their mouths stretched down, opening the same way the big one had before devouring Mom's head.

As Darryl lay there, five feet from his headless mother, he knew he couldn't let that happen. No matter what he witnessed in those woods, he couldn't sit there and watch those things eat something that looked like Mona.

He jumped to his feet and ran toward the bar. He flinched as he climbed over the top and had to avoid his mother's body. He couldn't avoid her blood on his hands or his knees as he scrambled.

He dropped to the floor and broke the rules, springing open the cabinet on the far right, grabbing the thing his mother told him never to touch.

"Hey! Put her down!" Spencer Hewitt shouted from the other side of the room. His internal clock must have told him it was time for another round, and setting his eyes on the things between himself and the bar, he spotted three dudes being rude to Mona.

Spencer grabbed the closest one by the shoulder and shook him. "I said put her down." His words slurred. "She's just a little girl."

The biker spun and closed its massive maw on Spencer's outstretched arm. Spencer watched the biker chew and swallow, and it was only when the stranger opened its mouth again that Spencer seemed to notice his missing forearm and the blood spraying from his stump.

Spencer screamed, and the biker chomped down on Spencer's face. The drunk's body dropped, and the top of his head tumbled on top of it. The biker chewed and crunched, blood running down his front, and turned back to the circle.

There was a boom, and a biker's head exploded. He collapsed beside the bar.

Darryl stumbled backward, the shotgun he pulled from the cabinet flying up and nearly smacking him in the face.

Red goo seeped from inside the headless biker. It flooded over the floor, revealing a hollow, meaty husk. It was all that was left of the thing that had looked so human.

The other bikers turned toward Darryl. They screamed.

Though Darryl was nearly deaf from the sound of the shotgun, he heard that scream without issue. The monster that had killed Spencer walked toward him, and Darryl raised the shotgun. He had done it once; he could do it again.

But when he pulled the trigger, nothing happened.

The biker extended his arm, and Darryl realized the problem. He had to pump it. He tried the pump, but it was stiff. He dropped to his knees, muzzled up, and pulled the pumper thing down. It expelled the empty shell, and, squeezing the stock between his knees, he chambered the next shell.

Darryl lifted the gun. He raised it toward the biker, but before he could aim it at the thing's head, the biker grabbed the barrel.

Darryl saw how this was going to go. He wouldn't be able to aim, and the thing would rip the gun from his grasp. Then it would eat his head.

Maybe he couldn't aim the thing like he wanted to, but he still had his hand on the gun.

Darryl pulled the trigger.

Another boom.

The blast took off the biker's arm and shoulder, and red ooze sprayed across the room. The biker dropped to the ground, twitching and shaking as more of the weird substance leaked from its hollow shell.

The biggest biker howled. It took Mona into a single hand, gripping her from the neck. It marched toward Darryl, the other hand out, and it leaned in before Darryl could pump the shotgun again.

It rose, holding both kids by the throat. It stretched its monstrous mouth wide, and Darryl knew this was the end.

He looked at Mona. He knew it wasn't her anymore, but it looked like her, and it reminded him of every moment they had had together. The games and the screams. The races and the treats. Cuddles on the couch as they watched TV when they were younger. He loved his sister. It only made sense they would die together—at least close to it.

He was ready to go limp and have his head removed—it seemed rather painless and quick from what he had seen—when something happened he wasn't expecting.

Mona gave him an understanding glance. It wasn't a Mona expression exactly, but something that was part Mona and part something else. It wasn't a smile, and not quite a smirk, but something in between, a message that she understood what he was thinking.

There was a flash, something so fast that Darryl wouldn't have seen it if he had blinked. Mona was suddenly gone, and a river of red slime was running up the biker's arm—more than running, it was devouring as it climbed.

The biker dropped Darryl, and the slime ate inch by inch, racing up the monster's limb. It reached the shoulder. It covered the head. It melted the giant man, and the man dropped to the ground.

Darryl jumped back, unsure of what was happening. He grabbed the shotgun, slid to his knees, pumped the weapon, and lifted it, aiming.

What he saw was Mona.

She smiled at him from the other side of the weapon. She closed her eyes, ready for him to shoot.

Darryl felt tears running down his face. He was crying, and he wasn't sure why. He was sure that he didn't want to shoot, no matter what this person was standing in front of him.

The gun fell from his shaky hands and clattered on the floor. Mona walked to him.

He closed his eyes. If he was going to die now, he didn't want to see it coming.

He felt lips on his cheek, the soft press of his sister's touch that he would have known no matter what was going on in the universe.

"I love you," she whispered.

"I love you." His words trembled.

When he opened his eyes, he was alone in the Dead Moose, alone in the world without his mom and his sister. But something told him he wouldn't be that way forever.

Cheers!

Alexandrea Christianson

"Hook and Gator Brewery! They make the beer with alligator!" Gilbert's eyes were wide with excitement. He loved finding breweries and dragging his friends along.

"Sick! Let's go!" Chuck jumped up from the couch.

"But *why* though?" Alison's face contorted as she nearly gagged. "That sounds disgusting!"

"Cool it, Alison. Just because you're a nurse doesn't mean we can't try fun and weird shit." Chuck held his hand out toward her. Alison rolled her eyes. She hated when he did that.

"I never said that. It has nothing to do with nursing. But beer doesn't have to be weird. It's like they're trying way too hard to be edgy." Alison was getting annoyed. "What the fuck would alligator do for beer?"

"Doesn't matter, come on! Let's go!" Gilbert had no sense of planning. He was always ready to try something new.

"Dude! It's Saturday and we ain't doing shit!"

"It's out in the middle of nowhere! It's a two-hour drive!" Alison was looking at her Google Maps.

"What are we doing?" Isabella looked up from her phone, having heard nothing.

The group had become friends in college and started going to a different brewery nearly every Friday. Now they had continued the trend after graduating and moving in together in a large bungalow.

"Fine, but we need to come back tonight. I'm on shift tomorrow." Alison stood and grabbed her bag.

They drove in the dark. Trees lined the dirt road looming over them. The headlights barely cut through the night as fog seeped from the trees like tendrils waiting to grab them.

"This is creepy. Like, I've seen this movie!" Isabella was in the front passenger seat leaning forward. The headlights created long shadows on the road.

Everyone had been quietly staring out the window. They all flinched at the pop and hiss of a can opening in the backseat.

Chuck chugged a beer, filling the car with the smell of alcohol.

"What the fuck, man! I can get in trouble for that!" Gilbert yelled and glared in the rearview mirror.

"Oh, please! We are in the middle of nowhere! Want one?"

Gilbert rolled his eyes and looked back at the road, thinking Chuck was right, but he wasn't in the mood to risk some backwoods cop harassing him. He immediately had a visual in his head: The cop leaning into the window, wearing aviators even at night and calling him Son. His mind wandered to what his company commander would say about him driving with an open container.

"There's a sign!" Isabella pointed and squinted. Everyone in the car peered forward. Gilbert slowed the car.

BEARDED TOOTH BREWERY 2 MILES! MUSHROOM BEER WITH ALLIGATOR!

TURN HERE!

"Oh wait, that's the wrong one." Gilbert scrunched his eyebrows.

"Bearded Tooth sounds interesting," Isabella said.

"That sign looks old!" Alison scrunched her eyebrows.

"So?" Chuck said.

"Well, what if it's closed?"

"Oh, lay off, Alison!" Chuck rolled his eyes and chugged a beer.

"What does GPS show?" Allison leaned forward between the front seats. Her need to take control was approaching overwhelming. "How many breweries around here use alligator?"

Gilbert squinted down at his phone.

"Stop!" Isabelle screamed.

Gilbert slammed on his brakes while looking up, following the order.

The car skidded to a stop on the dirt road, and the headlights were only feet away from a large orange and white roadblock sign. The dirt billowed up around the lights from the sudden stop. They damn near hit it. Everyone seemed to freeze for a moment as their heartbeats subsided.

Gilbert broke the silence. "That is not on the GPS."

"Whatever, man, let's just follow the other sign." Chuck cracked open another beer.

"Yeah, turn around. We can just take that last turn and follow the signs for that one that looks older."

"Wait, what? Who is to say that one is even open?" Isabella turned sideways in the passenger seat and looked at everyone. "No one thinks this is creepy?"

"Um, no, let's go!" Chuck said.

Gilbert threw the car in reverse and turned around.

"Is it closed?" Isabella did not like the look of the place.

There were no lights on, no other cars in the lot.

"Sumbitch!" Chuck threw an empty can out the window as the car sat idling.

As the can clanked on the blacktop, the entrance door slammed open, banging against the exterior. The gang watched in silence as a filthy old man gritting a cigar in his teeth grunted and heaved a tearing trash bag. A few pieces of debris fell on the porch. He coughed, then looked up and saw the headlights. He held up a hand at first to shield his eyes, then smiled and waved at them to come on in! He shoved the bag to the side of the door, turned, and went inside. The windows lit up from the inside as the old man appeared to reopen the brewery. A few neon signs flicked to life in the windows.

The gang watched in silence. It was a shack, appearing carefully held together by old, tattered posters and rusty nails.

"Whoa, that sign! Remember when Bud Light was only a dollar?" Gilbert laughed.

"Ugh, remember when we drank Bud Light back in the day?" Lucas patted Gilbert's shoulder.

"What the hell?" Alison leaned between the front seats, gaping at the shit hole before them.

"Yeah, this is so sketch." Isabella seemed afraid to even look at it.

"Oh, please guys, it's beer. It's fine! Dive bars are usually the best." Chuck threw open the back door of the car and jogged up the steps, disappearing inside!"

"Well, I will miss him." Alison sighed as she ran her finger across her throat indicating how he would die.

The group laughed.

"Hey, we have been to some dives. But we have also been places that ended up pretty bad ass. Let's go see. We can totally leave if we don't like it."

"I don't have cell service." Isabella held up her phone and waved it around. "This is like a clear sign we will die."

"No, it started out as a clear indication we will all die when we got in the car and drove out to the middle of nowhere."

"Ah, so it just keeps adding up. We will die tonight."

"Hey, we all agree this looks like a bad slasher movie. So, let's at least do it with a few beers!" Gilbert shook his head, smiled, then stepped out of the car.

Isabella and Alison sat in the car a bit longer.

"I just have a bad feeling," Alison said.

"Me too, but you always have a bad feeling. I just have it this one time."

"Ugh ... okay, let's just go to the door, look in, and then tell them we're leaving."

Isabella stared at her phone. She knew she only wanted to leave because she didn't have cell service.

As the girls arrived at the door, the guys were already seated at a table, and the old man was laughing, pulling on various taps, and filling pints.

The girls sighed, knowing leaving was no longer an option.

"Man! That one is awesome!" Chuck slammed the taster glass down. I'll take a pint of that!"

The old man smiled. "It's 12% ABV."

"Impossible! You can't even taste it!" Lucas took a long drink. He looked at the glass. "Yeah, this is gonna fuck me up!"

Alison scratched at her arm absentmindedly. "Yeah, this is pretty good." She felt a lot better, relaxed. Probably the buzz kicking in on their third round of beer.

The Bearded Tooth Brewery was run by the old man hosting them, Frank. He was a Vietnam vet that learned how to make beer back in Nam, he had said. He chose this small hole in the wall because he wanted to make beer but didn't necessarily want to work that hard. He walked with a limp but had not explained the cause. He told them how he had started out making batches of beer. Some that worked, and some that didn't. Then he came across the idea of brewing with mushrooms. His face lit up as he told everyone the detailed story and drank. Mushrooms gave the beer a subtle yet bolder taste.

Chuck stood to go to the bathroom. The room spun, and he dropped back into his chair. He scratched at the back of his neck. His actions went unnoticed as everyone listened to Frank, who seemed to make every story he told exceptionally interesting.

At one point, he diverted from talking about beer making and told a story about Nam. He even pulled a table on its side and peered over it to animate the story. He was clearly desensitized to what he had seen; however, everyone listening had a look of concern and strain on their face.

The evening wore on, and they continued drinking, laughing. Beers spilled, but most of the beer was consumed.

Chuck finally could not hold his bladder any longer and stumbled to the bathroom, holding onto the wall, his vision blurring. He smiled as he tried to figure out the sign on the two doors. He actually hated this part. The bar puts some pictures on the bathroom doors and you were never sure which one meant girl or boy.

He finally just chose the mushroom that was standing. The other mushroom was sitting. Surely, that was the difference? He hiccupped and pushed the door inwards.

The urinal on the wall told him he had made the right decision. He leaned his head back as he felt the relief on his bladder. He looked down to shake it off and noticed a spot on his penis just at the end near the urethra. "What the fuck?" He squinted, his drunken vision not helping. He ran his hand over it. It was raised. He shuddered at the thought of an STD. He didn't totally remember last weekend but was pretty sure he hadn't gotten laid. He picked at it. They were out in the middle of nowhere; maybe it was a tick? It didn't move. His heart thudded in his chest as he wondered what the hell it could be. Then he started losing his vision. There were dark spots covering his peripheral vision.

He braced his hand on the wall, trying to use his other hand to get his junk put away. If he was headed toward a blackout, he didn't want to be half-naked. He had never been blackout drunk before and had no idea what he might be in for.

Alison leaned forward, resting her elbow on the table. "But why alligator?"

Frank was taking a drink. He gulped, set his glass down, and started laughing. "Oh! I forgot about that! There is no alligator! I just say that to get people intrigued."

"Ha! Ha! That's smart man! Good marketing." Chuck held up his glass.

Frank tilted his head and shrugged his shoulders. "Or not."

Everyone laughed again.

"Hey, man you got something on your lip." Gilbert knew Isabella would flip shit if she knew something was on her face and no one told her. She scrunched her eyebrows and wiped her mouth with the back of her hand. She looked down, and there was a small brown streak across her skin.

"What the?" Isabella's face immediately went scarlet. She stood abruptly and walked down the hall to the bathroom. Her heart was racing. What *the fuck was brown and on her face?* She opened the first door and saw Lucas's back. "Sorry." She let the door close and went into the second room. The mirror was grungy, there was no toilet paper in the stall, and the hand towel was an actual towel. She shuddered. This place was disgusting. She was infuriated and wanted to leave. The faucet ran clear. Small favors, clean water. She used her fist to try to clean up the mirror when she saw a brown spot on the edge of her nose. "What the?"

Alison was trying to listen, but her eyelids were itchy. She didn't want to mess up her lashes, but it was starting to get unbearable. She tried several ways to get the itch but wondered if she needed to take off her lashes.

Isabella's hand trembled. The brown spot shot up, just a centimeter, and billowed a cap. She looked closer, terrified. It was a mushroom! "What the fuck?" She pinched her fingers over it and pulled. Her eyes filled with black dots. The pain was searing, like plucking a nose hair times a thousand. She felt her eyes watering.

She screamed, an earsplitting primal shriek. Her head spun, and she tumbled out of the bathroom, the door slamming into the wall. She tripped over something and toppled to the floor. She could barely see. She looked over her shoulder!

Lucas was crumpled on the floor. She could hear a loud wheezing. She thought it was him; that was his jacket. His face was covered in mushrooms! She tried to yell out to him. He moaned, and his breath squeaked. "Lucas, oh god! Help me!" Then she started coughing and hacking uncontrollably.

Screaming tore down the hall from the main area of the brewery. She tried to turn her head, but her vision was completely gone. She was blind! She coughed and felt something pushing on the back of her throat.

Gilbert took another long drink of his beer, then suddenly hacked uncontrollably. Frank limped over and pounded on his back. "Wrong pipe there, kid!" Frank laughed until a tickle in his throat turned it into an unrelenting cough. He wheezed a deep breath and hacked some more.

Alison stood up from the table and black filled her vision. She tried to blink it away, but her eyelashes were caught on something. She panicked and reached up, her fingers touching something, something coming out of her eyeball.

She looked over at Gilbert as mushrooms sprouted from his eyes.

Alison began coughing violently, and her vision went black.

As the sun broke the horizon and the fog began to burn off, two men in hazmat suits loaded a large road work barrier into the back of the truck then got back into the cab. The truck did a tree point turn around and headed down the side road. As they reached the brewery, men in hazmat suits carried out body bags. One called over the radio, "Every one of 'em, dead."

A loud bang caught everyone's attention as a man in a hazmat suit burst out of the brewery, ran to the field, and ripped off his hood, vomiting. Several men approached him cautiously.

He wiped his mouth and waved others off. "Sorry, sorry. It's the mushrooms growing out the eyes. I just can't handle the eyes."

Two men stood in a tent nearby, drinking coffee as they watched their men work. "Well..." Jim sighed and took a sip of coffee, watching the brewery with a wide smile. "Test two went well. I would like to conduct a few more before we go live."

"Yes, sir. The mushrooms do seem to follow the GI tract and the eyes." He shuddered, looking at his file from the last autopsy. "I am having trouble. They are always so young, the people in the tests."

"Damn it, I know. But ..." Jim paused and put his hand on Adam's shoulder. "This will save so many more young lives. Think about it, there will be less actual war for men to fight! A few lives here and this will save millions of soldiers' lives, biological warfare! Please try to stay focused on that." Jim turned and walked out of the tent.

Adam set down the folder and drank his coffee as he watched the men load the body bags in the large unmarked truck.

He coughed as he got a tickle in the back of his throat.

Original Artwork by Alexandrea Christianson

Serenity Box

MJ Mars

D onnie stood outside the side door to the old church, fighting the urge to run. The poster board at the front of the building which usually contained printouts of psalms or other bible quotes that meant little to him, now held the Serenity Prayer, along with an invitation for those who were struggling with drink to attend that evening's session.

Struggling was an understatement. Donnie's dependence on alcohol began as most people's do. A way to obtain a moment's peace. The chance to relax when every nerve ending in his body screamed. To switch off the echoes of his memories of Vietnam by sinking a few glasses of the good stuff, allowing him to sleep through the night rather than waking up every couple of hours screaming and clawing the bedclothes.

Either way, he was an impossible bed-fellow, and his wife had separated from him the previous year. That was when the drinking became more than just a relaxant. For a while, it was an obsession. A will he/won't he conundrum from the moment he opened his eyes in the morning to the inevitable chink of glass against glass, the relief when he poured and lifted 'just the one' to his lips and the battle of whether he might drink or not vanished. It was never 'just one.' He soon learned that was an impossible fight, the way he'd learned that waiting until 5 o'clock and feeling proud had been foolhardy. Now, he was lucky if he made it to midday.

And there was no pride in the delay anymore. Now, it was easier to simply acquiesce. Drinking had become as much a part of his morning routine as brushing his teeth or putting his pants on.

Inside the church hall, he could hear the gentle scrape of chairs being arranged in a circle. The door was open a crack, and the scent of too-strong and bitter coffee wafted out into the evening. If he went inside, he knew he would need to make the effort not to drink that night. The thought filled him with instant panic. Could he make it through an evening? It was highly doubtful. Then he would be faced with the crushing disappointment and guilt of letting every other desperate but willing face in that circle of chairs down.

He just wasn't ready, yet. Truly, deep down, he didn't feel as though it was possible.

Donnie turned to make a hasty retreat before anyone saw him and tried to usher him inside.

Stuffing his hands deep in his pockets, he hurried down the side path and out front. He wasn't driving, obviously (even in his worst moments, he chose not to drink drive. He'd been privy to far too much avoidable carnage during his time in the fire service prior to the war). Guilt was his main trigger for drinking, and the thought of smashing into a car full of kids or wiping out a pair of bright-eyed newlyweds on their way to the airport was too much for him to bear.

Needless to say, he didn't get out much.

But that was all right by Donnie. The liquor store and his couch were his best friends. He lived four blocks from the old church that held the AA meetings, so it wasn't a huge chore to wander over, hang out for a while, talk himself out of attending, and head back home. There was a bottle of Jack waiting for him under the sink. He'd tucked it away, shoved it deep behind a box of washing powder just in case he returned home from the meeting with a new mindset. He couldn't wait to get back to his couch. Just him, the safety of the four walls around him, and the peace of oblivion with his good friend, Jack.

A man was standing by the Serenity Prayer sign.

Shit. Donnie hoped it wasn't the host of the AA session. Didn't want to be collared by the do-gooder who had managed to fight off his own demons and wore the glistening sheen of renewed health on their face like an obnoxious badge of honour.

Shrouded in shadows, the man didn't look as though he was a beacon of health and self-control. He was hunched a little, the visible skin on his face that was illuminated by the streetlight pocked and dappled with sore-looking redness. Rather than being the host, Donnie guessed this was another sober-curious passerby, showing enough willingness to traverse the general area of the AA meeting without committing to actually setting foot inside. To do so would mean action would need to be taken. If you weren't ready, even stepping into the room was a pointless exercise.

Donnie felt a pang of deep regret when he reached the edge of the pathway to the exit. For a brief, fleeting moment, the safety of his living room couch and the bottle under his sink felt ominous and bleak. A rational moment of clarity fought through the panicked urgency of his need for alcohol, and he remembered momentarily why he'd come to the building that night. He turned back, longing to find the strength to hurry to the side door and plunge headfirst into the coffee-scented room with the circle of chairs.

It was no good.

The fear of even making it through one more hour sober overwhelmed him. With trembling hands hidden deep inside his coat, he moved on.

"It's not that easy, is it?" The stranger's voice was scratchy and, if not unfriendly, there was certainly no warmth there.

"A task for another day," Donnie told him, trying to sound jovial but startled at the weariness in his words. He was ready to change, he knew. If only his body and brain could get on the same page so he could at least begin to try.

"They peddle these meetings as though they're a magic wand or something. Truth is, it only works for a handful of people. If you ain't wired that way, it's never going to work for you."

It was nice to hear someone echoing the reasoning that Donnie had whenever he was toying with the idea of attending a meeting. He wasn't a chatty man. Never had been. The idea of sitting in a room and spilling his guts to a bunch of strangers—but people from his local area, who he might bump into at any point after—brought him out in nervous hives. Aside from that, he wasn't at all religious. After seeing the way some of his fellow soldiers had acted in Nam, he doubted there was any kind of a god looking out for a single soul on the planet. If there was, He was sure selective about who He deemed worth saving. And that just didn't sit right with Donnie.

"You're right about that." He gave the stranger a courteous smile, happy to hear his own sentiments echoed but still eager to get away. "We each need to find our own way of dealing with these things."

"I've got something that may help you," the man blurted, then reined himself back, waving his hand dismissively back at the church. "If this isn't your scene and you're looking for an easy way out of the pit."

An easy way? "Brother, there ain't no easy way out of this."

"See, that's what I thought, too. But I haven't touched a drop in six months. Trust me, you'll never catch me taking another sip in this lifetime."

Donnie wasn't born yesterday. He knew a potential scam when he saw one. And knew that the kind of person looking to make a quick buck off someone else's misery would likely target a hapless drunkard as a first port of call. Still, his interest was piqued. Damnit, as much as he didn't want to step foot in that AA meeting, he knew he needed some kind of help. Something had to give, and if he wasn't careful, it was set to be his liver. He exhaled as he spoke, making it clear he wasn't ready to tolerate any bullshit. "All right. I'll bite. Tell me what it is you want to tell me."

Chuckling, the stranger stepped closer. "I admire you being direct, so I'll offer you the same courtesy. Six months ago, I was offered a 'miracle cure' for my addiction. Like you, I thought it was a load of bullshit, dreamed up by scammers targeting the weakest customers in society."

"That pretty much nails it," Donnie confirmed, lifting his chin to show the man he wasn't going to stand around and get played.

"I hear you. So, I won't bullshit you any longer. You want the miracle cure? You got it. Don't, move along and you'll never see me again."

Donnie hesitated. He didn't believe in an instant fix, especially not for something as complex as trauma-fuelled addiction. But he knew in his heart he couldn't go on this way. His life was a broken merry-go-round revolving around a bottle that was destroying his health, his looks, and his already feeble sanity. He couldn't pretend it was helping him anymore. He was a broken man. There were two questions battling for answers: how much and how does it work? He asked the second first, knowing the answer would influence how well he regarded the response to the first.

The stranger scratched his cheek, and Donnie tried to politely avert his gaze from the flakes of skin that fluttered from his damaged flesh. While he knew the body could look briefly worse during detox, he figured six months was more than enough time for the impact of quitting to have dissipated. Whatever was wrong with the man must be a chronic condition, perhaps the cause of his drinking in the first place. Physical pain or mental pain, there was no denying that booze was a fixer, at least for a short time.

As the man spoke, his bottom lip cracked, a small line of blood forming in the centre. "Have you heard of those tablets that make you sick if you imbibe alcohol?"

Donnie sure had. He'd had a friend who was taking them and accidentally ordered a meal with unreduced red wine in the sauce. Poor guy had thrown up all over the restaurant and the screaming diners around him. Those pills made the taker violently, heinously ill if they so much as took a drop of liquor. Even with the knowledge of his friend's embarrassment, Donnie had considered requesting them from his doctor, but that had been before. Now, he knew taking the pills would have been pointless. If he wanted to blow chunks from taking alcohol, he'd just wait a little longer for the ulcer in his gut to get more inflamed. "I ain't interested in taking that shit," he snapped.

"It's not pills." The stranger spoke with calm detachment, no longer on the lookout for a hard sell. "You don't have to take any-thing."

Donnie snorted. "Is this some hippy wishful thinking nonsense? Because, if it is, you can kindly shove it where the sun don't shine." He'd been out of the house for far too long. His last sip was wearing off, and the tremors in his hands were worsening. A sheen of sweat bloomed on his brow, and irritation niggled his every last nerve.

With a brisk shake of his head, the stranger pulled a small, rectan-gular box from his pocket and held it out. "All you need to do is take this and open it in your house."

A hallucinogen? Donnie thought.

The man shook his hand a little, encouraging him to take the offering. "Just take it, man. Believe me. You'll never drink again after tonight if you do."

The words sank in deep, and Donnie felt like he was being offered a lifeline. "How much?"

"Just take it. Please. I don't need it anymore."

So, he did.

At home, Donnie went straight to the sink and ducked down into the cupboard, pulling out the bottle of Jack Daniels. It was like muscle memory, or a child going to grab their comfort blanket the moment they get home. Even having the bottle nearby eased the tightness in his shoulders and quelled the rising panic that grew inside him every evening.

He went to his trusty couch and set the bottle down on the table beside it, sinking down into the cushions. He held the small box in his lap, turning it over and over.

Now he was home, he could get a proper look at what he had been given. The box was small, the colour of faded olive, the softwood sides carved with elaborate patterns. The hinges were rusted, orange bleeding into the green. At the front of the box, a simple clasp held the lid down. He nudged it with his thumb, then hesitated.

Did he really want to quit cold turkey? Surely there was no way in hell the little container in his lap held an instant cure for alcoholism. But opening it was a step of intent, as it would have been if he'd set foot inside the AA meeting. Was it really that he didn't want to sit in a circle and talk about God in front of a room full of strangers?

Or was it that he wasn't ready to quit after all?

His hands shook, and he reached mindlessly for the bottle, his stomach churning and his chest thundering. He needed it. He couldn't live without it.

Fuck.

That, right there, was why he had to quit. He lowered the bottle and, before the urgent whisper in his brain could stop him, he opened the lid of the box.

Donnie wasn't sure what he expected, but it sure as hell wasn't what he found. It was...dust? A thick layer of dark powder sat in the base of the box, the sides coated in a fine layer of grey from where he'd turned it over and over. He poked a finger into the substance. It was course against his fingertip. He touched something solid and nudged it until it was sticking up from the powder. Disgusted, he wished he hadn't put his hands anywhere near it. It was a tooth, the four roots of the molar sticking up, mocking him.

Shaking his head, Donnie felt disappointment crush him. The guy outside the church was nothing but a whack job.

He closed the box and tossed it onto the table, rubbing his hand on his pants. For a while, he did nothing. Tried to sit with his feelings and get a hold of himself. If he'd gone to the lengths of taking a weird box from a stranger to quit drinking, perhaps tonight was the night he could make a start, all on his own. Right?

His resolve lasted just over fifteen minutes. By that point, the roaring in his ears and the itching of every nerve ending on his skin became too much to bear. His mind tormented him, throwing up snippets of memories: Donnie crouching in dirt with an empty cartridge, listening to enemy footsteps that were too close for comfort. Donnie listening to a screaming child, cruel laughter, and vulgar slurs. Donnie locked in a cell, not knowing what the next morning would bring. The alcohol knew just which scenes of his life would have him reaching for it. He was its slave, because he didn't know how to simply be without it.

Relenting, he unscrewed the lid of the Jack and took a hefty swallow.

The warm scorch of comfort coated his throat and hit his belly like a meteor going off, spreading easing numbness immediately through his screaming limbs. This was what he needed. It was all he ever needed. It was...

Agony.

A searing, twisting sensation exploded around his already swollen liver. It took his breath away, sent him hunching over, then rearing back in his chair as a heaviness bulged out from his middle. With tears streaming from his eyes, Donnie raked up his shirt and watched in petrified terror as a spinal column snaked across his front, an entity moving within him, its bony elbow poking out as it clawed once more at his liver, grasping it in both hands and squeezing.

Bourbon-tinted saliva dripped from Donnie's chin as he gasped and sobbed, eyes widening as the terrible creature that seemed as though it was growing from underneath his skin, slowly eased its way out of his body, a gray, skeletal form with a pale webbing of skin and sunken, yellowed eyes that peered up at Donnie's own with unhidden glee at causing his pain. The hands remained inside him while the beast crouched like a malformed hairless cat. At the last moment, it yanked its arms, twisting once more, wringing out the internal organ that had already been put through so much.

The spectral hands released and tugged away, leaving Donnie in the room alone, his palm swiping across his belly in search of blood or torn flesh but finding nothing but the soft and malleable paleness of his hair-spattered torso.

A hallucination, he reasoned. He needed more booze to make sure it didn't happen again.

But when he reached his hand for the bottle, something in his brain pleaded with him to halt. The terror was still raw, as was the dull, aching throb that stayed within, just below his ribcage.

Donnie went to bed, hoping the mercy of sleep would take the dreadful daily decision away from him. Every time he closed his eyes, he recalled the terror of the creature that crawled out of him, its eyes so like the ones that stared back at him in the mirror.

The pain had gone, now, and all that gnawed inside him was the desire to drink. To his own frustration, the fear of the vision hadn't spooked him hard enough to leave the damn bottle where it was, or even to pour it down the sink. In fact, he'd mindlessly brought it with him to bed, holding its neck like a Victorian carrying a candlestick to light their way. It taunted him from his bedside table, now. It sat, tall, proud, and gleaming in the moonlight, towering over a splayed paperback that was coated in dust, half-read before Donnie's nights usually involved him passing out when his head hit the pillow.

There was an idea, he thought. He could pick up the book and commence reading until he fell asleep. He'd remembered enjoying it, all those months ago. Hadn't stopped due to disinterest or a loss of the plot. He simply became too drunk to read.

The realisation shamed him. He raked a hand over his face and propped himself up on his pillows. This was as good a time as any to change his habits, he told himself. He'd start reading again, would read til dawn and get straight up if he had to. Keep himself distracted.

But, when he reached over with the intention of picking up the book, his muscle memory sent his hand passing over the flattened novel and to the glass neck of the bottle.

It felt so good in his hand. So right.

There was no consciousness in these moments, only a deep, visceral need that took over every aspect of the humanity in his brain. He gulped at the honey-brown liquid, the friendly fire coating his throat in its welcome hug.

Donnie's relief was short-lived.

A gnarled gray hand with stubby, dirt-edged nails, reached up and slapped the mattress beside him. From the side of the bed, a strange, guttural voice began to warble, a gleeful dirge that sounded a little like an old man doing an imitation of a toddler's mindless, happy chatter.

Shrinking away from the hand, Donnie tried to slide to the other side of the bed and make a dash for it, but terror had rendered his limbs momentarily useless. That, combined with the groggy, floundering motions of a man in the beginnings of withdrawal, meant that before Donnie could make a move, the ghoul was already beside him.

This second encounter allowed Donnie more time to process its appearance. It had strands of yellowed hair streaking across a balding pate, the colour of the hair matching the sclera of its eyes. The irises were the same chocolate brown of Donnie's own, and it dawned on him just how similar the entity's bone structure was to his.

It pounced, digging its spectral hands once more into the depths of his entrails. Donnie screamed and writhed on the covers, sweat soaking the sheets as the ghoul took gleeful pleasure in grabbing and twisting his bowels, tugging at his engorged liver, and poking his kidneys. The ordeal went on for some time, the stench emanating from the creature that of stale piss and sun-baked excrement. The agony went on and on, the pain sending fireworks across Donnie's vision. He tried to focus on the ceiling, anything to take his eyes away from the foul creature that looked so much like him in many ways, but the torture was relentless. There was nothing he could do to distract himself.

Even in Nam, having splinters pushed up under his nails and into the soft, nerve-filled pad of his fingertips hadn't broken his resolve. He'd gritted his teeth, focused on a point on the wall, and turned his mind off, knowing he was in full control.

Control was something Donnie had given up long ago.

The ghoul climbed higher, its fingers raking along Donnie's torso, somehow trailing inside his flesh from its second knuckle down. His lungs tickled, and he wheezed at the touch, his bronchi strained and irritated by the sudden interference. At his collarbones, the monster yanked its fingers out with a slurping sound and placed its palms on Donnie's cheeks. It breathed heavily in his face, and its foul breath scorched his skin, flaying off the top layer and leaving him tingling, like an unexpected sunburn. "Don't you want a drink?" it wheezed. With a burst of laughter, it vanished.

Screaming, Donnie snatched up the half-empty bourbon bottle and flung it at the wall. It smashed, the sound ringing in his ears barely audible over his own screams.

Six months later

Claire hovered outside the church, smoking a cigarette. She should go in. She *should* go in. But she wouldn't. Fuck, she knew it as soon as she'd pulled on her sneakers and headed out the door. She may as well have gone straight to the kitchen and poured a mug of red wine. Who was she kidding?

She turned to leave and almost bumped into a man hunched up near the sign, the godawful Serenity Prayer that made her want to burn the whole place to the ground.

"It's not that easy, is it?" the stranger said, giving her a small smile.

He had kind eyes, chocolate brown, and they were bright, the way hers used to be. She figured he was about to sell her a promise of hope, and resisted the urge to tell him to go fuck himself. There was still something of the desperate about him, however, and it made her want to stay a little longer, out of politeness. His face looked sore, the skin peeling as though it was healing from a burn.

The man reached into his pocket and took out a small, carved box. He looked as though he was pondering whether to tell her a story, smoothing his other hand over his thinning, yellow hair and tilting his head from side to side. Eventually, he held the box out with a sigh of deep relief.

"Just take it," he said. "I don't need it anymore."

Don't Knock Back

Mike Salt

Ethan wasn't supposed to stop. Not in this town, not this late. But the rain had turned the highway into a smear of lights and reflections, and when he saw the glowing COLD BEER sign bleeding through the mist, he figured a quick drink wouldn't hurt.

He slowly pulled his car into the parking lot and surveyed his surroundings. He had never been through this town. Ethan was always hesitant when he was someplace new; however, this had become a part of his life. Traveling from small town to small town with his phone, tripod, and mic. He loved the freedom of being a social media influencer. The fact he got paid to travel was still insane to him, but he wasn't about to waste it. He was on the road whenever he could be. Checking out haunted hotels, Airbnbs, museums, hell, he even stayed the night in a haunted restaurant once.

The bar sat squat and tired at the end of a forgotten side road, tucked between shuttered storefronts and old pickup trucks that probably hadn't moved in decades.

A place that looked like it had stories and probably too many of them. The brick building was nothing special; if it weren't for the glowing neon signs out front, Ethan wouldn't have even noticed it. Through the downpour, he made out the name of the bar: Whiskey-Town.

Ethan grabbed his backpack, checked that he still had its contents, and tucked it over his shoulder. This wasn't the first bar he had landed in while waiting for his next stop. Usually the b-roll of the surrounding areas played well in his videos. Any opportunity to make content was an opportunity to make money.

Plus, more than once he got free drinks by sharing the name of the bar and some good shots of the life inside.

This didn't look like it would be one of those bars.

Ethan sprinted out of the car and covered his head from the rain, struggling to pull open the door to the bar before stumbling inside.

Whiskey-Town was warmer than he expected. Not cozy—just warm, like someone left the heat running and never bothered to adjust it. There were twelve other people in total.

Ten at the bar.

One hunched over a booth.

The bartender.

They all looked up when he walked in. Not suspicious, not surprised. Just ... aware.

"Sit anywhere," the bartender said. A woman in her early forties, sleeves rolled, a tattoo of a kraken wrapped around her forearm. She wiped down the counter even though it didn't need it.

The bar was similar to any other small town hole in the wall. The walls were plastered with various attempts at jokes. Neon lights shone from a juke box in the corner; Nelly rapping Country Grammar echoed in the small building. Behind the bar was a taxidermy jackalope with a trucker hat on its stuffed head. The bar had large cooler cabinets full of various beer bottles and cans. Sitting on some shelves were an array of standard name brand liquors. Between them, a steel door that had an exit sign above it. A piece of paper was taped to the door that said "Go away".

Ethan took the stool second from the end. Two seats down, a big guy with a gray beard and an oil-stained ball cap nodded once, then went back to sipping from a short glass.

"You look like you've had a night," the bartender said.

Ethan nodded. "Just needed somewhere dry."

"Dry as in sober, or dry as in not drowning?"

"Both," he said, half-smiling.

"You don't come in here for the former," she said as she cracked a cap off a bottle of beer without asking. Ethan grabbed the bottle and inspected the label. It simply said: BEER. The liquid inside was dark and hoppy. "Name's Mara. If you need anything, just holler."

He was halfway through his drink when it happened.

Knock.

Just one.

Loud and deliberate.

It came from the back of the bar—through the door between the cabinets of beer and shelves of liquor. The bar wasn't big, Ethan would guess it ended right there at the door with the giant exit sign.

Ethan froze.

But the others? They cheered.

"Hell yeah!" someone called out. A skinny guy in a denim vest clinked his shot glass against the bar.

"First one!" said another.

Everyone—everyone–took a shot. Even the guy in the booth stood up, lifted his glass to the sky, and slammed it back before sitting down like it hurt to move.

Ethan blinked. "Okay," he said slowly with a shy giggle, "what just happened?"

Mara grinned and poured whiskey in a shot glass. "That? That's our little tradition."

She slid the shot to Ethan.

"Someone knocking?"

"Every night. Like clockwork. Always one to start. Nobody's ever out there. Used to freak folks out. Now it means the party's on," Mara said with a grin.

"Just ... one knock?"

"Yep. One to get us going. Second one comes later, usually around midnight. We drink for both. That's how it works."

He watched as everyone settled again, drinks in hand, casual laughter returning like someone had pressed play on a paused moment. It was so expected and familiar that the locals didn't even recognize it happened after it was done.

"Isn't that kind of creepy?" Ethan asked.

The bartender shrugged. "Only if you think too hard about it," she said.

Ethan chuckled uneasily, raised his glass, and shot it back.

The whiskey settled into Ethan's bones like flames curling up on firewood.

Warm, slow-burning.

It reminded him of swiping his fathers whiskey and sneaking out to a party in high school. It wasn't good whiskey, bottom shelf. It was all his father ever drank.

Ethan felt the alcohol flow through his body, the stress of driving through sideways rain finally bleeding out of his shoulders. He was relaxing, he could feel it.

The storm couldn't have happened at a better time. He needed the break anyway.

"You're not from around here," said the woman three stools down.

Ethan turned.

She looked to be mid-thirties, curly brown hair pulled back beneath a faded green beanie. Her jacket was oversized and patched with various band logos.

He smiled, "Was it the soaked jacket or the general confusion vibe?"

"Why not both?" She said, "Name's Jodie."

"Ethan."

They shook hands. Hers cold but steady. She gripped Ethan's hand like they were old friends and smiled at him.

He ordered another drink, this time something with a proper label, and turned slightly to face her. "So what's the deal with the knocking thing? You all just... go along with it?"

Jodie grinned and leaned in close like she was sharing a secret. "It's tradition. Weird one, yeah, but it grows on you."

"Does it always happen at the same time?"

"The first one, yeah. Second one's a little more unpredictable. Depends on the night. The vibe. It's usually around midnight, but sometimes it comes later. My guess: It's about how many people are here or who is here or whatever." She tapped her shot glass with a finger. "But it always comes."

Ethan glanced toward the back door, then back to her.

"You know its just the bartender fucking with you guys, right?" he said.

Jodie nodded. "Doubt it. I've seen it happen when no one was behind the bar. I've seen it happen when the bar was bare. I was even walking around out back once, down the alley smoking a cigarette, and it happened. Trust me ... it's not any of us."

Ethan smiled and nodded.

After a few sips of his beer, he turned to her. "You know, I'm actually kind of glad I stopped here," Ethan said as he sipped his beer.

"Most people aren't," she said, chuckling. "What brings you through?"

"I do travel content. Social media stuff. YouTube, Reels, TikTok, that whole mess."

"Like a vlogger?" Jodie asked.

He winced at the word. It felt cringeworthy. He didn't consider what he did as *vlogging*, but when you broke it down to it ... it kind of was.

"Sort of. But less 'what's up, guys!' and more scenic hikes and haunted bed & breakfasts. I was on my way to one tonight actually. Little coastal spot near the bay. But the storm got bad, and ... here I am."

"Well, your journey led you somewhere interesting."

"Tell me about it," Ethan said. "Think anyone would mind if I get the next knock on video? Like, can we time it right?"

Jodie's eyes lit up. "Seriously?"

"Yeah. Might make a great b-roll. I've got a pretty big following. People love weird local legends. Especially if there's a drinking game involved."

She sipped her drink and tilted her head. "You'd post about this place?"

"I tag everything. It's kind of the deal."

"Well, if this becomes your most viewed video, I want credit."

"You got it." Ethan laughed. "Mind giving me a heads-up when you think it's close?"

Jodie nodded, smiling. "Sure. It's usually about a couple hours after the first. We've got some time. It's unpredictable, but if you are okay having your camera rolling, you'll get it."

"Guarantee it will happen?"

"Like a fucking clock." Jodie smiled.

So they talked.

About travel, about places she'd never been but wanted to see. About the old highway that ran parallel to the coast and how no one really used it anymore. She told him the town didn't even show up on most maps–hadn't for years.

"It's like we're a glitch," she said, raising her glass. "Cheers to being nowhere."

Somewhere along the bar, a patron hollered back, "To nowhere!"

Ethan smiled as people clinked glasses and bottles and drank to it.

Eventually, after a handful of hours, her eyes flicked toward the clock behind the bar. "Almost time," she whispered. "Feel it in my teeth."

"In your teeth?"

"You heard me," she smiled.

Ethan pulled a small tripod from his bag and popped it open on the edge of the bar. His phone clicked into place. The red record light blinked alive. He adjusted the angle, set it to a wide lens, and angled it down the bar. "Alright," he whispered, grin wide and stretching from ear to ear. "Let's catch a ghost."

"Spooky," Jodie said as she waved her fingers in front of the camera. She adjusted her hair and sat up straight. Jodie leaned her elbow on the bar, eyes trained on the back.

The camera continued to roll.

Ethan leaned back in his stool and continued to converse with Jodie. It was nice to have someone to talk to. It was hard on the road. That was one thing that he hated about his job: Being alone. Everyone he met was behind a camera, and the conversations were all about the location. No real human connection.

Not with Jodie.

She smiled.

She laughed.

She shared stories with him.

He knew it was only ten or so minutes since he started rolling, but the seconds flew by as they talked. It was exciting. It reminded him of a date, although it was clearly not. Talking. Flirting. Smiling.

It was nice.

While Jodie let out a large laugh, she leaned over and braced herself on his knee.

The bar went quiet. Not silent, but lower. Softer. As if the whole place knew something was coming.

Then ...

Knock. Knock.

Two clear raps.

Sharp.

Measured.

Right on cue.

The bar erupted.

"Second one!" someone shouted.

"Bottoms up!"

Glasses clinked. Laughter rolled through the room. Ethan glanced over at his phone, eyes wide and a smile plastered across his face. "Got it," he said, beaming. "Fuck yes!"

He raised a hand up and knocked it on the bar twice.

Knock. Knock.

He turned to Jodie, who was already raising her shot glass.

"To social media and old ghosts," she said.

Ethan tapped his glass to hers and drank.

He smiled and turned as one of the older men in the bar approached.

"Shouldn't ov dun that," he mumbled.

"Excuse me?" Ethan asked as his smile dropped.

"Shouldn't ov knocked back. Yew don't wanner do that," he said as he stroked a hand through his long beard and stumbled.

"OK, Rick," the bartender said as she walked around the bar.

"Yew don't knock back!" he screamed. "Ittsa rule!"

"Sorry," the bartender said to Ethan as she approached the man and gently grabbed him by the shoulders. "He's a little drunk. I should have cut him off."

"Ner! Im not dat drunk. I-I-m I'm just leaving," Rick said as he was turned by the bartender towards the doors.

"I'm gonna call a cab and get you home," Ethan heard her saying to him as they walked. He watched them the entire way until they were out of the building.

He turned back to Jodie, "What the fuck was that?"

Jodie took a drink from her glass and shrugged. "The local drunk."

"I can see that. What was he going on about?"

Jodie laughed, "Just some superstition. I don't even think about it, otherwise I would have mentioned it to you."

"What? Mentioned what?"

"There is this old superstition that if a ghost knocks, you don't knock back or you invite it in," she said. "It's kind of a rule, but no one really cares so it is kind of unspoken, I guess."

"Oh," Ethan said.

"Yeah."

"And I–"

Jodie knocked twice on the bar.

Ethan smiled at her.

Knock-knock from down the bar as the man in the denim jacket pounded on the wood.

Knock-knock, another man knocked beside him.

Laughter followed by more knocking.

Before he knew it, the entire bar was smiling and knocking on the bar.

"Looks like a lot of rule breakers here tonight,' Ethan said with a laugh while looking at the camera. It was going to be great for content.

"Welcome to Whiskey-town," she said as she raised a glass.

They talked like old friends who hadn't talked in years.

Jodie told Ethan about the time a sinkhole swallowed half her backyard and how she kept the gnome it nearly took as a good luck charm.

He told her about the time he got locked in a crypt overnight during a "Haunted Stay" series in New Orleans.

She laughed until she snorted, then hid her face in her hands.

"So what do you actually do?" Ethan asked, eyeing the bottom of his bottle.

"Professionally?" she said, lifting her brows. "I guess I disappoint my family."

"Relatable."

She smirked and leaned in. "But when I'm not doing that, I fix clocks. Old ones. Antique stuff."

"No way."

"Yeah. Like your grandma's ticking war relics. The ones that chime at the worst times," Jodie said. "I've always loved bringing something beautiful back to life."

"I like that," Ethan said.

"Thanks," she said. "What about you, Internet Boy? You just film yourself walking through abandoned houses and drinking lattes?"

"That's ... accurate," he said, pretending to be offended. "Except it's more like walking through abandoned houses *while* drinking lattes."

She laughed, and it lingered between them for a beat too long.

Ethan glanced at the clock above the bar, its hour hand tipping at one.

"Damn," Ethan said. "It's almost one."

Jodie leaned back slightly, watching him.

"I should probably get going," he said. "Storm's slowed down, and I've got an early check-in."

She tilted her head.

"You sure?"

"Yeah," Ethan confirmed, sliding off the stool. "That bed and breakfast's only another hour out. If I don't leave now, I'll crash on some backroad and end up an urban legend."

He tossed a couple bills on the counter and gave Mara a wave. The bartender nodded and smiled.

Jodie stood too. "Well, it was nice talking. Really."

"You too," he placed his bag on the stool and opened the zipper. "You should follow me on whatever social media you have." He reached out for his phone still on the tripod. "I'd love to stay in touch."

"Okay," Jodie smiled and pushed loose hair back around her hair.

Knock. Knock. Knock.

Three.

Sharp and hollow.

Ethan froze, mid-placing the phone in the backpack.

The whole bar did too.

No cheers this time.

No raised glasses.

Just a heavy silence that slid across the room like a spilled drink.

Ethan turned back slowly. The regulars weren't smiling. A few stared at each other. One guy near the end of the bar mumbled something under his breath and left the bar.

"What was that?" Ethan asked, trying to keep his tone light with a smile.

Jodie didn't answer right away.

Her lips parted slightly, eyes flicking toward the back door. Her shoulders had tensed, just enough for him to notice.

"That ... doesn't happen," she finally said, her voice soft. Unsure.

"What do you me—"

"There's never a third."

Ethan laughed once, a small, nervous *ha*.

"Okay, well—maybe you've got a bonus ghost tonight. Should I film it?"

Ethan pulled his camera back out of his bag and placed it on the bar.

No one laughed with him.

Ethan stayed.

Not because he wanted to. Not exactly. But because the room hadn't returned to normal. Not really. There was still something thick in the air, like fog just below eye level. It pressed on the chest. Made you drink slower. Ethan was positive he got that third knock on his recording. He even got some of the fear on the people's faces. He couldn't leave yet.

The video wasn't finished.

He sat back down.

Jodie watched him with raised brows, like even she hadn't expected him to stay.

"You're recording still?" she asked.

Ethan tapped his phone. The blinking red dot in the corner of the screen hadn't stopped since the second knock. "Always rolling. Best stuff comes unplanned," he said.

"People are gonna think you faked this," she nodded slowly and gave a small smile.

"Yeah. But they'll click," Ethan said. "They'll leave a comment. Engagement is engagement, baby. Fuck 'em."

The bar tried to move on.

Small conversations sparked up again, but they were softer. Half-laughed jokes, unfinished sentences. The guy in the hoodie left without finishing his beer. A woman with short hair flagged Mara for her tab and walked out into the scattered rain without putting her coat on.

One by one, people trickled out.

Fewer and fewer at the bar now.

Ethan checked the time.

1:38 a.m.

He let out a long breath. "Alright," he said. "I really should go. I've pushed it enough."

Jodie's face fell just a little.

Knock. Knock. Knock. Knock.

Four.

Louder than usual.

The room froze again.

No one spoke for a full five seconds. Just the low hum of the cooler, and the faint clink of glasses being set on the bar.

"That's four," Ethan whispered.

"You can't leave now," she whispered.

He stared at her.

"There's never been four," she said. Her eyes were shining, wide with a strange mix of nervousness and awe. "This is ... *new*."

Ethan hesitated, then slowly pulled his phone off the tripod and turned it on her.

"Mind saying that again?"

She smiled.

"There's never been four knocks. It's kinda exciting, isn't it?"

He turned the camera on himself. "Alright, folks," he said to the phone, "I was about to hit the road, but this bar ... this little off-the-map watering hole in the middle of nowhere ... just got a fourth knock. The locals are buzzing. No one's ever heard a fourth before. No one in this town ever knocks. It's forbidden. You go to a neighbor's door, you don't knock. You just yell until someone shows up."

"You're stupid," Jodie laughed and took a sip of her beer.

"Seriously," Ethan continued to talk to the camera, "if you knock—straight to jail. They lock you up. Lickidy-split."

"Lickidy-split?" Jodie asked.

"I can feel it in my teeth," Ethan said in a mocking tone.

Beer shot from Jodie's mouth as she laughed. "Fuck you!"

He turned the camera back toward the thinning crowd. "Let's see—"

Knock. Knock. Knock. Knock. Knock.

Five.

This time, someone began to clap.

Then another person—one of the older guys—laughed. A quick bark that turned into something almost joyful.

Playful.

It was fun again.

"Oh hell!" he shouted. "This is history, baby!"

Jodie raised her glass. "Fifth time's the new charm!"

A round of cheers followed.

People toasted, laughed. They slid empty shot glasses to Mara, and she slid them back with the brown liquid inside. The people yelled and talked fast.

Ethan panned the phone around the room.

"Okay," he said, catching his own excited smile in the reflection behind the bar. "This is turning into something wild. I'm gonna start talking to people."

He clicked the camera to selfie mode and moved to the first guy, the one with the gray beard.

"How long you been coming here?" Ethan asked.

"Too long," the man replied, his voice gravelly. "Never seen any-thing like this."

"What do you think it is?"

The man shrugged. "Ghost. Trickster. Hell, maybe it's just the bar itself trying to be remembered."

Ethan moved down the line.

Everyone had a theory.

One woman thought it was aliens.

Another said it was a "local spirit with a drinking problem."

Everyone laughed and listened to each other answer Ethan.

"Do you think it'll go to six?" Ethan asked Jodie, pointing the camera at her.

She bit her lip, eyes on the back of the bar. "I kinda hope it does."

She laughed excitedly.

And then—as if answering her challenge.

Knock. Knock. Knock. Knock. Knock. Knock.

Six.

Louder this time.

Loud enough Ethan felt it reverberate off the bar.

People roared.

Glasses slammed.

Cheers erupted.

One guy even whistled and called out, "Lucky number six, baby!"

The lights flickered.

Just for a second. But it was enough. Ethan felt the air get sucked out of the room. Tension built. The laughs stopped. The cheering dimmed.

Ethan lowered his phone.

Jodie looked at him, face flushed from drink and fear. "That was weird," she said. "Six. That's the most knocks ever."

The entire bar waited for more knocking.

Seven knocks.

It almost felt inevitable.

What came instead was a dull thud.

From the other side of the bar.

Not the door.

Thud.

Thud.

Thud.

Repeatedly. Slowly. Deliberately.

The crowd quieted.

The sound continued.

Thud.

Thud.

Thud.

Ethan edged around the bar, slowly.

At the far end, near the wall, a man he hadn't paid attention to even during his interview was hunched over the wood. His head was tilted forward, face down, and he was banging it against the bar.

Thud.

Thud.

Everyone was watching him now.

Mara leaned across the counter. "Charlie?" she asked.

He didn't respond.

"Charlie—stop that, you're bleeding," Mara said as she tried to push his head back.

Blood was already running down the man's nose. More with each impact.

He wasn't reacting.

Just slamming his skull into the bar.

Over and over.

And then, as he lifted his head, Ethan saw his eyes.

Eyes rolled back. Just white.

He smiled as he slammed his head down.

Thud.

Thud.

The crowd hesitated at first, unsure of what to do. The sound of his skull cracking against the bar rang through the room, heavy and slow, like a drumbeat that wouldn't die.

Thud.

Thud.

"Charlie!" someone shouted.

Charlie didn't react. Blood pooled beneath his chin.

Someone tried to grab his arm, but it was too late. The thudding continued, slower now, deliberate. Harder.

The moment his skull cracked open with a sickening *pop*, the room went dead silent.

Charlie's body slumped forward, lifeless.

For a second, no one moved.

"Did that really just happen?" someone whispered.

Ethan couldn't look away.

The blood had started to pool on the bar in front of Charlie, streaking into the cracks in the wood. He saw the shattered bones beneath the man's skin, and something in his stomach twisted violently.

Should they call an ambulance?

But before anyone could say anything else, Mara, from across the bar, lifted her head and slammed it down against the bar.

It happened too quickly for Ethan to process.

She lifted her face toward the bar, and then she lowered her head toward the surface suddenly and violently.

Thud.

Thud.

The same rhythm.

The same violent, hollow knock.

This time, people screamed.

"No! Don't do it!" someone shouted.

But it was too late. Mara didn't stop.

Thud.

Thud.

Some moved around the bar and were trying to help, pulling her away, but the blood was already pooling in a grotesque mess around her head. She slammed her head down, stronger than those trying to stop her.

Her head met the wood, over and over, harder with each impact. Her skull cracked open with a sickening *pop*, blood spilling out like dark syrup onto the counter. She went limp.

The crowd was paralyzed. They could only watch as her body collapsed, lifeless.

Ethan's stomach churned.

His heart hammered in his chest.

The gray-bearded man Ethan had interviewed earlier looked down at the bloody mess and turned and ran away.

He stopped.

The older man looked at the crowd and grinned. A dark, wide grin that didn't match the fear in his eyes. He was trembling, but there was something else in that smile.

He cocked his head back and sprinted to the bar.

Thud.

Thud.

Thud.

The same horrible rhythm.

His skull cracked open after the third hit. It wasn't as slow, as calculated, as Charlie's. No, this was powerful and violent.

The room was a mix of shouts and gasps. Some people tried to pull him back. One person threw a glass at the wall, as if that would shatter the curse.

But it was futile.

The man fell dead.

A beat of silence.

And then, just as his body slumped forward, another person, this time a young woman, stood up from her stool.

"No," someone whispered as she grabbed her friend's arm, tears rolling down her face.

But it was too late.

She lifted her head.

Thud.

Thud.

Thud.

As another head met the bar, Ethan realized that whatever was happening wasn't going to stop. That this was something they couldn't control.

Ethan couldn't breathe.

His throat was tight. His legs felt weak.

There was only one thought in his head: *I need to get out.*

He turned quickly, grabbed his phone, and grabbed Jodie by her elbow.

The two of them stumbled toward the door, but his feet didn't move fast enough. The sound of a large *thump* behind him made him freeze.

He turned back.

The woman had gone down, her head cracked open just like the others.

Ethan pulled Jodie's arm, but she didn't budge. He looked over at her, Jodie's eyes locked on him. There was something darker in them now, something hollow. Something different.

Something mean.

She smiled. A quiet smile, but it was more sinister than anything.

"Jodie—"

Before he could say another word, she raised her head in a cocking back motion and ripped her elbow free from Ethan. In one swift flow, she sprinted to the bar and threw her head down.

Thud.

Thud.

Thud.

Ethan lurched forward, instinct kicking in.

"No! Jodie, stop!"

But she didn't.

She couldn't.

Thud.

Her skull cracked open, her body crumpling with a sickening wet thud onto the bar, her blood mixing with the pool already gathering around the other dead bodies.

Ethan's knees buckled beneath him, he felt light-headed.

And then, just as he thought his heart would stop altogether, he felt something ... a presence—cold, dark, gnawing.

His head started to throb.

A pulse of agony in his temples. His skull began to ache. His thoughts faltered.

Thud.

Thud.

He was holding his breath, trying to pull himself together. This couldn't be happening. This wasn't him.

But his head tilted forward.

No.

No.

No, he repeated in his mind with each slam.

His body moved.

Thud.

The sound echoed through his mind, through his body. It bounced around in his skull and filtered out through the growing crack in his skull.

His head slammed into the bar.

The last thing he saw was Jodie's face, her cold smile still grinning from the floor.

Then it all went black.

Bar & Grill

Joe Scipione

"Excuse me," I said to the first person I saw on the darkened roadway. I'd been walking for a while with no memory of how I got there or where I was going. "Where does this road lead?"

"If you're here," the woman looked me up and down as if she was judging me for being lost on this narrow road cutting through dense forest. "Then the only place you could be headed is the Bar & Grill. It's up ahead on your left. Just keep walking, man. You can't miss it."

"Bar & Grill?" I said. "It doesn't ring a bell."

"No, no. It wouldn't. Just keep going. Trust me."

She continued past me, back down the way I had come. And I set off in the opposite direction. As I walked away from her, I could feel her eyes on me as we both went our separate ways. I felt her looking. Somehow, I knew she was watching me, but I refused to turn and look back at her.

I wished I could remember who I was or how I got there. Nevertheless, at least I had a destination, and maybe some answers were there as well. The Bar & Grill. It sounded harmless enough. Though this area didn't seem like the best location for a restaurant. The forest was thick, and there weren't many people passing by. Maybe the answers I needed were at The Bar & Grill. If I was supposed to be going there, maybe someone who knew me was there and could tell me who I was.

I traveled on down the road, tripping occasionally on the potholes and tree roots that had burst up through the pavement.

I felt my pockets for something—anything—that might give me a clue as to who I was. There was no wallet in my pockets, no phone. I had nothing but the clothes I was wearing. As for my clothes, they didn't provide much information either, a dark t-shirt, a pair of jeans, and a dark colored hoodie.

The trees closed in around me as the road narrowed. They towered above me and felt like they were going to fall down and crush me at the slightest breeze. Still, I walked on, my eyes focused ahead, looking for this Bar & Grill or for another person who might be more helpful than the last.

Soon the old, cracked pavement beneath my feet was gone, and the road became two worn, dirt ruts through a dense forest. I started to lose hope. The woman who told me about the Bar & Grill might have been on something. Had she been drunk? High? Maybe she was just an asshole who just liked to mess with people and tell them about a Bar & Grill in the middle of the woods to see if she could get them to believe her.

I considered stopping and turning around. It was more likely the answers about my identity and what happened to me were behind me in the direction I came from and not in front of me at some mysterious Bar & Grill. The night was at its darkest, and I had all but stopped, intent on turning around when I saw a faint red glow originating from somewhere through the trees and on the other side of a hill off to my left

I looked back at the road I'd already traversed, then at the red light, which didn't seem all that far off. It was worth going off the road to check it out versus retracing my steps. I tugged down on my hoodie, turned off the road, and went up the hill to see if I could find the source of the red glow.

I don't know what I was expecting, but an actual Bar & Grill wasn't it. It was, however, exactly what I saw when I reached the crest of the small hill and looked down the rocky embankment.

The building wasn't facing me, so when I looked at it, only the side was visible. From that angle, however, I could see the red neon sign that must have been on the front of the building. I couldn't read it from where I was, so I didn't know the name of the place.

"Holy shit," I said. I took a few steps forward, letting my feet slide down the dirt and rock-covered hill that led to the Bar & Grill. I half-slid, half-walked down the hill until I got to the flat ground at the bottom. When I got there, I gave a glance back up at where I'd come from, then looked around for the front door to the place.

The Bar & Grill was made from a dark red brick and was not much taller than me with a flat roof. It was one of those places you could tell had a low ceiling without ever stepping inside. The windows on the sides had neon lights advertising various beer brands but the light emanating from those paled in comparison to the massive red neon light on the front of the place. I looked up as I circled around to the front, eager to find out the name of the Bar & Grill. As I got there, the name came into view, and I couldn't help but smile. Even in my current state, knowing next to nothing about myself, my life, or how I ended up at a bar in the middle of the woods, it was hard not to find amusement in a bar called "Satan's Bar & Grill."

I pulled open the right side of the wooden double door and expected to get hit with a barrage of 'bar-noise'—music, shouting, sports on TV, the crack of pool balls. There was none of that. Instead, it was an eerie quiet that made the place seem empty.

It wasn't empty, but close to it. At a booth along one side was a man with his head in his hands staring at an empty plate. He could have been crying, but I couldn't get a good look at his face to say for certain. At a table near the back of the place, there was a man and a woman talking with a few drinks in front of them, but their voices were low, and I couldn't hear them. Whatever they were talking about, it seemed important. On the other side was the bar itself, which stretched from the front wall all the way to the back. Behind the bar was a woman dressed all in black. She had her back to the door, and I didn't think she'd seen me enter.

Since all the seats at the bar were empty and the bartender appeared to be the only employee of the place, I went over and sat on one of the stools.

"Something to drink?" the bartender said without turning around. Maybe she *had* seen me come in.

"Um, a beer I guess," I said. "Whatever is coldest."

She pulled the tap and filled a glass with beer before turning around and setting it in front of me.

"How's it going today?" she asked. She smiled, but there was something strange to her smile. Something out of place.

"Not that great actually," I took a sip of the beer and realized I couldn't remember ever drinking a beer before. I didn't like the taste but took another sip before continuing. "I don't know how I got here, actually. Don't remember who I am. I just found myself on that road out there a little while ago. I know it sounds pretty crazy."

"It's not crazy for this place," she said. "In fact, you fit right in. A lot of people come in here not knowing who they are or how they got here."

"Really?"

"It's sort of unique to this place. I'd explain everything to you, but usually it helps if you drink a little first. The drink will help with your memory. Finish that and see how you feel."

"What kind of place is this?" I started to rise up off the stool, but the woman reached out and put her hand on mine.

"It's okay," she said. "Don't worry. Have faith. Things will be all right. Just finish the drink and let's talk then. Take as much time as you need."

She turned and left the bar area, leaving me alone with the drink in front of me. I sat there and stared at the glass, trying to figure out if what she'd said was real or just bullshit. The drink looked like any other drink. How could it make my memories return? I spun the glass in a circle a few times, watching the carbonation rise to the top and create a light foam.

I didn't know who I was or why I was there. The answers I wanted sat right there in front of me ... possibly. I needed to take the chance.

"Fuck it," I said. I picked up the glass, put it to my lips, and drank the entire thing down. I didn't know if I was the kind of person who chugged beers or not, but that day, I was one of the best to ever do it. It felt more like pouring the golden liquid down my throat as opposed to drinking it. When the glass was empty, I sat there waiting for a change and trying to remember the life I'd forgotten.

Nothing came.

As I suspected, this was all bullshit. This bartender was either having fun with me because she thought I was kidding, or she was just an asshole.

From the corner of my eye, though, I saw movement in the darkened corner of the room. I turned my attention there, trying to make my vision cut through the shadow. There was nothing there. I turned to look for the bartender, but couldn't see her, and there was movement again. This time it was behind me, just out of sight as if someone was walking up to me. I turned the other way to see who it was. There was no one there. When I returned to the empty glass in front of me, the bartender was back.

"You're seeing them, yeah?" she said. Her eyes stared into mine like daggers.

"There's nothing there," I stammered and looked back down at the corner of the room just to make sure what I was saying was correct.

"No," she smiled, her eyes still locked on mine. "They're there. They just don't exist completely in this realm so you can't quite see them. But you will. Don't worry about a thing. It will be over soon."

"What? What do you mean?"

She said nothing and took my empty glass. She refilled it with beer and set it down in front of me.

"Those are yours," she said. "Your memories. The reasons you're here. Drink this down and it will be over sooner. Don't and they will take their time, I promise you."

"Take their time. What do you mean?"

"Drink it now," her voice was deeper then before. Her eyes glowed a dark crimson. Her skin became tight against cheekbones. Her tongue flitted against her lips as she grew taller, standing over me, looking down at me, her features almost unrecognizable to what they were when I first spoke to her.

I didn't move, shocked by what I was seeing and everything that was happening around me.

"Drink," the bartender-demon before me growled in my face.

I felt my pants dampen, and warm urine dripped down my leg. I couldn't take my eyes off the monster, yet I could somehow see the glass full of beer in my periphery. Still, I couldn't have forced myself to take a drink even if I wanted to. I was frozen in fear.

"Drink," she demanded again.

Something released in me, and I was able to get the semblance of a word out.

"What—what are you?" I said, though I wasn't certain how clear the words sounded through the fear-induced sniveling. My hands didn't move, and all the creature wanted from me was for me to take a drink. Since I wasn't doing that, other forces took control. From behind me, hands emerged from the barstool. Two came out and encircled my arms and chest, pinning me to the back of the chair. Before I had time to react, two more were thrust out the sides of the seat and wrapped themselves around my thighs, making it impossible for me to get up or even move.

I struggled against the hands nonetheless, but it did no good. I couldn't move. The hands held me tight and with each twitch and twist of my body they only squeezed harder, clamping me tighter to the stool.

"Let me go, I want to go home," I screeched. As soon as I opened my mouth, a fifth hand burst from the back of the barstool. Four boney, ash-flavored fingers found their way into my mouth and pulled my jaw down. I screamed louder and tried to close my mouth. As with the hands holding me to the chair, they were too strong for me to do anything and if I forced my teeth together any harder I feared I'd snap my jaw in half.

The bartender-demon wasted no time and with my mouth held wide open and my tongue thrashing back and forth, she poured the second beer down my gullet. At first, I tried not to swallow, breathing out through my mouth causing some of the liquid to splash out. When I did that, another hand appeared from nowhere and pinched my nose closed. Bartender-demon poured more into my mouth and with no way to breathe, I had no choice but to swallow it down or die—though maybe I was set to die either way.

I gagged and coughed and choked until all the beer was gone.

"Release him," the bartender-demon said as I swallowed the last bit. The hands fell away and disappeared as if they had never been there. I collapsed out of the stool and down to the floor, which was wet with a mixture of spilled beer and my urine.

I gasped and coughed some more.

"What do you want from me?" I whimpered, unable to lift myself up from the fetal position I'd taken.

"It's not me," the bartender-demon said. "You wanted your memories, and *he* wanted you."

"Who is he?" I asked, trying to gain some modicum of composure. "And I still don't remember anything."

"You will," the bartender-demon laughed. "Just wait and watch."

I didn't have to wait long. As much as I didn't want to, I kept my eyes open, watching my surroundings from my spot on the floor. I still had little inspiration to get up. There was movement again just out of my main field of vision. I could see it yet not see it. This time, however, when I shifted my gaze toward the movement, I saw the thing that was moving. It was not much bigger than a large cat, but it was hairless with reddish-black scales running from its head to the end of its long tail. The tail was at least twice as long as the creature and was straight out behind it as it moved. Its claws clacked on the floor as it came toward me, and its short snout was pulled back, revealing teeth that seemed too large for the mouth, which was dripping and frothing.

It came right at me. I struggled to get to my feet and put some distance between myself and the creature. Before I could get up, though, there was a second creature, then a third and a fourth, all coming toward me, surrounding me too fast for me to think about making an escape.

When the first creature got close, it hissed and leapt at me. Its mouth was open, claws out in front of it. The creature lunged at my face. I put my hands up hoping to block its attack, but it was too late. The creature buried its claws in my cheek and forearms. The lacerations burned like fire. I screamed, and there was a second impact followed by a thunderbolt of pain exploding at the back of my neck and shoulders. Then another impact and another. Things happened too fast for me to make sense of it. I could only feel the hot fire of pain in my head and neck and hear the hissing and heavy breathing of these hellish creatures.

They were all over me, explosions of white, hot pain burst and tore their way through my head and face as I was ripped apart. Then, as fast as the creatures came at me, the pain stopped.

I was dead. I was certain of it. The world was black. There was no more feeling. Those creatures had taken the life I couldn't even remember from me.

But I was wrong.

They hadn't killed me. They'd simply returned my memories.

Jason. My name was Jason. My whole life came back into focus. Growing up as a kid. My parents. My sisters. My wife. My kids. How could I have forgotten them? It wasn't just people I saw, it was events too. Everything I'd ever done. The good things. And the bad things too. Waves of emotions passed over me one at a time, different thoughts and feelings with each memory as they came. I barely had time to process a memory before another came and took its place. By the time I was done I was overwhelmed having experienced a lifetime of memories all at once. I groaned and rolled over, feeling a hard coldness against my cheek. My eyes opened. I was back on the floor of the Bar & Grill.

I scrambled to my feet screaming as I ran my hands over my head. There were no wounds on my face, no blood. Nothing.

"They were your memories," the bartender-demon said, still standing and watching from behind the bar. She had returned to her human appearance, though her voice was still that of a demon. "They were never real. The return of memories can be terrible. Those monsters can be terrible as well."

"I-I have to leave," I said. "My wife, Katie, we were in an accident. I have to get back to her."

The bartender-demon watched as I walked toward the door but said nothing. What was this place? I still didn't understand, but I knew my wife had been injured in the crash. I could see it plain as day. I had been left unscathed and just walked away like I didn't care. My indifference was probably due to memory loss, but still, I should have done something.

I pulled the door to leave, but it was locked. I yanked harder, then tried the other side of the double doors. That was locked as well. Neither side would budge.

"What the fuck?" I said and turned back to look at the bartender-demon, but she was gone. The entire place was empty. The Satan's Bar & Grill looked nothing like what it had when I first arrived. The windows were gone, as were the tables and chairs and the neon lights. I was standing inside an old, windowless shed. The floor was dirt, and there were piles of dried leaves in corners.

"Let me out," I shouted and pulled again at the door. It wouldn't move. "Please, I have to help my wife."

In the far corner—the darkest corner—the small pile of leaves rustled.

"There is good news," a voice called out from all around me. It was deep—much deeper than the bartender-demon's voice. This was someone else.

"What?" I said. "Who are you?"

"The good news," the voice carried on as if it hadn't heard my questions. Or more likely, it, hadn't cared, "is that Katie has survived."

The pile of leaves rustled again. I stared at it, watching for more movement waiting for those creatures to come at me for a second time.

"You, Jason, did not," the voice said. The leaves shook and flipped up into the air as if a huge gust of wind had somehow entered the building and scattered them. I jumped back, and it was only then that the words, the voice had spoken registered in my head.

"What do you—" I stopped speaking because from the corner where the leaves had been emerged a giant beast.

It crawled out of the shadows, arms first pushing itself out of the darkness. This beast was brown and covered in dirt as if it had actually been living in the soil beneath my feet. It was massive, and as it entered the small room, it stood, rising up at least four feet taller than me. On either side of its head were two horns, coming out to the side and then curling down on either side of its face. The horns were caked in dirt. Leaves fell off them as the thing moved. It seemed as though the beast was nude though due to the dirt which caked its flesh, I couldn't see much of its skin.

"You know what I am," the beast said. "You know you died, Jason. You did not survive the crash. You also know that you've been a piece of shit for most of your life. You know who I am and you know why I'm here."

"I-I changed. I made myself better," I stammered thinking back to all of the shitty things I did in my younger years.

"It doesn't change anything," the Devil said to me then. "Now is the time. You are done with this world."

The Devil pointed toward the dark corner from which he had emerged.

"This doesn't have to be painful," the Devil said. "But it can be."

I stepped toward the corner. I wanted to cry but didn't want to give the Devil the satisfaction of knowing I was a broken man.

"Face the corner," the Devil said. "I'll do the rest."

I stood in the corner of the building, facing the dark shadow, and thought about my life. I thought I'd done enough to escape this everlasting torment, but I hadn't. I hadn't done enough to change my destiny. Maybe I never could.

"What, what do I do now?" I asked.

"Nothing," came the reply and a strong hand shoved me hard in the back. I fell down into the dirt and leaves.

And then I kept falling.

Linger Longer Lounge

Ben Young

N othing but static.

Jamie pressed the *SEEK* button over and over, but the radio—as if in direct protest of his insistence—still returned nothing but static. He looked to his girlfriend, Stacey, in the passenger seat. "Is the GPS back yet?" he asked.

She shook her head, shimmying her pixie cut, holding the phone up for him to see. "No, nothing," she said.

"We can't be that far from the edge of the park," he said, while aware that they weren't exactly driving through the couple-hundred-acres kind of park. This was Mount Rainier National Park, for fuck's sake. One of the last great wildernesses in the continental US. Without the GPS to orient themselves, they could be hours from any type of structure.

The gas tank sat at an anxiety-inducing low, a hairsbreadth above the 'E' mark, and the uneven road conditions caused him to eek by under fifteen mph, winding ever onward through the massive trees.

It was both gorgeous and endless.

Strange to think in these modern times how remote some places could still be. How easily you can find yourself lost and cut off. And when it happened, it was surprisingly hard to avoid losing your grip on sanity. Part of him knew they'd be fine if they just kept going. It was no more complicated than that. But the voice questioning this (*Exactly how much more gas is there? How many more miles can we make it?*) was getting louder by the minute.

Stacey had warned him before they started driving this morning, too. If he voiced his concerns to her now, he would be opening himself up to some well-earned criticism.

The sun was dipping behind the horizon, and the dark was gathering, emerging cloud-like from the tree trunks surrounding them. They came around another sharp bend to see the single lane road branching for the first time in at least thirty minutes.

Only a minor change in scenery, but it was grounding nonetheless. Jamie breathed a bit easier.

A hand-painted sign with a right-facing arrow stood at the fork and declared:

Linger Longer Lounge
2 miles ahead

Jamie was faced with a decision then. It wasn't their destination, and his rational mind told him that the destination couldn't be that much further away. Certainly not impossibly far away. Certainly not ... Right?

Should he turn, or keep going?

His eyes swept over the gas gauge nervously, without pausing, refusing—like a skeptical bird—to settle there.

Maybe at this bar or whatever it was, they'd have a map. Or someone could tell him how far until the edge of the forest. Suddenly the need to know if they had enough gas left outweighed the uncertainty of turning off the road to follow that sign.

He slowed and made the turn.

"What are you doing?" Stacey asked. "That's not our route."

Time to confess. "I'm not sure we're even still on the right route," he said. "Or how much further. And the gas gauge is getting kind of low. It's only two miles. Let's stop and stretch our legs and see if someone can tell us where we are."

Luckily, she didn't protest. "Okay," Stacey said.

The two miles spurred behind them quickly, perhaps an exaggerated distance. Blacktop gave way to gravel, and at its end, there stood a small, boxy, rustic building. Linger Longer Lounge marked above the door in red neon. It had only enough space for a couple cars to park, but there were no other vehicles. No windows, either. The road ended here.

"Cool name, but I don't think it's open," Stacey said.

A worm of panic twisted in Jamie's gut. Had he just cost them some four-ish miles when they were already low on gas?

"Stay here, I'll check," he said, before opening the door and stepping out.

"I'll come with you," she answered.

The front door was heavy, but unlocked. The lounge's interior was dim and smoky. And crowded.

On a quick scan, Jamie clocked at least eight people. One behind the bar, four seated on stools with their drinks adjacent. One leaning on a full-size juke box next to the bar and a second beside them. Two more near a pool table in the far corner. All of their backs were to Jamie, with the exception of the bartender.

Swing music poured from the jukebox, lending an odd sense of time displacement to the ambience of the small room.

The door clapped shut loudly, and everyone in the place turned to look at Jamie and Stacey.

Stacey gasped.

Something about the ... suddenness of it. The wideness of their eyes. All of them turning together. The air felt charged with muted hostility, warning Jamie they shouldn't have entered.

Was this some kind of private bar? For a motorcycle gang or something like that? He had seen no signs on the outside except the red neon one with the place's name. No other vehicles, and he would have noticed a platoon of motorcycles.

Wanting to make this as quick as possible, not wanting to ... linger any longer ... he tried to shed the unwelcome stares from all these strangers and approached the bar. Everyone else seemed to return to their previous state then, accepting the newcomers. Ignoring their disruption.

The bartender was an older man, wearing thick glasses, and ... was there something familiar about him? Felt that way, but Jamie couldn't place a finger on why.

"Excuse me," he said. "We could use a little help."

"Now that you're here," the bartender said, blinking slow and heavy behind his inch-thick lenses, "might as well stay for a drink." He motioned toward two empty stools. "On the house." Jamie noticed a few dark stains on his tan shirt.

"Oh," Jamie said. "That's kind of you, but ... we're in a bit of a hurry."

The bartender chuckled. He muttered something while turning away. To Jamie it sounded like "maybe you were" but the music picked up at the same time and obscured it.

Hoping to keep focused, he said, "We don't mean to bother anyone, but could you tell me how far to the nearest gas station?"

The bartender didn't answer. He busied himself mixing drinks and then set them in front of his newest customers. For Jamie, an Old-Fashioned. For Stacey, a Gin and Tonic with lime.

Jamie narrowed his eyes. "How'd you—"

The bartender smiled and said, "I always know."

"Listen, we really can't stay," Jamie said.

Again, the bartender chuckled. "I respectfully disagree," he said. Then he walked away, toward the jukebox.

"What an odd man," Stacey said. "Don't think I've ever met a pushy bartender, but I guess he has to take whatever business he can get out here."

"Let's just ask someone else," Jamie said. He turned left, to the woman on the next stool. "Excuse me." She appeared to be half-asleep, head hung close to the bar's surface, fingers wrapped around the handle of a nearly empty beer mug. Was there ... was there something familiar about her too? No, too hard to even see in here. Mind playing tricks.

"Excuse me," he repeated.

She looked at him only long enough for him to glimpse her face but didn't respond. Re-hung her head.

Jamie walked past her to the man seated on the other side. "Sir?" he said. The man gave no response, so Jamie tapped him on the shoulder. "Sir, excuse me?"

The man turned, and he was definitely familiar. Someone Jamie recognized but couldn't place. Hard lines in his face. Close-set eyes, sunk deep in the sockets.

"Look," the man said. "Maybe no one else has the balls to tell you this, but there's no avoiding it."

"I don't—" Jamie started.

"Might as well get comfortable," the man said, cutting him off. "You're here now."

"But we're just passing through," Stacey said from behind Jamie. "Can you give us directions?"

The man shook his head. "You're not going anywhere, miss."

"Hey," Jamie said. It felt like a threat, and he had to respond. "If you don't want to help us that's fine, but we're leaving."

The man only stared, which pushed that sense of familiarity in Jamie's mind. "Do ... do I know you?" Jamie asked.

The man gave no answer still, turned back to his drink.

"Jamie, let's just go," Stacey said. She sounded worried. Jamie thought about the gas gauge and decided to try once more.

He went to the pool table and addressed the two men there. Both had their backs turned again.

"Hey," he said. "I'm sorry to bother you guys, but I just need to know how far until the edge of the park. Can you tell me, please? Then we'll be on our way."

The man closest to him, wearing a blue trucker hat, turned to respond. Jamie gasped.

He knew this man, there was no doubt.

"Uncle Gary?" he said.

"Hey kid," the man answered.

Jamie could only stutter. "You ... h-how ... no ..."

"Been a long time," Uncle Gary added. "Sorry you ended up in here. But you might as well get comfortable."

You're dead, Jamie thought. *You died when I was a kid*. But the words wouldn't leave his body. Only a pained choking sound escaped.

What the hell was this place?

"Jamie," Stacey said. "What's going on?"

Realization came then. The other people he'd spoken to in here, he knew them all.

"What's happening?" Stacey asked. "Can we just go now?"

Jamie barely heard her, though. Lost in memories. The bartender, with his thick glasses and stained shirt, was the first person Jamie had ever seen dead. His father's barber. Dad would bring Jamie, and he'd sit and watch while the guy (Al? Was that his name?) would flick the scissors, clipping here and there, and smoking a cigar. His shirts were always stained, and Jamie would wonder how he could be so precise with those coke-bottle glasses on. But Dad wouldn't trust anyone else to do the job, so he must have been good at it.

He'd died of a heart attack when Jamie was around nine, and Dad made them all go to the funeral. The first one Jamie had ever attended.

The woman at the bar looked like his third-grade teacher who'd been struck by a city bus and killed the summer after he'd been in her class. The man next to her resembled Jamie's first boss, who had been crushed by a dump truck bed while trying to fix a leak in the hydraulics.

And now, Uncle Gary. Who'd been like a second father until stomach cancer had first decimated and then taken him away.

Everyone in here was dead, and Jamie had been to all their funerals.

"I don't … don't understand," he said, his mind sputtering like a failing engine. A wave of dizziness hit him, and he put a hand onto the pool table to catch himself. "I don't … No. No. No."

"What?" Stacey asked. "What's wrong?"

Again, Jamie didn't register her words. He rushed for the door.

"I'm afraid it's too late for that," the bartender (Al?) called to him, projecting his words over the continuous music from the jukebox. "Once you're in here, it's too late."

"What the fuck is this place?" Jamie shouted.

Al (?) shrugged. "Don't have any answers for you, kid. Don't know how long it's been, how this place came to be, or what you did that landed you here. But … none of us can leave. We're all just kind of, waiting."

"Waiting for what?" Jamie asked. "Don't have a clue, kid. I'm real sorry."

"Jamie," Stacey said, her voice painted with concern now too. "Where'd the door go?"

"It … it was here," he said. Only, he was staring at an uninterrupted wall of brick. "It was right here."

The music played on, bold and brassy.

The billiard balls clinked together.

"Where'd the door go?!" Jamie shouted. "Where'd the fucking door go?!"

The bartender clicked his tongue behind them.

Everyone lingered longer.

The Godfall Taproom

Cassandra Celia

As remembered by Bigby, German Shepherd, Good Boy, Survivor

T he first time I spoke like a man, the sound didn't come from my throat so much as claw its way out—wet and broken, like bark peeling from a tree that had stood too long in the rain, softened by rot. The voice was wrong, too deep and too slow, bubbling up through my chest like something dredged from beneath a stagnant pond.

It didn't belong to me. Not really.

Not to Bigby the dog, who once ran through forests at Al's side, tongue lolling, tail high, the wind in our fur and laughter in the trees. Not to Bigby, who knew every command, who watched the world with wide, honest eyes, who waited by the door every evening until the truck's engine announced his friend had come home.

No, this voice was something *else*. Older than I was. Older than dogs. It tasted like smoke and old leaves. Like memories you try to bury but keep rising in the night, scratching at the door. It felt... borrowed. Like I'd dug it up. Or worse, like it had *always* been there, waiting for the right moment to slip through my teeth.

I used it anyway, because the door had been left *open*.

Al never leaves the door open. Not in spring, when the fog clings low and thick like breath on a window. Not at night, when the woods lean too close. But he'd been strange all day, looking past me. Kept humming the same hollow tune, over and over, like something was singing it through him. I watched like a guardian, but I couldn't pinpoint what was amiss. Just something different, something *wrong*.

He said he was going out for a drink.

"Stay, Bigby," Al murmured, and scratched behind my ears without meeting my eyes. He didn't close the door behind him.

The hinges gave a long, aching groan as the cabin door swayed back and forth. The air shifted. Curtains near the window lifted gently, stirred by a breeze that shouldn't have been there.

It wasn't the kind of wind that prickled your skin or carried the clean bite of pine and night. This wind slithered low, brushing along the floorboards like a snake seeking warmth. It carried with it a damp heat, the kind that clung to fur and crawled into your nose like steam rising from rotted wood.

It smelled *wrong*. *Wrong wrong*. Like the earth turned over in places where things had been buried too long, or the breath of something that had lain still for years, then woke up hungry.

My ears flattened. My hackles rose. I lifted my snout from my crossed paws, and it took far too long to move my old, achy bones from the hardwood floor. But for Al, I would do anything.

Every muscle tensed as the air stilled around me. Something had already arrived. Right under my nose. And it took Al with it.

I left our home, our safe space, while the darkness slithered in behind me and the door swung, beckoning it in.

The lane found *me*. I wasn't looking for it, I was looking for my friend, of course.

I know the woods. Every stone, every trail. But this road—this narrow, dark stretch of bone-colored gravel and lichen-slick roots—it found me. My paws knew the way, like they'd walked it in another life, under a colder sky. It split off from the county road. No lights. No sounds.

I knew something in here was calling for my friend, drawing him into the woods. It drew me in too, pulling me along by an invisible string tied to each foot, but I followed anyway.

The further I went, the deeper everything sank:; sight, sound, smell. The pines began to sweat sap that glistened like blood. The air smelled like rain on stone and meat left too long in sunless places.

There were no birds. No frogs. Just the sound of the trees, whispering in a language I couldn't understand; words like cracks and tears in fabric. The sky narrowed, *watched.*

And then, there it was. The bar.

It didn't rise from the earth so much as grow from it, slumped between two black-trunked trees, their bark flayed in long ribbons. The structure pulsed. Not visibly, but in the way you feel a heartbeat inside a room before you hear it.

The building looked built from forgetting, wood warped with damp memories, windows fogged with stories that never finished being told. The sign overhead flickered with dying neon: LL TAP, the rest eaten away by time, or maybe teeth. Al's truck was there, alone and ticking. Still warm. There was no music, no laughter. Just the amber glow leaking through glass, and something that pulsed beneath it.

I stepped forward. The door opened for me.

The air inside was heavy. Sweet. Clinging. It wrapped around my snout and slipped down my throat like syrup made of nightmares. It smelled of singed fur and scorched leather, and tasted like old milk. The floor was sticky beneath my pads; not from spilled drinks, but from something wetter. Blood.

Al sat at the bar. Back straight. Eyes wide. His hands trembled around a glass of ink-black liquid that never rippled. I watched as his fingers twitched, just once, like he was trying to remember how to move.

The bartender leaned close—his lips brushing Al's ear like he was murmuring something intimate and awful. Then he turned to me and smiled. My tail lowered, and the growl that settled in my stomach manifested into bared teeth.

He wore the suggestion of a human shape, as if someone had whispered the idea of a man into the dark and let it fester there. But his face moved, not with expressions, not with the rise and fall of emotion, but like decisions being made behind a curtain. Subtle shifts, half-formed choices. His skin twitched as though trying to reject the form it had been given, shimmered like heat off asphalt, and fought—violently, hopelessly—to settle on a single truth.

His eyes were too wide, stretched beyond comfort, like they once belonged to something that needed to see in every direction at once. The bartender's mouth was too narrow, clenched and trying to hold something back. And his fingers, too many of them and too long, twitched each on its own rhythm, like a scatter of spiders sensing prey nearby, or testing the air for weakness.

"You came," he said, the smile still taut on his lips. It was everywhere, all at once. His voice came from the walls, from the floorboards, from the mirror behind the bar. It came from beneath the floor, deeper still.

That's when it happened.

I spoke. Not barked. Not whined. Spoke. The words dragged themselves out, bitter and wet, something dead finally surfacing.

"Where's my friend?"

The bartender's grin cracked wider, stretching across his face like a seam tearing open under pressure. I heard it splinter, an audible, brittle sound, dry wood giving way or ice fracturing beneath a boot. It wasn't just a smile anymore but something else entirely, one that had no business belonging to a human face.

The corners of his mouth crept toward his ears, too slow, too deliberate, pulled from the inside by invisible hooks. His teeth showed, not just in a flash, but in full, as though they were being presented and offered. I didn't know if the sound came from his skin or his bones, but it stuck in my ears.

"He's not yours anymore," the bartender turned to face Al. His lips moved, repeating the same tune he'd been humming all day, but there was no recognition beyond that within his glazed-over eyes.

"He came here. Of his own accord. He's being shown the truth. That's all this place offers to those who hear the song beneath the world. That's all that's left."

It wasn't a song. It was a *summons.* The melody of something vast and sleeping. Something he didn't mean to answer. Something Al couldn't seem to resist.

"I'm taking him home."

"You can't," the bartender said. "Not without seeing. Not without drinking."

He placed a bowl before me. Dark liquid; not a drink, not water, but something that moved when I blinked, and stilled when I stared.

"You want to follow him? You want to bring him back? Drink."

And I did.

I drank the bowl dry, and the world opened. Not like a book, but like a wound.

My mind split. My body fell away. I was falling without falling; plunging sideways through time, through before. Through the long sleep of Earth. Through the dreams of the god that slumbers beneath the soil. I saw it. Its body is the roots of trees. Its breath is the wind through the leaves. Its dreams are the fog that rolls in thick and silent. It has no name, not one spoken or safe.

And it heard Al. Worse—it answered.

I saw him walk the lane in the dream. I saw him reach the bar in the belly of the beast. I saw the dogs. So many dogs.

I came back with a scream. Not a bark. Not a word. A tear in sound. Whatever it sounded like, it snapped my friend from his trance. Al looked at me. Really looked.

"Bigby?" he whispered, eyes wide.

"We have to go."

The bartender's fingers lengthened, unfurling into tendrils of darkness rooting into the walls. "He's seen now," he hissed. "He belongs."

"No."

"You all come here thinking you can resist," it said. "But you forget, you were built for this. Flesh made to hold fear. Minds made to carry it." The bar pulsed. The walls sighed. And from the shadows... other dogs.

Some looked like me. Most didn't. Dogs that moved wrong, that breathed in jerks, that blinked with the wrong rhythm. Dogs with milky eyes and twisted legs. One had a jaw unhinged and twitching. Another had no mouth at all, just a stitched snout.

They emerged like echoes. Some had too many eyes. Some none. Some had fur that shifted like shadow, or barked sounds that weren't barks.

They sat at booths, on stools, beneath tables. Some stared into empty glasses. Some lapped from bowls filled with things that shimmered like oil on a hot road.

They did not bark. They did not wag. They watched.

"I came for Al. I will bring him home."

The others moved; not with menace, but inevitability. A slow, shuffling tide of eyes and teeth and fur, of things that once were dogs and something else now. A mutt with ribs like fence posts leaned close, breath like grave moss. *"You drank, and you came back. Not all do."*

"I didn't drink for me," I growled.

"No. You drank against yourself. That's different."

Al trembled beside me, hands clenched to his head. "Make it stop. Make it—please, Bigby, I don't—I didn't mean—"

The dogs pressed in, forming a circle around us, their shapes distorting like wet ink on paper. I looked at Al, his eyes no longer glazed, no longer distant. Terrified, yes, but present.

"I heard it," he said. "I heard something underneath. It promised I wouldn't feel alone. It promised peace."

"It lied," I said, the words thick with smoke.

The bartender's form unraveled like thread pulled from a fraying coat. His human mask sloughed off, slithered across the bar, curling inward like burned paper. In his place rose something like a tree. Tall, skinless, branching. Its face split open in a vertical grin that went all the way down.

"You cannot save what has already opened the door," it hissed. "He let me in. You let me in. You drank from the bowl. You carry the echo."

"I do," I said. *"But I carry it so he doesn't have to."*

And I howled.

It was not a sound the bar had heard before. It was not worship or surrender. It was grief. Old and bright. A sound for running under the stars and sleeping by fires. For waiting by doors. For watching over the one you love, even when they stop watching back.

The howl split the air like lightning through still water. It echoed in the rafters and cracked the neon sign. It made the dogs stir, one by one, lifting their heads. Eyes cleared. Tails thumped once, slow. Their shapes flickered, like the memory of who they'd been reached up through the soil and touched them again.

The bartender screamed, the kind of scream that comes from a mouth not made for sound. He lunged, but the dogs moved. They moved for me.

They surrounded us—Al and I—teeth bared not in threat, but in defense. Barking now. Real barking. And I saw it then, not anger, but a choice.

They'd remembered too late. I hadn't.

I turned, pressing my body to Al's. *"Run,"* I said.

For a moment, the bar fought to hold us. The door stretched further away with each step we took, like the hallway of a dream. The walls buckled, the booths bled shadows. But we pushed on, leaving the dogs who'd sacrificed themselves for us, behind.

The stitched-snout dog lunged at the bar itself, tearing into it with bone-white teeth. The bloodhound bayed like thunder. They fought for me. For the chance I still had. For the choice I'd made.

We reached the door, and the moment we passed through, it closed. Not with a slam, but like an eyelid, soft and final.

Behind it, I heard the song break.

We didn't speak for a long time. Al and I sat in the bed of his truck, parked just off the gravel road that now looked like any other trail. The stars above didn't blink.

Eventually, he said, "I was gonna drink again tonight."

I looked at him.

"I wasn't going out for just one," he whispered. "I didn't want to feel anything. It just... hurt."

I rested my head on his lap. He scratched behind my ears.

"I think I understand now," he said. "What it wanted. What it was."

"It feeds on forgetting," I murmured. He nodded.

"But you didn't forget."

I thumped my tail once. *"Never."*

#

Al never asked what I'd become. Never flinched at my voice, though I used it sparingly. Sometimes we talk in silence. Sometimes we listen to the wind together.

But we never leave the door open. Not anymore.

Because the god beneath the earth still sleeps. And it remembers the sound of our names.

BIGBY'S FINAL RULES

(etched into the cabin door in claw marks)
If the wind smells like burnt fur, stay inside.
If the door opens on its own, don't follow it.
If you hear barking from beneath the ground, don't answer.
If they offer you a drink, don't.
If you hear your name called from far away…
…it's not Al.

Ahoy, Matey!
Viggy Parr Hampton

"Ahoy, matey!"

Lance barely stifles a scream as a deep voice bellows out of the pirate in front of him.

Stormy, the head bartender, laughs. "Don't worry about it. Captain Eddie gets everyone at least once."

"Captain Eddie?" Lance asks, craning his neck to look up at the six-and-a-half-foot-tall pirate. The animatronic stares back at him, ocean-blue eyes wide. Its face is too large, the size and shape of a massive dinner plate, and its nose is a bulbous tuber. Within the nest of its long, dark beard, its pale pink lips look like earthworms, pulled back into a leering grin. Some people have resting bitch face, but Captain Eddie seems to have resting creep face.

"Well, his official name is Captain Edward Balboa, but most of us just call him Captain Eddie."

Lance swallows hard. "Um," he stammers. "Where did he... where did he come from?" The rest of the pirate's body is thick and solid, swathed in black, white, and red, with a gold-buckled belt and disproportionately enormous black boots. He should be ridiculous, like something out of a Spirit Halloween store, but he's not. He's... unsettling.

"No one really knows," Stormy says. "Velma bought the bar from the original owners back in 1975, and Captain Eddie came with the place."

Lance shakes his head a little, trying to dislodge the creeping dread. He doesn't want to look silly in front of Stormy—she's pretty hot, after all. "Got it. Well, he's very... on theme."

Stormy laughs. "Can't have a pirate-themed bar without a pirate, huh?"

"Right," Lance says, laughing along with her, but it feels forced.

"Okay, so, a few things," Stormy says, getting down to business. She gives him the spiel she's probably given dozens of times to new employees, and Lance starts to calm down... but then she finishes with, "Oh, and one last thing. Don't be in here by yourself after closing."

Lance's stomach drops. "Right. Why?"

Stormy shrugs. "This is Savannah, man. Everything is haunted."

"Seriously?" Lance asks. He expects her to laugh again and tell him this is just part of some newbie hazing ritual.

"Seriously," she says, but the way she waggles her fingers at him signals otherwise. "Ghosts are real."

Lance has no plans to stay at his job after hours anyway, so he's not concerned about possible ghosts... although the thought raises goose pimples on his upper arms. He hopes she can't see them.

He's about to ask another question when Captain Eddie lets loose with, "Welcome to Pirate's Cove!"

Over the next few weeks, Lance acclimates to his life at Pirate's Cove. He even forms some tenuous friendships with a few of the regulars, and he's not entirely sure, but he thinks he and Stormy might have some potential.

He's even come to appreciate Captain Eddie, though he still finds him off-putting. Since he started, he's heard a few more of the Captain's gems:

"Shiver me timbers!"

"Don't get shanghaied!"

"Argh!"

"Now you'll have to walk the plank!"

The Captain's stock phrases should make him seem more silly, but when business is slow or it's dark outside, Lance can't help but imagine new phrases slipping out of the Captain's plasticky mouth. Once, when he whipped around to look at the pirate, he swore he saw those marine-blue eyes staring straight at him.

Of course, that's all nonsense, Lance knows that—but he also knows trying to control your feelings isn't always easy, or even possible. Why else would he have left Birmingham after his mother's death? He wanted a clean slate somewhere new, somewhere nobody knew he had a dead mom and no dad. He wanted—and still wants—to recreate himself as the kind of person he wants to be, not the kind of person weighed down by a tragic history.

"Last call," Stormy yells out over the Saturday night crowd. It's nearly three in the morning, and Lance's head is starting to pound along with the jaunty music. Pirate's Cove is a popular spot, and he loves the atmosphere most of the time, but right now, all he wants to do is go back to his studio apartment and sleep for the next twelve hours.

Half an hour later, drunk patrons are stumbling out of the bar, and Stormy and the rest of the Pirate's Cove crew are cleaning up, preparing to close for the night.

"So, Lance," Stormy says, elbowing him in the ribs as they both work to wipe down the bar. "It's been a month, right? How are things?"

Lance pauses, considering. There's the more comforting answer: "Things are great, I'm loving it here, what an awesome place." Then, there's the more honest answer: "This isn't what I thought it would be, I'm lonely a lot of the time, and I miss my mom."

His actual answer falls somewhere in the middle. "Good. Getting used to everything, you know, but I'm liking it so far."

Stormy smiles. "Good. If you need anything, you let me know, okay?"

He smiles back, wondering if she really means it, or if that's just something she says to all the new hires. "Sure," he says.

When they've finished all their closing duties, the crew files out onto the sidewalk, and Stormy locks up. The others drift off toward their homes, but Stormy lingers with Lance, and they start to walk side by side down the street. This is something new, and Lance's palms start to sweat.

"Maybe I can show you around town sometime," she says. "Help you get more comfortable."

Lance has to clench his teeth to hide the goofy grin that wants to erupt across his face. Is she asking him out? Should he have asked her out first? "That would be awesome," he manages lamely.

She giggles. "Maybe I should give you my number?"

Shit! He should have asked her for that a long time ago. What is wrong with him?

"Yeah, for sure," he says, reaching into his pocket for his phone. It's not there.

"Fuck," he mumbles, sticking both hands deep into his pockets, digging for his phone.

"What is it?" Stormy asks.

"I think I left my phone at the bar," he says, scowling.

"No biggie," Stormy says.

"Ugh," Lance says. He doesn't have a laptop, so without that phone, he feels naked, vulnerable. He uses it for everything from online banking to watching porn, and the thought of going even twenty-four hours without it makes him shiver. "I really need to get it."

"Don't worry," Stormy says, stopping. "I'll go with you. It's okay."

Lance nods gratefully as they turn and walk the short distance back to Pirate's Cove.

When they arrive, Stormy unlocks the heavy wooden door.

"Thanks," Lance says, pulling it open and stepping inside.

"You want me to come with you?" she says, pulling a pack of cigarettes out of her purse.

He does, badly, but he doesn't want to look scared in front of her. Plus, she clearly has something she'd rather be doing than babysitting him.

"No, I'll be in and out," he says.

"Don't let the ghosts get you!" she says as she flicks her lighter and brings it to her cigarette.

"Right," he mumbles, slipping inside and letting the door close behind him.

His phone is right where he left it, in his cubby in the back room. He darts in as quickly as possible, grabs the damned phone, and stuffs it into his pocket.

It's dark in the bar, even with the moonlight filtering through the windows, and when he hears the footsteps, he's relieved.

"I wasn't scared, you know," he says.

No one responds.

"Are you fucking with me?" he says, desperately hoping Stormy will jump out from behind the bar and yell "Boo!" He'd take a jump scare over anything else.

But what exactly might that "anything else" be?

"Stormy?" he calls out, passing the bar, barstools flipped upside down and placed on top for the night.

There's another loud set of footsteps. The wood floor groans, and Lance reflexively grabs his crotch to keep from wetting himself. What is he so afraid of?

"Time to walk the plank!" a deep voice bellows, and Lance's entire body goes rigid. He's paralyzed at the end of the bar, wishing he could squeeze his eyes shut but also terrified to be stuck in the darkness.

The footsteps continue, and they're getting closer.

As Lance stares, a shaft of moonlight is broken by two enormous black boots. A microsecond later, Captain Eddie appears, plunging the room into darkness. When he shifts to take another step forward, the light breaks over him again, and Lance sees that even his walk is strange—bowlegged and uncanny.

"Jesus fuck," Lance whispers, finally losing the battle with his bladder. Warm urine gushes down his legs, pooling in his shoes.

Lance wills his body to move, to run, but he stays rooted to the spot, shaking uncontrollably.

The pirate closes the distance between them in two large strides, and the last thing Lance hears before he plunges into the abyss is, "I'm taking you to Davy Jones's Locker, Lance!"

When awareness returns to Lance, he feels inflated, heavy, bogged down, as though he has the worst hangover of his life. It's too bright in here, too loud. What the fuck did he do last night?

People are talking around him, but he has to really focus to understand what they're saying.

Is that... Stormy?

"I'm glad you made it out of here alive last night," Stormy says.

Why can't he remember?

He tries to blink, but his eyes feel as though they've been covered with coarse sand. He smells plastic and hot metal, a nauseating combination. Jesus, he's never drinking again.

"Wouldn't have missed a night with you for anything," a voice says, and he recognizes that one, too, but... it's not possible.

With a concerted act of willpower, he forces his vision to clear.

He instantly wishes he hadn't.

He's looking down at the bar from somewhere high up, too high. He can see Stormy behind the bar, a rosy blush in her cheeks. Across from her, it's... no, it can't be...

"I told you the ghost was a load of bullshit," Lance's body says, smirking at Stormy over the polished wood of the bar.

What the fuck is happening?

Lance's body turns to face him, lowering an eyelid in a wink.

He tries to pry open his rubbery lips to scream, but two words escape instead.

"Ahoy, matey!"

Looks That Kill

R.E. Sargent

The music thundered, forcing the patrons to raise their voices above the noise to be heard. The thunk of glasses hitting on the bar, the clack of pool balls colliding against one another, and the whooping and hollering when a dart hit a bull's-eye all added to the din.

Smoke curled through the air like ghostly fingers, dimming the neon signs and veiling the bar in a haze. The Devil's Tacklebox—most patrons simply referred to it as "The Box"—was fairly packed as it was every Friday night. Every barstool had an ass attached to it, and every pool table was surrounded by groups of four or more. The three pinball machines in the corner blinged and flashed as the players tried to rack up the highest scores. A burly man in a western shirt, Wranglers, and a baseball cap drained his third ball right down the center of the playfield; his attempts to save it by flapping the flippers like a duck in flight were to no avail. He slammed his fist down on the machine, grabbed his beer, and joined his friends at their table near the back of the bar.

Lizzy Haley selected K4 on the jukebox, her last selection of five. Bon Jovi's "Wild is the Wind" blasted out from the various speakers that were located strategically around the bar. Anticipating one of her songs coming on next, she turned away from the jukebox and surveyed the crowd, taking a long draw off of her Michelob Ultra. Her seat at the end of the bar still stood empty—Sandi, the bartender, wouldn't let any of the asshats in the place take her spot. She headed back to her seat, dodging out of the way before narrowly missing the backward thrust of a pool cue to her right breast. Bon Jovi ended, and one of her songs started. Jesse James Dupree's vocals belted out the question, when would it rain.

Lizzy slid onto her stool, downed the rest of her beer, and held the empty bottle in the air, catching Sandi's attention. Sandi nodded at her from the other end of the bar, finished up with her customer, reached into the bar back cooler and pulled out a new bottle, snapped off the lid, and placed it on a fresh napkin in front of Lizzy.

"Here you go, gorgeous."

"Thanks, Sandi. Flattery will get you everywhere." Lizzy laid a twenty down on the bar. "Keep the change."

"Thanks, Sweetie," Sandi purred. She picked up the twenty, rang up the beer, put the bill in the register, took out the change, and stuffed it into a beer pitcher on the back bar counter. Turning back to Lizzy, she said, "Where's your girl tonight?" Sandi was referring to Lizzy's best friend Hailey.

"Your guess is as good as mine. She was supposed to meet me here at seven. She's not answering her cell either. Go figure."

"How long are you going to wait for her?"

"Not sure. I'm in a drinking mood, though, so with or without her bitch ass, I'm hanging out."

"I'll keep the beers flowing."

"You fucking better!" Lizzy flashed her a big smile, her teeth almost too perfect, too white.

"I probably should mention... since Hailey isn't here to watch your back... don't turn around now, but the three guys at the table in the corner have been watching you closely. I think they like what they see."

"Ugh. Why is it always me? Can't a girl just enjoy drinks without being eye-fucked all night long?"

Sandi laughed. "Have you seen yourself, girl? Beautiful blond hair and those damn ice-blue eyes. And you probably weigh a buck-ten soaking wet."

"One twenty-two, thankyouverymuch."

"Either way, you're the hottest girl in the bar. You should try frumping it up a little bit when you come in."

Lizzy laughed. "I'll keep that in mind for next time. Anyway, how are tips tonight?"

"Really good!" Sandi leaned forward toward Lizzy and set her breasts on the bar, her low-cut shirt exposing the ample cleavage. "I use my secret weapons to my advantage. Great tits equal great tips!"

Lizzy smiled, her eyes sparkling. "I mean, if you got 'em, flaunt 'em!"

"Right?"

A man sitting at the middle of the bar called Sandi over.

"Gotta go, girl. Have fun!"

"Gonna try," Lizzy said, sliding off her stool and making her way over to the empty *Playboy* pinball machine that sat in the corner.

She set her beer on the small ledge that ran the length of the wall and slipped two quarters into the slot. When she hit the play button, the machine sounded its musical notes and popped the ball up onto the playfield. Lizzy pulled back the plunger and set the ball in play. It remained in play for several minutes before it drained down the side. Halfway through the play of her second ball, she noticed a person standing nearby out of her peripheral vision, watching. She didn't look up but continued to play. When the second ball slipped between the flippers, she slightly glanced to the side and saw one of the guys from the table—the guys Sandi had warned her about. Without saying anything, Lizzy played her third ball, and when her game was over, she grabbed her beer and tried to slip by him.

"Nice score," he said. She stopped and gave him a once-over. He seemed to be in shape, probably mid-thirties, blue-and-white flannel shirt, Levi's and boots. Nothing struck her as creepy about him, and he had a kind face.

"Thanks. It's all yours." Lizzy started to walk back to her stool at the bar.

"Buy you a drink?"

She stopped, turned. "I'm good. Thank you."

The man smiled. "I don't bite. I'm not looking to get in your pants... just would love to talk to you for a bit."

Lizzy hesitated. "Um... I appreciate it, but I'm meeting my friend here."

He turned to look at the bar. "Looks like she is running late."

"Yeah," Lizzy said. "She should be here soon though."

"One beer. If she shows up, I'll vamoose back to my table."

Lizzy cocked her head and paused for a moment. While she wasn't in the mood for company, she also didn't want to come across as a bitch.

"One beer. C'mon."

Lizzy walked toward her seat at the bar.

"What's your name?" he asked, following her.

She turned her head slightly. "Lizzy. You?"

"Doug."

They got to the bar, and Lizzy sat down while Doug found a recently abandoned stool farther down the bar and dragged it close to hers. "Looks That Kill" by Motley Crüe was blasting over the speakers, one of her picks.

"Bartender, can you please get the lady another beer, and I'll have what she's having?"

Sandi turned and looked at Doug, then Lizzy, her right eyebrow arched quizzically. Lizzy nodded, and Sandi grabbed two beers out of the cooler, popping the caps and setting them down before each of them.

"Glass?" she asked Doug.

"Nope. Thanks."

He grabbed his bottle and took a swig. "So, Lizzy, this is my first time here. Is this the hotspot for this town?"

"One of them. It's a pretty small town, but there is another bar toward the other end that gets pretty busy also. Seems like most of the regulars jump back and forth between the two."

"Well, it looks like I picked the right one."

Lizzy ignored his compliment.

"So, are you just passing through? What brings you and your boys"—she motioned with the tip of her bottle toward the table with the other two men—"to town?"

"We were actually on a hunting trip, but are on our way home."

"I hope you guys aren't gonna hit the road again tonight."

"No. We rented a little cabin nearby for the night. Heading out in the morning."

"I take it you didn't get anything?"

"Nope. But it was still great to hang with the boys and get away from the job, the wife... you know the drill."

"Not really. I'm not married... nothing to really get away from."

"Sounds promising."

Lizzy squinted at him and looked him in the eyes. "Not for you it doesn't. You just said you're married. I don't do married men... but then again, it's one beer, remember?"

"I remember. It's just that you are so fucking hot. And it'd just be one night. You'd never see me again. C'mon, it'd be fun... break up the monotony of using your vibrator all the time. Whatdaya say, Lizzy? Want to get out of here and go back to your place?"

Lizzy's gaze turned to steel. "I think we're done here."

Doug's mouth dropped open, clearly not expecting a rejection to his not-so-smooth invitation.

"Oh c'mon. Girls like you don't come to bars like this all dolled up unless you are down to fuck. I'm just cutting out the bullshit all-night banter. If it's not me, it'll be one of these other guys here. Facts. Might as well make it me... I'm packing way more than you are probably used to."

"Is there a problem here?" Hailey said, approaching the two. Lizzy hadn't even seen her enter the bar.

"Mind your business, bitch," Doug snapped, his tone gruff, the nice-guy routine clearly over.

"That's it! Get the fuck away from us, you asshole," Lizzy yelled.

"I'd listen to her," Hailey said, her stare icy.

Sandi noticed what was going on and hightailed it to the end of the bar.

"What's happening here?" she asked, concern etched into her tone.

"This guy was just going back to his table," Lizzy said, clearly not leaving room for negotiation.

Doug stood there, glaring at all three of them.

"Maybe she didn't make herself clear, dude," Sandi said, her voice lowered, her words coming out through gritted teeth. "Go back to your table, or I'll have the bouncer remove you and your friends. Now go!"

Doug looked from one to the other, started to say something, thought better of it, and turned and left, going back to the table. They watched as he told his friends about the situation. All eyes were on the girls.

"Want me to bounce them, Lizzy?" Sandi asked.

"No, fuck them. We're leaving. Hailey, want to head down to The Gulch?"

"Yeah... let's go. Who is that creep?"

"Your guess is as good as mine. Where the hell were you, anyway?"

"Ugh. Sorry! I laid down for a quick nap before I came here... I was exhausted. Work has been a bitch this week. I overslept."

"Well, at least you showed up when it mattered."

Lizzy turned toward Sandi. "Thanks, girl. Be safe."

"No worries. I keep a gun in my purse just in case. Let those bastards try something."

Lizzy and Hailey laughed, gave one final glance at the table full of guys—who were incidentally all still glaring at them—and walked out the door.

Lizzy and Hailey licked the salt off their hands, tossed back the shots of tequila, and simultaneously popped the lime wedges in their mouths and sucked the juice out. Both followed the lime with a swig of beer. Hailey stuck out her tongue and made a face, and Lizzy laughed.

"Remind me why we are doing shots of this shit again?" Hailey asked. "You'd think we'd have learned our lesson after last time."

"Yeah, but last time, it wasn't just one shot." Lizzy smiled.

"Yeah, more like six."

"Shit, for all I remember, it could've been sixteen."

"Definitely not tonight," Hailey said. She looked at the time on her phone. "I should probably get going soon. I promised my mom I'd drive up and see her tomorrow. It's two hours each way, so I don't want to get too late of a start."

"Yeah, I probably should call it a night too. It's good to get out, but I'm exhausted as fuck. Work has been a hell-hole this week."

Lizzy glanced around the bar, trying to find the server amongst the patrons. The bar was at about seventy-five percent capacity... not quite as busy as The Box. She finally spotted the server, Stef, coming out of the kitchen area, caught her attention, and waved her over.

"Ladies! Another round of shots?"

"Tempting," Lizzy said, laughing. "Better cash me out though… before I drink the bar dry." Lizzy handed her credit card to Stef.

"Thanks, doll," Stef said. "I'll be right back."

Hailey held three twenty-dollar bills out toward Lizzy.

"Nope. I got it tonight," Lizzy told her, pushing the money away.

"Didn't you get it last time too? You're making me feel like a freeloader."

Lizzy laughed. "Stop! You know I like to treat my BFF when I can. Besides, you know I made out pretty well in the divorce, so I'm not hurting for money."

"Okay, fine, but next time, I'm buying!" Hailey insisted.

"Deal."

Outside, Lizzy walked Hailey to her car, and they chatted a little more before they left, Hailey in the driver's seat and Lizzy hanging on the driver's door for support. She felt buzzed, but she knew she was okay to drive.

"Hey, I just noticed you're matchy tonight!" Lizzy said, pulling on Hailey's orange tank top as she tried to match it against the car's paint color.

"You know it's my favorite color."

"It looks good on you."

Hailey smiled.

When they had said their goodbyes, Lizzy leaned in the car and hugged Hailey, and straightening up, she shut the door for her, made a waving motion with just her fingers, blew her a kiss, and stepped back and watched as Hailey backed out of the parking spot. Lizzy admired the Orange Challenger—she had always been a fan of the older ones—and remembered that Hailey had offered to let her drive it anytime she wanted. She would definitely take her up on that next time they were together.

Hailey made her way to the driveway of the parking lot. As she exited, a truck exited from the other entrance farther down the lot, and Hailey had to punch the accelerator to keep from getting hit. Lizzy smiled as the Challenger tires barked on the asphalt and Hailey pulled away from the lifted king cab Ford 350 that had pulled out at the same time.

Lizzy watched the taillights disappear around the curve in the road several hundred feet down the windy asphalt. The truck was right behind her, which made sense since The Gulch was pretty much at the edge of town. The only people that lived the other direction either lived one town over or owned one of the parcels of land with double-digit acreage in between.

Lizzy made her way to her vehicle, a black Toyota 4Runner. Inside, she put on her seatbelt, plugged her phone into the charging cable, started the vehicle, and pulled out of the lot. She was tired and looking forward to her soft bed and Groot, her German Shepherd that she knew was going to cuddle the shit out of her.

She lived a few miles from The Gulch, and the drive home was uneventful. She was lucky enough to live on a half-acre parcel, so her neighbors weren't right on top of her. As she drove down her long driveway, Groot jumped up on the couch, which was positioned under the front window, his tongue hanging out and his tail flipping back and forth so dangerously fast that it would surely knock things off of shelves and tables if he got close enough.

Inside, Groot molested her until he got his fill of petting and scratches behind the ears.

Before she got ready for bed, she let Groot out in the fenced back yard to relieve himself and burn off some energy before bed. Lizzy emptied her jeans pockets and put everything on the dresser, changed into shorts and a white tank top, brushed her teeth, plugged in her phone, and placed it on her nightstand. The screen lit up, and she noticed it was twelve thirty in the morning. She definitely needed to get in bed and try to catch five hours or so of sleep.

She let Groot back inside, and he lapped at the cool water in the dish. The weather outside was perfect, not too hot or cold, but Groot had been running around at full speed in the yard doing zoomies, so he had worked up a thirst.

"Try to leave some of the water in the bowl," Lizzy said, laughing. She grabbed a paper towel and wiped all the splattered water up off of the laminate floor.

In bed, Lizzy pulled the covers up to her chin, and Groot jumped up on the bed, turned around a few times, and plopped beside her.

The alcohol made her even more tired, and she was out within minutes.

In her dream, her phone rang. She tried to find it, but no matter where she looked, it wasn't there. The sound tricked her and was everywhere and nowhere all at once. It eluded her, and then the sound stopped. She lost focus, and the dream shifted to her at the zoo watching a giraffe, but the sound started up again. The ringing came from within the giraffe. How could that be? Why was the giraffe ringing?

The ringing pierced her dream like a needle slipping into skin—everywhere, nowhere, impossible to silence.

Finally, the shrill tone brought her awake, and she realized the phone had been going off for a while. Was it her alarm? She shook her head to clear it and reached for the phone. It went silent. How long had it been ringing?

Lizzy picked up the phone and tried to read the display through blurry eyes. She squinted to make out the display. Three missed calls. Not good. Someone really was trying hard to reach her. She rubbed her eyes more and looked again. Not three missed calls. Eight! Eight missed calls! Frantically, she fumbled to unlock the screen and look at the history. They were all from Hailey.

Lizzy pushed the button to call her back. The call went straight to voicemail. Lizzy tried again and then two more times with the same result. She looked at her phone again and saw a red "3" over the message icon. Her stomach tightened, a slow, rising tide of dread she couldn't swallow down, and she knew, with everything she had, that something was wrong—terribly wrong.

She clicked on the icon and then the third message down, which would have been left first. She needed to know as much information as she could gather in the order things happened.

Hailey wasn't a drama queen, and Lizzy couldn't ever think of a time Hailey had blown up her phone. Whatever was happening must be real bad. Bile started rising up the back of Lizzy's throat.

The first message started playing.

"LIZZY! WHY AREN'T YOU ANSWERING ME? PLEASE CALL ME BACK! HURRY!" Lizzy could hear Hailey take quick breaths. "They disappeared outside... oh God... please, Lizzy, please help me!"

The message ended, and a chill shot up Lizzy's spine. She shuddered, wondering who Hailey was talking about. She pressed the button to call Hailey back. It again went straight to voicemail.

Birch Hollow was a safe town. Hailey had grown up there. The most dangerous thing she had encountered was the boys in her high school and an occasional wild animal that ventured into town. Her parents' only child, her dad had raised her like a boy, and she knew how to hunt, fish, and fight as well as any man, or better. Her mom had died when she was seven, so it was just her and Dad, until his untimely passing a few years prior. He had left her the house and she stayed there, grasping at each and every memory it held.

Hailey was a transplant. Moved to town with her husband Steve five years back and fell in love with it. Unfortunately, Steve had fallen for Rachel, the waitress at the local diner, and when Hailey received a tip that Steve had slipped, tripped, and "accidentally" stuck his dick in Rachel, she was done. She kicked him out, and shortly after, Steve and Rachel disappeared.

Lizzy's first time meeting Hailey was almost what those in the movie business refer to as a "meet cute" with one exception—they weren't romantically attracted to each other but had adored each other from the start and had immediately become besties. They were both shopping at the Piggly Wiggly, which was the only full grocery store in town. Lizzy was debating on what kind of dessert to get her father for dinner that night as a special treat. Hailey was standing nearby trying to decide what to get to help celebrate her and Steve's wedding anniversary. Both remained indecisive for a few minutes, neither paying attention to the other, until they both reached for the last strawberry-topped cheesecake at the same time.

Hailey had been kind enough to insist that Lizzy take the cheese-cake for her father, and later, they had both chuckled over the incident, glad that Lizzy's father got it and that fuckstick Steve didn't.

Lizzy played the second message.

"OH GOD, LIZZY! Please pick up! I don't have much time. They're going to be back any second!"

Lizzy heard deep sobs escape in bursts from Hailey's lungs, the sound of her gasping for air, the sucking of snot.

"Please..." Hailey whispered. "I need you, bestie..."

The message stopped. Lizzy shot out of bed, pulled a pair of jeans, a t-shirt, and her tennis shoes on. She realized she didn't know what was happening and where she needed to go to rescue Hailey. She tried to call Hailey back again and wasn't successful. Lizzy clicked on the last message. It had been left fifteen minutes prior.

The voice was merely a whisper, crackling like something buried, clawing its way through static, trying to reach her from the grave. Lizzy had to strain to hear it, even after turning the volume on her phone all the way up.

"Liz... girl... where— Why aren't you answering? I can't... I'm so scared. It hurts so bad. So bad. They keep coming back. I know they're going to kill me. I feel it in my bones. I wish... wish you... that you were here."

A low wail pierced the room over the speaker.

"I know you would save me... you'd kill these fuckers. All three... I know you would."

Hailey sucked in air.

"It may be too late for me, my friend. But please, Lizzy... if you get this, please find me. You'll always be my girl. And if it is... if it's too fucking late, find them. It's the fuckers from the bar, Lizzy. They followed me. Attacked me. I'm in... it's... shit, I dunno. Like a cabin. They fucked me up bad, girl. Really fucking bad. I... I love you, Liz."

Lizzy felt her face flush as her blood pressure soared and a slow burn crept through her veins. Part of her wanted to cry and the other part—her protective side—wanted to maim. She kept listening in hopes of hearing something else, but her phone was silent. She looked at it and realized the message had ended. There were no other messages, and Hailey had stopped calling. She also wasn't answering.

Lizzy didn't want to dissect what that meant, because she knew her mind would conjure up the worst possible outcome.

Lizzy called one final time with the same result. Voicemail. Grabbing the keys to her 4Runner, she rushed out the door. She absolutely had to find Hailey before it was too late.

Lizzy tore down the dirt road, her speed extreme enough that the back of her vehicle fishtailed when she went around curves. She felt lucky that she was skilled enough to keep the vehicle on the road, her corrections to the skids purely instinctual.

If she remembered correctly, the cabins she was thinking about were a few miles down this road, nested in the tall trees. She'd only been out this way a couple times, the last being several years ago. The cabins were all owned by the same person who owned a big chunk of land out there.

They rented them to people on vacation, hunters, honeymooners, basically anyone that was looking for a place to stay in a small town that wanted more than a motel room had to offer.

As she drove, she watched for lights or other vehicles. The darkness consumed everything, stretched out in all directions, thick and absolute, her headlights the only savior to the inky blackness. A couple miles farther and she saw the light of a few sodium-vapor lamps that lit up the ground below them but cast shadows throughout the area. The cabins stood like tombstones under the sodium lights, silent, empty, and watching. She saw no vehicles present, adding to the eeriness.

Lizzy continued toward the cabins and spotted a sign before she got to the first one.

CLOSED UNTIL FURTHER NOTICE

Odd.

She couldn't understand why the cabins would be closed. She had remembered them as having year-round availability. She drove by the sign, rolled down her window, and started around the loop that serviced all eight cabins. As she drove by each one, she slowed down and carefully scrutinized the front, looking for any signs. Lights. Vehicles. Personal property. She listened. Nothing.

She pulled up in front of one cabin, got out, and tried the door. Locked. Back in the car, she went to the next one and repeated the process. Same results.

Lizzy went to the back of her 4Runner, raised the hatch, and pulled her five hundred lumens flashlight from the side storage cubby. She flicked it on, and the beam sliced through the shadows like Dexter sliced through flesh. The darkness fell away, and Lizzy swept the beam back and forth among the cabins and up and down the road. Finally, she pointed the beam toward the treed area and looked for anything amiss. She saw no signs of any life. Hailey was not there.

Lizzy turned off the light and climbed back in the vehicle. The phone messages played back through her head, and she shuddered. She thought about Hailey and how she had been through so much. Her friend needed her, and Lizzy couldn't find her, and the worst part was she had no idea where to look.

Goose bumps formed on her arms, and she locked the doors out of instinct. She looked around at her surroundings but couldn't make out hardly anything. She willed herself to drive but had no idea where to go. Hailey had mentioned a cabin. And if the assholes from the bar were the ones that had her, they had also mentioned renting a cabin for the night. All signs pointed to the fact that Hailey and her captors should be there somewhere. But they weren't.

Lizzy racked her brain, trying to figure out where to go to help her girl. She thought about calling nine-one-one, but she didn't know what to tell them anyway. She didn't know what rental cabins Hailey could possibly be at.

These can't be the only ones.

The thought hit her like a freight train. She was a local, and these cabins were the only ones she knew about, but there had to be more.

Lizzy picked her phone up off the passenger seat. No messages and no more missed calls. She felt her stomach flop, and she choked back the urge to lose anything that was still there from the night before. She brought back up her recent calls and clicked on Hailey's number again as she rolled down the windows and listened. Silence. Once again, the voicemail picked up, and Lizzy disconnected.

She pulled up the Safari app and googled "birch hollow cabins for rent," and the top result was for the cabins she was currently sitting at. She scrolled through the list and saw cabins for neighboring towns, but that wouldn't make sense considering they were at The Box. Those other small towns up or down the highway were far away and also had their own bars. As a last-ditch effort, she pulled up a vacation home rental site and put in her town's name. A dozen or so vacation home rentals or single room rentals popped up. She filtered the search down to show cabins, and one result remained on the screen.

"Welch Cabins. Huh."

Lizzy quickly read through the description. It appeared the host owned two cabins on an acre, and they could be rented out together or separately. That had to be the place. She scoured the property information for a clue as to where they were located, but she was well aware that you never really got the address of a vacation rental until after you paid. She tried googling "Welch Cabins Birch Hollow," and no results that were connected in any way were returned.

As a last-ditch effort, she checked availability for that night. It was still the wee hours of the morning, long before most people were stirring. But if the guy was telling the truth, they'd be leaving later in the day and going back home to their wives and families, telling stories that conveniently left out doing brutal things to a strange female in another town.

Both cabins were available that night with check in at four p.m. The booking profile advertised an "Instant Booking," so Lizzy hoped that information would automatically be sent to her and that she would not have to wait until daylight to get information on her reservation.

Lizzy booked the cheaper cabin for one night and went to the pay screen. She entered her card information and got the confirmation screen.

Flipping over to her email, she refreshed it, looking for a confirmation email. She saw nothing. She tried Hailey one more time, and it rang through to voicemail again. She refreshed again and again. Nothing. Her reservation may have been set, but she wouldn't get any information on the booking until someone that owned the property damn well pleased. She was at a dead end. She had nothing left but to call the police and hope they could help.

As she gave her email one last refresh before calling nine-one-one, an email popped in. It was an auto-generated email from Welch Cabins thanking her for booking. She rapidly scanned the email until she came to the information she was looking for. The property address. Entering it into the GPS, Lizzy put the 4Runner in gear and tore off into the night.

The cabins were located toward the far edge of town... ironically fairly close to The Devil's Tacklebox. When she turned off the main highway, GPS told her she still had four miles to go, so the cabins were set back away from the in-town houses by a couple miles. As she worked her way deeper into the open country, she wondered how she would be able to get close to the cabins if the men were still there. A mile out, she cut the lights and drove incredibly slow, the sound of the tires crunching the gravel broadcast through the still night air like a guitar riff at a rock concert.

When she was almost at the cabins, she pulled the 4Runner between some trees, grabbed her phone, and started toward them on foot. She kept to the sides of the road where the weeds and foliage absorbed the sounds of her approach.

Although the night was dark, and the trees lining the road made it shadowy, she was able to make out enough to stay on track.

When she rounded the final bend in the road, she saw lights and knew she had arrived. She could make out the two cabins—which stood approximately a hundred feet apart—by the light that peeked around the edges of the blinds. A Ford 350 truck was parked in front of one of the cabins.

Lizzy stayed in the shadows and tried to let her eyes adjust to the landscape. She surveyed the entire area but did not see Hailey's car.

That would make sense since there was no way Hailey drove out here of her own free will. They would have had to have grabbed her somewhere else and brought her back here, if she was even here.

Lizzy paused, a knot in her stomach. Yes, the guys were pigs, at least the one she had talked to, and probably all of them, but did that mean they would attack a person? What was her plan of action? Would she just go pound on the door and demand they give her friend back? Bust down the door? She couldn't just go accuse people in the middle of the night of doing the unspeakable without proof. Yes, the voicemails were some sort of proof—proof that something nefarious had happened to Hailey. But she had no proof that the guys from the bar were involved. Hell, she didn't even know if the people staying at the cabin were the same guys, although the Ford F350 certainly looked like the same one she saw pulling out of The Gulch's parking lot. She paused, hiding in the shadows, unsure of what her next move was.

Lizzy sat behind a huge tree at the edge of the clearing. Her heart beat quickly, adrenaline coursing through her veins. Her heart shredded as she thought about Hailey and what she had gone through... what she still may be going through. The stillness of the night was interrupted by loud laughter. It was coming from inside. It was time to call the police and let the chips fall where they may.

She removed her phone from her back pocket and brought up the dial pad when she noticed it.

No service.

The impossibility of the situation sliced through her like a chainsaw. She was helpless and had no idea what she could do for her friend. Then she made up her mind. She would try to get verification Hailey was there. A visual of some kind. Maybe she could see through one of the windows.

She slipped from her safe haven behind the tree and circled back behind the cabin, taking care not to step on a stick or some other object that might alert the men inside. The first window was covered by solid curtains, and although she could tell there were lights on in the room beyond, she could not see inside. The next window had blinds. Although they were shut, she could make out some clothes strewn across a bed through the slight gap at the bottom. She couldn't make out any movement or any signs of Hailey.

She crept her way around the side of the cabin, noticed no windows, and made her way around to the front side, the end opposite the front door. She noticed another window—possibly a bedroom, or maybe a living room. The inky black of night was not easily dispelled by the fraction of light sifting through the blinds. Her breath caught in her throat as she inched her way toward the window, approaching cautiously. She could not see the ground in front of her, and she tested her footsteps before she put full pressure on her feet. The solid object was unexpected, and her foot came down on it at a strange angle, her ankle twisting in the process, pitching her body toward the house. She was unaware of her muffled yelp as her head crashed into the window, shattering it, leaving her in an unconscious mound at the base of the windowsill.

Lizzy awoke, confused, her head feeling like a freight train had plowed through it. She touched her forehead, and it felt sticky. Pulling her hand away, she noticed the coagulated blood on her fingertips. She felt cold and then noticed her surroundings. She was in a living room, obviously inside the cabin. Above the large television was a taxidermy mount for a ten-point buck. She noticed brown leather furniture and rustic end tables and an enormous live slab coffee table. Her mind drifted to wondering where the men were. She had to find Hailey and get out of there. It was when she tried to stand up—and only after her ankle buckled and tossed her back to the ground—that she realized she was naked. The only clothing on her body were her socks.

Lizzy's mind raced, the realization setting in. She performed a mental examination of her body. Massive headache from nosediving into the window—she remembered that one. Ankle on fire from twisting it on a rock or whatever the fuck that had been. And then she felt it. The burn, the rawness at her center. She felt ripped, torn, shredded from both sides.

Lizzy shoved her right hand between her legs, and her worst fear was realized. She knew the substance there, and from the feel of it, it was from more than one of them.

Tears involuntarily squirted out of the corner of her eyes as a wild groan started to rise up out of her chest. She pulled it back, internally yelling at herself to shut the fuck up. Tears and screams would only make things worse for her.

There is no time to be weak. Dad raised you as a fucking survivor. So fucking survive already.

Lizzy painstakingly pulled herself up to her knees and put her good foot flat on the floor. She paused, listened through the pain. She could hear muffled conversation out of earshot. It appeared to be coming from out front. She stood up the best she could and hopped over to the window closest to the front door. She couldn't make out the conversation, but she heard three distinct voices, snippets of sentences wafting through the glass.

"...stupid bitch..."

"...too late..."

"...tore that... fine as..."

"...do we do..."

"...have to deal..."

Lizzy envisioned them out there, proud of their conquests, cigarettes hanging out of their mouths. She fought back her purge.

MOVE WHILE YOU CAN, her brain screamed at her.

The cabin was fairly small, and besides the living area and kitchen, it appeared that the bedrooms were on the other end of the home. Lizzy hopped/limped/shuffled toward the bedrooms to look for Hailey. When she got to the first bedroom, she found only a couple bags. No sign of her girl. The second bedroom was the same. A Winchester rifle was propped in the corner. A duffle bag sat on the bed with clothes spilling out of it. Lizzy pulled a pair of jeans from the bag and slipped them on. They slid down her hips. From the floor, she grabbed a pair of tennis shoes and pulled the laces out, quickly threading them through the belt loops, cinching the makeshift belt tight around her waist, and then she bent over and rolled the pant legs up several times. She spotted a hoodie in the bag as well and grabbed it, slipping it over her bare torso.

She had no idea where her clothes were, but she wasn't going to pass up on grabbing what she could when she could.

Knowing she was living on borrowed time, she stumbled to the third bedroom. The room was in disarray, the covers ripped off the bed, stains on the sheets, a lamp toppled from its nightstand. Lizzy wondered if this was the room that she had been assaulted in. Or worse, Hailey. Lizzy moved around the side of the bed, and then she spotted it. The orange tank top, the front of it ripped almost in half. Lizzy's heart felt like it started beating backward, jackhammer-like. Inside, she felt like releasing a torrential downpour of tears, but she was in survival mode. There'd be time to cry later. For now, she had to get out of there.

Hailey had been there, of that she was certain. But she obviously had been moved somewhere. Lizzy had checked all the rooms.

Taking a deep breath, Lizzy hobbled for the bedroom door and peeked around the corner toward the front door. The men were still outside, but she knew her luck wouldn't hold out much longer. Loud laughter sliced through the log wall and into her heart.

Knowing her survival would hinge on getting free, she tried to formulate a plan. It would be impossible to sneak out past them with there being only one door in the cabin, so she would have to hide. A door off the side of the kitchen caught her eye. It had to be a pantry. She doubted these fuckers were cooking anything, so maybe the space would be safe. She pulled herself over to the room and popped the door open, slipping inside. It was pitch black, no light sneaking in from other parts of the house. Lizzy felt for a wall switch, finally discovering one on the wall.

The flood of light sliced through the blackness, but nothing could prepare her for what she found. The room wasn't a pantry at all. It appeared to be a laundry room. In the middle, spilled onto the rough wood plank floor, lay Hailey, her body a roadmap of ruin—cut, bruised, and painted in the sick hues of a slow, cruel death. Lizzy moved around to the side to look at her face, her eyes open, lifeless, her mouth partially open as if in mid-scream. Her neck was covered in blood, and upon closer inspection, Lizzy noticed it had been slashed. She lay in a pool of her own blood.

Lizzy thought back to the phone messages left by Hailey. She had still been alive at the time. They had used her, hurt her, fucked her up beyond comprehension, and then the sick motherfuckers had killed her. Her Hailey. Her best fucking friend.

Lizzy saw red and hobbled out of the laundry room as quickly as she could, her plan to hide no longer a valid option. She made her way back to the bedroom and grabbed the Winchester, which had somehow not even registered with her when she had originally noticed it.

In the living room, she cracked the action slightly, noticing the shell was in place. When she closed it, as if on cue, the front door opened. Lizzy didn't hesitate, bringing the rifle up to her shoulder and squeezing the trigger. A hole opened up in the man's chest, and he collapsed to the ground. Before they understood what was happening, the second man stumbled over the fallen man and fell into the cabin, trying to recover and roll into a squatting and then standing position. By the time he was on his feet, it was too late. Lizzy had already cycled the bolt and squeezed a round off at his head. The bullet hit its mark, and brain matter splattered across its trajectory path.

"HOLY FUCK," was all Lizzy heard before the last guy—incidentally, the one that had hit on her in the bar—rushed through the door and tackled her. She landed on her back with him on top of her, and she gasped as she tried to get breath back into her lungs.

"Fucking bitch!" he yelled as he swung at her face with both hands, connecting twice before she was able to grab his arm, twist it, and roll over with it underneath her. His scream ripped through the cabin as he was forced to roll off of her. Lizzy forgot about the pain and went after the only thing she had control of. His arm. She put all her strength into twisting it, his screaming almost bursting her eardrums. Finally, she heard a loud pop and knew she had dislocated it.

The pain fueled his rage, and he ripped his body away from her, pulling his arm free.

"I should have fucking killed you when I had the chance."

"Bet you're feeling kind of stupid now," she said as she lunged at him, her thumb aimed at his right eye. She had always wondered what it would sound like to destroy someone's eyeball, and she got her answer as she dug her thumb in as hard as she could, and it exploded like a grape, the POP a sound she would never forget. She felt her finger go inside, like she was finger-fucking his eyeball, and then she curled her thumb around the optical nerve and tugged the entire thing free from the socket. The man let out a cry of rage, and as he did, his destroyed optic swung freely like a pendulum keeping time, a macabre countdown.

The man was able to pull himself to his feet, and he landed three kicks directly on her ribs, the force cracking the bone like a stick underfoot. White blazing light shot through Lizzy's vision as she tried to cry out, and then when she tried to focus on what was coming at her next, she didn't see him. She swiveled her head back and forth and looked at the space, and he wasn't there. It was then she heard the roar of the truck's engine coming to life.

Lizzy tried to get to her feet and fell down, but her rage fueled her, and she half stumbled, half ran, out the front door. She picked up a large rock without thinking and fired it at the back of the truck as it tore down the road, the back window taking the impact. Then she watched as the truck disappeared around the curve in the road.

Unsure of what to do, her instinct took over and she limped—rocks poking at her semi-exposed feet—to her 4Runner as quickly as she could, starting it and slamming it into reverse. Luckily, she had the foresight to leave the key fob in the cupholder.

While Lizzy had only driven the road once before—earlier tonight—she took off at high speeds, hoping to catch up with the Ford. For several minutes, she thought she had lost him until she rounded a corner and saw his taillights ahead. The sight of his truck fueled her rage even more, and she pressed down the accelerator all the way.

Ahead, she saw that the road had curved around to the left and the Ford had navigated the curve and was heading at a forty-five-degree angle from her. She estimated it would take her several seconds to get to the curve, and then she would still have to catch up to him. Instinct took over, and she ripped the steering wheel to the left, launching the Toyota off the rutty dirt road and into the brush and rocks of the natural landscape. Her vehicle shrieked as the bushes scratched pinstriping down the side, but nothing mattered at this point. She floored the gas pedal as the vehicle bounced over rocks and bushes, her deepest fear at the moment being the possibility of hitting a large boulder.

Her cross-country trek gave her the advantage she needed, and she watched as she kept getting closer, her attempts at intercepting him working. Then, with one last slamming down of the pedal, her SUV lurched as it popped back onto the roadway, catching the Ford truck in the left rear corner, spinning him around at a high rate of speed, his forward momentum too much for the vehicle, and as if in slow motion, she watched the truck roll over several times sideways down the dirt road before slamming into the side of a huge tree with a sickly crunch.

Lizzy stopped her vehicle and got out, the one good headlight shining on the crushed Ford. She limped to the driver's door, the dust dancing through the air, the light filtering through it giving it a strobing effect. She crouched down and peered inside, the truck upside down, the driver clearly hurt, dazed. But, unfortunately, alive.

He stared at her with his remaining eye, fear projecting, his lip trembling. His mutilated eyeball still hung free in front of his face.

"Ple—ase," he begged.

"Please what?" she snarled, looking down and seeing the broken glass from the side mirror laying on the ground.

"P—please... don't."

Lizzy reached for the largest sliver of the broken glass and stopped beside the open window of the truck, the man's body contorted into an odd position.

Lizzy spit at him. "Like I told you earlier tonight, Doug, I think we're done here. This one's for Hailey."

With that, she drew the glass across his throat as he tried to say something, but all that came out was a gurgle.

Lizzy pulled her body onto a rock by the side of the road and sat, watching, his life slowly fading from his eyes.

EPILOGUE

Lizzy carried the plastic stick out to the kitchen and set it on the counter. It had been eight weeks—eight long and grueling weeks of recovery. Between the sprained ankle, the three cracked ribs, the black eyes, the violation to her womanhood, and the cuts and bruises all over her body, she had been in a lot of pain. But the physical pain couldn't hold a candle to the pain on the inside. The pain of losing Hailey. The realization that maybe if she had heard Hailey's phone call and answered it, just maybe, Hailey might still be alive.

The guilt permeated her soul like poison, her attempts to reason with herself futile. Add to that survivor's guilt and she was one fucked-up mess. She definitely saw therapy in her future.

She looked at the clock on the microwave. Three minutes had passed. Lizzy picked up the stick and looked at it. Two pink lines.

"Fuck my life."

It had been two months since the attack. All three men had died. Somehow, they had cleared her of all charges. Yet she wasn't clear at all. She had a murderer's baby growing inside her.

Her soul cracked, and her badass resolve faded away. She had always felt like she could handle anything. But this. BUT FUCKING THIS!

Lizzy walked over to the butcher block and pulled out the carving knife, studying it intently. What happened that fateful night two months prior was out of her control, but tonight... tonight, she would take that control back.

Authors

Clay McLeod Chapman writes books, comic books, YA and middlegrade books, as well as for film and television. *Wake Up and Open Your Eyes* is his most recent novel. You can find him at www.claymcleodchapman.com.

Christina Henry is a horror and dark fantasy author whose works include THE HOUSE THAT HORROR BUILT, GOOD GIRLS DON'T DIE, HORSEMAN, NEAR THE BONE, THE GHOST TREE, THE GIRL IN RED, THE MERMAID, LOST BOY, the CHRONICLES OF ALICE series (ALICE, RED QUEEN and LOOKING GLASS) and the seven-book urban fantasy BLACK WINGS series.

Her short stories have been featured in the anthologies HOWL, ELEMENTAL FORCES, CURSED, TWICE CURSED, GIVING THE DEVIL HIS DUE and KICKING IT.

She enjoys running long distances, reading anything she can get her hands on and watching movies with samurai, zombies and/or subtitles in her spare time. She lives in Chicago with her husband and son.

You can visit her on the web at:
www.christinahenry.net
BlueSky: @christinahenry.bsky.social
Threads: authorChristinaHenry
Instagram: authorChristinaHenry
Goodreads: goodreads.com/CHenryAuthor

Lance Dale was born and raised in Wisconsin and is the author of Title Pending: A Collection of Short Fiction. His stories have been included in several anthologies, and he is an avid fan of extreme metal music, horror movies, and books of all genres. He spends most of his time hanging out with his amazing wife and two children, dog, and two psychotic cats near La Crosse, Wisconsin.

Cassandra Celia (she/they) is a Maryland bookseller, turned author. They write horror, weird fic, and dark fic, such as THE ELRIC UNDOING, and their latest release, HOUSE OF HARROW. Cassandra obsesses over stories with love, death, ambiguous endings, and everything in between. In their books, they take inspiration from haunting art and media, and they absolutely love writing about angry, scorned women.

Brandon Eldridge is a fiction writer and author of BEINGS, and THE ESTABLISHMENT. His third novel, WHERE SHADOWS SLEEP, will be released July of 2025. Born and raised in Indiana, Brandon fell in love with reading and writing in high school, where he would write short stories in several genres. He earned both a bachelor's degree in Business and MBA from Indiana Wesleyan University. He lives in Fishers, Indiana, with his wife and two children.

C S Jones is an award winning writer from Wrexham, North Wales, who holds a prestigious 10 meter swimming certificate, along with the Bookstagram Debut Author of the Year 2024. Often mistaken for an escaped mental patient, he has been writing for only a short time, his recent massively inflated sense of self finally winning out over the years of overwhelming laziness. A keen horror enthusiast, he has finally decided to give back to a community that has provided so much, whether that be in his writing or general appearance. Initially a timid child, he was scared of anything and everything, including Ghostbusters 2 - insisting his parents record over it immediately. If he can make you feel even a modicum of that terror, then mission accomplished. I, I mean, he, hope's you enjoy.

Ben Young lives in the Cincinnati, OH area with his family and dogs, where he is currently working on more stories which may or may not ever see the light of day. He does not enjoy writing about himself, especially in the third person like this. Find him online at www.benyoungstories.com

Steven Pajak, a Chicago-based author, crafts stories that explore the depths of horror and the human psyche. With a pen that dances on the edges of darkness, Steven brings to life tales that challenge, terrify, and linger in the minds of readers. Drawing inspiration from the urban tapestry of Chicago, his work merges the pulse of city life with the eerie quiet of the shadows lurking within the darkest corners of our minds. Steven invites you into a world where fear meets courage, and the journey through his imagination proves as haunting as it is unforgettable.

Ruthann Jagge is from Upstate NY, where October is otherworldly. Work as an author includes a novella, a co-authored novel, reviews, articles, and short stories featured in successful anthologies. Her memorable characters and settings incorporate elements of folklore, Gothic, horror, and fantasy. She enjoys discussing the creative process in interviews and on professional panels. Work for release in 2025 includes a Southern Gothic horromantasy, a sequel, and several invitational projects. Extensive travel and backyard superstitions influence her work. Other passions include cooking, sewing, and dancing with her demons. She currently lives on a rural cattle ranch in Texas with her husband and his animals. A large, blended family keeps her sane most of the time.

Member HWA/SSAG

Andrew Najberg is the author of *The Mobius Door* (Wicked House Publishing, 2023), *Gollitok* (Wicked House Publishing, 2023), *The Neverborn Thief* (Crystal Cove Publishing, 2025), *In Those Fading Stars* (Crystal Lake Publishing, 2024), *Try Not to Die In the Shadowlands* (Vincere Press, 2024), *Extinction Dream* (Wicked House Publishing, 2025), and the forthcoming *Paradise Falls* (Co-authored with Patrick Reuman, Wicked House Publishing, 2025) and *Dead Hearts Eat the Light* (Wicked House Publishing, 2026). His short fiction has appeared in *Fusion Fragment, Khoreo, Translunar Travelers Lounge, Utopia Science Fiction, Prose Online, Psychopomp Review, Solar Press Horror Anthology,* and more. Currently, he teaches for the University of Tennessee at Chattanooga.

Robert Essig is the author of thirty books including Baby Fights, This Damned House, Disco Rice, and Master of Bodies, which was nominated for a Splatterpunk Award. He has published over 125 short stories and edited three anthologies. Robert lives with his family in East Tennessee where ticks are hard at work trying to kill him.

Viggy Parr Hampton, MPH is an epidemiologist, content marketing strategist, host of the podcast "Horror Humor Hunger," and the author of *A Cold Night for Alligators, Much Too Vulgar,* and *The Rotting Room.* She is a graduate of Georgetown University and Emory University's Rollins School of Public Health. Connect with her at her website, http://www.viggyhampton.com , or on Instagram @viggyparrhampton.

Alexandrea Christianson lives in the mid-west with her husband and three dogs. She has an avid love for reading books, and creating artwork! She has written four books with the most recent being *Zombies: Dead Clown Apocalypse.*

D E McCluskey was born in 1973, in Liverpool, England. He is the author of novels, graphic novels and comics. He lives with his daughter (an author in her own right (at the age of 8) with her children's adventure The Hangry Hamster), his partner, her daughter, and a sausage dog called Ted.

R.E. Sargent is the author of several novels, as well as a handful of novelettes. R.E.'s novels include Relative Terror and The Fury-Scorned series.

At a young age, R.E. fell in love with books. While many of the other kids were playing sports, he was reading as many books as he could. He quickly got hooked on mysteries and suspense. It was his love of books and storytelling that led to his passion for writing. One of his biggest inspirations is Dean Koontz.

R.E. currently lives in Oregon with his wife and their two fur-children, Riley and Mason. Riley is a Chocolate Lab and Mason is a Bernese Mountain Dog.

Jay Bower is a horror author living outside St. Louis, MO in the forest of Southern Illinois. He spends his time reading, writing, and convincing his wife the dark stories he writes do not involve her.

Elizabeth J. Brown was born in Kent, England. This probably explains her obsession with tea and cake. She currently writes the Brimstone Chorus series - dark fantasy horror featuring demons, witches and a whole host of things that go bump in the night.

Mike Salt was born once... But then immediately raised by wolves. He spent the majority of his childhood fighting to survive in the forest. Cold. Alone. Mike learned English by snatching various paperbacks from campsites and off hikers. He is feral. He is in need of a bath. Don't trust him. But read his work. It's fine.

It's fine.

Paul Avery Tindol is an East Texas horror author. Paul has been writing stories since he could pick up a pencil, and obsessed with all things spooky since his babysitter showed him *A Nightmare on Elm Street*. His known works include *Hunting Snipe: and Other Notes on the East Texas Cattle Mutilations*, *This House Will Never Be Warm*, *There's Something Upstairs*, and *In The Pines*, as well as multiple short stories that's have also been featured on podcasts like Creepy, NoSleep, and Someone Just Like You.

Elizabeth Devecchi is a member of the Horror Writer's Association, Rocky Mountain Fiction Writers, Castle Rock Writers and Italian American Writers Association. She currently resides in Colorado with her family, which includes an ever-changing menagerie of pets and "guest creatures."

Upcoming releases include short tech-gone-wrong horror story "A Corporate Family," to appear in Rabid Otter's upcoming anthology *Error Code*, edited by Zaq Cass; short horror story "Open House," to appear in a Running Wild Press anthology in 2025; and debut thriller/suspense novel, *A Twist of the Lens*, to be published by Wicked House Publishing in mid-2025.

MJ Mars is a geek, ghoul, and horror enthusiast living in Lancaster, UK. Her debut novel, ***The Suffering***, was published by Wicked House in 2023. When she isn't writing, you'll find MJ playing pool, trying to skateboard (badly), or listening to rock music. She owes every success to her mis-spent youth.

Short story collection, ***We've Already Gone Too Far*** out now! Coming in 2025: ***The Fovea Experiments***, a second novel to be published by Wicked House. MJ is currently working on a sequel to ***The Suffering***.

Join her on Twitter @MJMars, Instagram /mjmarsauthor, and her Facebook page, MJ Mars Author.

Raised on Goosebumps, the horror section at Blockbuster, and other things he shouldn't have been exposed to at eight years old, ***Sean McDonough*** is a fresh new voice in horror fiction. His books evoke a sense of gleeful gruesomeness and dark humor, perfect for keeping the Halloween spirit alive all year long.

William F. Gray is the bestselling author *THE DEVIL WITHIN US ALL*, a small town horror novel inspired by the evil average people are capable of on an everyday basis. Taking cues from his own experience and the world at large, Gray creates horror that attempts to worm itself into your heart as well as your mind. His self-published *debut THE MAN BEHIND THE DOOR* tackles themes such as grief, trauma, and addiction through the lens of a ghost story, the main character of which is inspired by his own late father, while his latest effort

OUR FATHERS' BURDEN is Appalachian horror that focuses on the stigma that still surrounds mental health issues, especially amongst men.

He currently lives in West Virginia with his wife, son, and daughter while working as a Lead Pharmacy Technician. His hobbies include reading, playing video games with his wife, and playing music.

D.W. Hitz loves the outdoors and enjoys making it a background character in his work. He devours stories in all mediums. He enjoys writing in the genres of Horror, Supernatural/Paranormal Thriller, and Science Fiction/Fantasy. He aspires to tell stories that thrill the heart and stimulate the imagination.

When not writing, D.W. enjoys spending time with his family, hiking, camping, and playing with the dogs.

Editors

Joey Powell is the Owner & Operator of Mad Axe Media, where he manages cover and interior design and publicity. He is also an award-winning author and actor. His upcoming published work includes *Squirming All the Way Up*, an anti-fascist horror novella from Madness Heart Press.

Nico Bell is the Editor-in-Chief of Mad Axe Media. She is also the author of *Static Screams* and the co-editor of Publishers Weekly Book-Life's Best of 2024 *Diet Riot: A Fatterpunk Anthology*. She adapted her award winning novella *Food Fright* into a screenplay which was a finalist in the Killer Nashville Claymore Awards (2024).

When she isn't writing or editing, she is wrangling her dog, Egg, and trying to maintain her sanity.

www.ingramcontent.com/pod-product-compliance
Lightning Source LLC
Chambersburg PA
CBHW031031310726
48969CB00007B/1939